WILL

WILL

Timothy P. Munkeby

Minneapolis

ISBN 13: 9781945769221

Library of Congress Catalog Number: 2016956008
Printed in the United States of America
First Printing: 2016
20 19 18 17 16 5 4 3 2 1

Cover design by Emily Mahon
Interior design by Patrick Maloney
Typeset in Minion Pro

Published by W.I. Creative Publishing, an imprint of Wise Ink Creative Publishing.

W.I. Creative Publishing
837 Glenwood Avenue
wiseinkpub.com
To order, visit seattlebookcompany.com or call (734)426-6248.
Reseller discounts available.

For my grandson Will, who I believe will become a Peewee.

We are but visitors on this planet for ninety or a hundred years at the most. During that period, we must try to do something good, something useful with our lives. If you contribute to other people's happiness, you'll find the true goal, the true meaning of life.

—Dalai Lama XIV

[Ok, a little heavy, maybe, but tell me that's not hard to argue with?]

We want you to grow up in a world better than ours today.

—Mark Zuckerberg and Priscilla Chan
in an open letter to their newborn daughter

[From what I hear they're certainly trying . . . don't we all want a better world? Especially if you have children and grand- and great-grandchildren. I sure do. It's why I wrote this book.]

Only a life lived for others is a life worthwhile.

—Albert Einstein

[I don’t think we should listen to this guy; he wasn’t too smart.]

Complexity is the harbor of scoundrels.

—Unknown

[Keep it simple. Some things are pretty obvious.]

CHAPTER ONE

Sept. 30

Today was a day to die for. A rare Indian summer day. Relief. A nice, warm sun after several frickin' miserable days of trying to steal a painless breath. A kiss from the cold, such an intimate pain. The colors so remarkably vibrant: red, yellow, orange, gold. Especially the fading luster of the tamaracks. The breeze so crisp it could break. I'd rather be outside than in, but more and more I don't feel good outside, especially knowing what's coming. The concept of living as long as possible does not exist in nature. After procreating and nourishing, breath is no longer necessary . . . only the satisfaction of hunger. This may sound disconcerting, but it gives me solace

I know you knew and understood. Thanks, big guy, for

handling it the way you did. You are going to make it all worthwhile. Really, dude, you will. There were times I almost believed that maybe I'd be . . . ah, well. Wasn't likely, huh? But it it's frustrating, I have to admit. But what can you do? This newest pain a bleak harbinger I'm afraid . . . like the tamaracks losing their needles.

So, sorry for getting a little maudlin there, but on this day to die for I've decided to start my last will and testament. I've been reading the Dalai Lama. I like this guy. Smart. He says that if you have willpower, you can accomplish anything. Since you appear to be lacking in this area, I hereby will you mine. I've left it to you. Bequeathed it to you. Got it? Here's my first item you'll be needing my willpower to take care of:

Item #1: Peace in the world. Don't roll your eyes. I realize that's what the beauty queen always wishes for, making her appear simple-minded to cynics. But, really, she's just being honest and optimistic, like me. Yes, I realize the beauty queen has a reason for optimism. The world's her pearl. My oyster may seem empty to most . . . like to my tormentors, including my mother, unfortunately. But because of you I have hope. That's my pearl: hope.

I realize your first order of business won't entail the United Nations, but eventually you'll have to straighten them out. I don't know what they do, but it doesn't appear they've been effective in their mission of world peace. Not even close.

They'll tell you that achieving world peace is too complex, so keep it frickin' simple for them. I realize there are no easy answers, but SOMEBODY HAS TO DO SOMETHING! The direction the world seems to be moving in now is toward apocalypse it seems. How absurd; "holy" interpreted to mean, "kill everybody." What the shit! People just don't seem to trust each other anymore. There's a cold wind in the branches, blowing hard and slow . . . the fading leaves trying hard to hang on. "A hard rain's gonna fall" and "slow train a-coming" as Dylan said . . . etc., etc.

Einstein wrote, "Peace cannot be kept by force; it can only be achieved by understanding." "Understanding" – a synonym for "education." You gonna argue with Einstein? Yet ignorance is winning! The war happening in our cities is bad enough, but IS and the other terrorist assholes have caused a divide of trust around the world. It's really irritating. I know you realize, in spite of your attempt at apathy, that all the horror going on in the world, as well as here in the US of A, will only escalate, exponentially, if things don't turn around. Right? But it's pretty obvious it's going to take a unified effort by the world at large if we're going to move toward a universal understanding and arrive at any semblance of peace in the world. (Quit shaking your head. No, it's not going to happen overnight, but the more of the world that's at peace, the better the world will be for our children. Yes, that's "our" I imagine you now realize.) If they're going to call themselves the "United Nations," they definitely need a kick in the ass to get going. I don't know anybody with a bigger boot than you.

I can just see your face. "Right!" you'll be crying. "Not a chance, Shrimp!" Well, sorry for this little diatribe, but it's my will and I know you. A hint: the Dalai Lama, who's pretty hard to argue with, says we need "truth, reason, and human solidarity" to fix things. Sounds good to me.

Speaking of solidarity, I hear mother hollering downstairs. Must be supper. More to come. Sorry.

WILLY ALWAYS SLUNK LIKE A SHADOW down the hallway in the morning before classes started. Slipped into his usual seat in the corner, back row, for homeroom. Peewee, his best friend, rarely got to school before second hour and left before sixth. Those times, before second and after fifth, were the dangerous times. Any of a number of guys, and one girl—Big Betty—could find him. The most common game, especially before school, was stuffing Wee Willy in his locker. Willy just let them. No sense in fighting it. That would be even more embarrassing. He just climbed in when an asshole decided to have some fun, hoping that not seeming to be bothered might eventually take the fun away. When Peewee arrived after first hour, the first order of business was to check Willy's locker to make sure he wasn't in it. Anyone needing to mess with Willy did it when Peewee wasn't around.

Peewee had failed his senior year. Twice. Hard to pass when only attending four out of six classes. He refused to go to his first-hour World History class. Said there was too much bullshit going on in the world that he wanted nothing to do with. He already got an earful of world history almost daily from his well-read, well-informed, and surprisingly radical and iconoclastic little friend anyway. Sixth hour was an elective—he said he elected to go do something else. Peewee was completely bald—always had been since birth . . . some odd disease—yet had a dense, impressive growth of beard by ninth grade. Nobody but Willy knew why he didn't just drop out of high school. Get his GED or whatever.

The football coach hated Peewee because, being six foot

nine, two eighty, and the fastest kid in school—he could mean a state championship. The basketball coach drooled over what his presence under the basket could mean . . . a state championship, of course. The baseball coach was incensed. He had seen Peewee playing pick-up games. He could hit the ball out of sight—literally. The coach noticed that he never threw the ball as hard as he could because, it seemed, he was afraid he would hurt somebody. They all, with championships looming in ulterior fields and courts of their brains, tried to convince him that he could be famous, rich, make millions of dollars in any sport he chose. But Peewee, very politely, declined.

The principal was in a quandary. He looked up to him, both literally and figuratively, and admired him. Peewee was the nicest guy—always respectful and smart—yet he appeared to have no aspirations, like graduating. The principal had no idea what to do with him, nor did he understand why Peewee hung around high school. He thought he should encourage him to drop out, but he didn't have the heart, and the teachers of the classes Peewee chose to attend enjoyed having him in class. While in most schools students tried to gain the respect of their teachers, in Oak Grove High School the teachers wanted to gain Peewee's respect. They all knew Peewee was extraordinary. No one knew what to do with him, except Willy.

No one could quite accept the fact that a wild-haired, wise-ass, lisping little shrimp was and always had been Peewee's best friend. It just didn't compute to them. When Peewee would find Willy stuffed in his locker, he'd pull his four-foot-seven friend out and demand to know who had done it this time. Willy would never say. Or when Peewee'd swing by to see Willy after his first hour and find him soaking wet, a Dr. Pepper or something having been poured over his disheveled noggin, he'd beg Willy to tell him who the perpetrator was. But Willy would never give him or her or them up. Willy knew that if Peewee avenged him, someone would get hurt, and it wouldn't be Peewee of course. Willy didn't want to put Peewee in that predicament. So Willy mostly stayed as invisible as he could, like a tiny, innocuous haunt, only showing his real persona, his wit, his personality when Peewee was around. Nobody, nobody bothered him when Peewee was around.

Willy wished he were Peewee. He envisioned Peewee as a massive Dalai Lama. Although he frequently couldn't help himself, he did try to resist pressing Peewee to make more of himself, trying to get him more involved in world issues; Peewee didn't like it. Willy would ask Peewee things like what the devil did he think the United Nations did or accomplished? But Peewee was not in the least bit interested in talking about the UN. Why did Willy think he skipped World History class? But Willy knew if he were Peewee, he'd accomplish great things. Things that needed to be done. Things that he thought Peewee could do . . . if he wanted.

The bell rang and Willy headed to his first hour class—World History. He found his seat, back corner, same as homeroom. He slid down in his desk to be hidden by the back in front of him and closed his eyes, drifting off, a smile on his face as the lecture on turmoil in Africa began . . .

PEEWEE INTERRUPTED THE UNITED NATIONS General Session. He strolled confidently up to the moderator who was facing out at semicircular rows of previously bored but now surprised faces. He stood next to the moderator, a smallish four-foot-seven

Asian, and smiled out at the nations' representatives. Everyone, including the moderator, froze. Time seemed to stand still. Peewee smiled down at the moderator, a charming, but disarming smile, and picked up the microphone that had been poised in front of the now quiescent, quaint man.

Peewee's stature, his imposing presence, captured everyone's full, unwavering attention. His bare dome shone like a beacon in the lights of the assembly hall, his magnificent beard and regal posture commanding not only their attention but acquiescence.

"Pardon me, gentlemen and ladies," he spoke with authority into the microphone, which translated his words into the native language of each of the assembled representatives. "I have one initial question to ask. If your answer is 'yes,' I will leave you to whatever it is you do. Before you respond, though, I would like to remind you that several hundred young girls in Africa have been kidnapped by extremist guerrillas, most likely to be used in the sex trade. Nothing much seems to have been done about attempting to return them to their families? I'm sure you've heard?"

Peewee glared out at rows of incredulous faces until their eyes dropped.

"If your answer to my question is no, I ask you for a few moments of your time. Please write your answer down."

Each member, as if mesmerized almost into a trance, obediently picked up their pens. A chorus of clicks, like a choir of caged crickets, resounded in the hall. Peewee's voice boomed, brazen and strong: "Do you feel the United Nations has been as successful as it should be in promoting, inducing, and sustaining fairness to all and peace in the world?" He gave them a moment. Almost simultaneously echoing through the hall was the slight slap of pens set back down, each microphone magnifying any sounds, including a cacophony of barely audible grunts and sighs.

"Thank you, esteemed representatives. Would those of you who wrote 'yes' please raise your hands."

Not a paw was lifted. Not a breath was heard. Not a head was turned. All eyes were riveted on the imposing figure standing next to the moderator.

"Well, then, let's get started," Peewee said, with surprising assurance for an interloper. "Please write down the word 'politics' . . . all of you—please."

One hundred ninety-four heads bobbed.

"Now cross the word out . . . no, put a firm 'X' through the word. Thank you. Now write 'economics' . . . thank you. Now 'X' that word out."

Peewee waited until all eyes were back on him. "One last word that may be telling. Some of you may have difficulty writing this one down, much less 'X'-ing it out. 'Oppress' . . . no, let's be more universal in our language—for clarity's sake—please write 'Bully.'" Barely audible puffs filled the microphones like fly farts.

Peewee surveyed the faces. "I see some of you have not written that word. Those of you that have, please 'X' it out . . . twice.

"Ah," Peewee said, smiling almost condescendingly. "I see several of you still have refused to write that word, much less 'X' it out. Are we defensive about the word 'bully'? Afraid to, maybe, be considered a bully? I see China, Great Britain, Russia, and the United States of America, among others, have assumed defensive postures. Being an American myself, may I ask the representative for the US of A why she has resisted writing 'bully' down?"

"Fool!" exploded a firm, not-so-feminine exhortation. "I

don't know who the hell you think you are, but I can see where this is heading. Why don't you take your insinuating questions and get the hell out of the way. Let us get on with things."

"Hmm . . . that certainly resembles something a bully might say." Again there were startled gasps, more like chicken farts this time, resounded in the room. "But, Madam, I'm sure your intentions are otherwise?" The stern madam uncrossed her arms and rose up, erect.

"Just what are you up to? What is this ridiculous game of writing words and," she behumphed into the mic, "X-ing them out? Maintaining peace in the world, in case you don't realize, is a highly complex problem, dependent on economics and politics, you blithering fool. Just what are you implying?"

"I'm implying we can simplify the 'complex' problem. Do you feel, Madam and esteemed delegates, that the UN can operate successfully in, as you dubiously coined, 'maintaining' peace, if you and the other delegates have to answer not to your own consciences but to the politicians and economic pundits in your countries? Might you agree that each country's political and economic desires might be in conflict with what's best for humanity?"

"I have no idea what you're talking about," the US delegate responded.

"Let's take a look at slavery, for an example: good for the economy, not so good for humanity. I assume you'd agree? I believe some economies in many parts of the world still rationalize slavery? You say you want me to get the hell out of the way so you can get on with things? Are you going to 'get on with' finding those kidnapped young schoolgirls, likely now sex slaves in Nigeria? A bunch of farmers armed with pitchforks and shovels are out looking for them. What chance will they have against the rifles, mortars, tanks, and bombs of the extremists who kidnapped the girls?"

"That's the obligation of their country's government to get them back!" the representative from France hurled into his microphone.

"Oh, I see," Peewee responded. He surveyed the room. "Would all of you who feel the girls' government will get them back please raise your hands."

The hand of the spirited Frenchman spiked high in the air. When he looked around and found no other hands raised, his hand slowly dropped.

"Hmm," Peewee said, raising his brows. "Not only has the government of that forlorn country not attempted to find and protect these girls from a horrendous fate, but it has also refused help from countries that offered. Would the representative from Nigeria like to respond?"

A clearing of a throat echoed in the large hall. "If we accept help from a specific country, they will expect things from us in return."

"You don't mean to imply it's 'political'? Political blackmail to be exact? What are the lives of a few hundred young females worth in the potpourri of world politics? Is that what you're saying?"

"Those . . . extremists as you called them . . . aren't all Nigerians!" the Nigerian representative exhorted. "They are criminals, composed of guerrillas from across many borders, using weapons developed in your United States and other countries . . . countries we don't trust, by the way."

Peewee perused the silent room, shaking his head. "Yes—trust. And, so, it appears it is not pragmatic for any individual country to get involved. Too much blame, suspicion, and *mis*-trust. But an impartial, unified effort from the rest of the world sounds like the ticket. A force composed of all the countries on the planet to stop atrocities by criminals or misguided fanatics? Know any organizations like this?"

Peewee held the microphone down to the moderator. "We have condemned their actions," he claimed proudly.

Peewee placed his hand over his heart. "No!" he exclaimed. "You condemned their actions? I just bet they're shaking in their combat boots."

"I find your cynicism embarrassing," the US representative, now seated but erect like she was poised on a stick, admonished. "The United States will be aligning itself with Syrian rebels to contain IS, Boko Haram, and other terrorist groups."

"Aligning with rebels to gain peace? That only makes contorted sense in the, would you say, 'complex' world of politics? Align with Syrian rebels rather than the current corrupt government? Might the rebels be just as corrupt if they gain power? But with the rebels in power it might serve the US's current political and economic desires for a while? Is that it? I'd ask the assembly if trying to impose regime change, even trying to militarily force democracy, isn't an act of 'bullying'—imposing by force?

"And then there's Russia, who is, apparently, using IS as a ploy to bomb these rebels, supporting the current cheesy dictator that the US is trying to get rid of. So, rather than unite, we don't trust each other due to self-serving political posturing. There's that all-important word again: trust. Again, it would appear we need a global partnership unaffiliated with the economic or political pandering of individual countries."

"Economic and political alliances are needed to defeat our enemies." The US representative postured as if speaking to a child. "Alliances are currently underway in the Arab states to fight terrorism. It is very complicated. I don't suspect you understand."

Peewee grinned. "Well, Mom, sorry it's so complicated and I am so naïve. I bet none of these Arab countries will have any political or economic agendas of their own? Countries that have been fighting since the beginning of time? Think these alliances will work?

"If I might take an example from history: prior to World War II, the US allied politically with Stalin. In retrospect, is Stalin, a dictator that murdered more people than Hitler—his own countrymen to boot—the example of a leader we might be proud to have aligned with? A good fellow was this Stalin? Hmm? Been pals with the Russians ever since?"

"It was necessary!" she shouted, banging her purse on the table.

"Oh, but that is my point. I'm implying that war is not necessary to peace . . . it's rather a paradox. Might we have solved a short-term problem with Stalin but created a cold, long-term one?

"It would be safe to say, I'd wager, that we cannot kill our way out of a war with the Islamic State. Like crushing an anthill: more will always take their place. Ignorance, I might suggest, is actually the enemy around the world . . . including in the US. But the enemies are certainly not these masses of poor, hungry, hopeless men and women. Dealing with educating and feeding the poor is a global problem, requiring a worldwide solution . . . and the long-term solution is not killing. What these poor, hungry, brainwashed civilians need is stability and security . . . by way of providing them with education, not guns.

"But don't get me wrong," Peewee implored. "Any country that has ever attempted to colonize, and I doubt we have few innocents in this room, was a bully, forcibly imposing its will. I certainly don't want to get into it now, but Ukraine probably agrees that bullying is still going on."

"We're imposing economic sanctions on Russia!" the US representative interjected.

"By 'we' I assume you mean the US? Now, you are complicating the matter . . . some countries support the US, some Russia—most likely for their own political and economic reasons? The East vs. the West. The EU vs. Asia . . . whatever. Divisive, not unifying. It's not a political issue. It's not an economic issue. It's a worldwide solidarity issue, and it needs to be solved by a unified world by means of a united organization that stands together. Would the delegate from Russia like to comment?"

The Russian crossed his arms. "No comment," he guffawed.

"Well, I didn't think I was being that humorous, sir. Thank you. I was afraid there for a second you were going to take your shoe off."

The Russian lost his laugh at the reference to Khrushchev's shoe-pounding escapade.

"And we can't have the US and seemingly innocuous countries like Sweden, for example, selling arms to terrorists. How absurd. Again, an issue that's obviously based on self-serving economics, not creating accord but discord, not unity of purpose but disharmony."

A soft Scandinavian-sounding gasp, like a herring burp, escaped a microphone.

"We have to put humanity before economics if we are ever to trust each other," Peewee continued.

"But certainly economics is significant to the world, especially to developing countries?" the representative from China interjected.

Peewee gazed toward the man seated primly in his chair and bowed his head politely. "I believe China's attempt at limiting the number of children a family can have was motivated by short-term and, it seems, shortsighted economic gain?

"I doubt the killing of female babies to gain economic supremacy would be condoned by Buddha? Not to mention the quandary of having a civilization that, by 2020, will have thirty million more males than qualified bearing partners. What's that going to do to the future economy of China . . . much less the state of mind of all those hapless males?" (What will China think of transgendering? Peewee resisted a smile at the thought.)

There was silence in the room.

"Please, my intention is not to be divisive—much the opposite. But if you each have your own selfish agenda, there will always be mistrust. Would you please write above the word 'politics,' 'truth.' Truth should be the primary tactic the UN utilizes. It's quite simple: if you are not truthful with each other, you'll never be effective. If you are not here to honestly seek peace in the world, you simply do not belong here.

"Above the word 'economics,' please write 'reason.' If the decisions you attempt to arrive at are based on self-interest, is this reasonable? How can you ever agree?

"And, above the word 'bully,' please write 'human solidarity.' If you, as representatives of your countries, don't have unity of purpose, we have no chance of attaining peace in the world. The representatives of the United Nations must represent the world, not their individual countries.

"Consequently, in bold, capital letters, please write 'action'!"

"It's not that simple," the delegate from the United States spouted. "Once again you illustrate your naïveté. Solving world problems is very complex."

"I agree, Madam. Wars have changed. In the past we, each country, knew who we were fighting. Heck, the British, in America's war for independence, even wore red and walked in a straight line, like they lost the flip of a coin or something, so the Americans could tell who they were shooting at and take good aim. Americans were the ones that hid behind rocks and trees . . . and they won. How can you fight an enemy you can't discern? What's simple and what I really don't understand, though, is why we can't learn from experience: Korea, Vietnam, Iraq, Afghanistan . . . wars that can't be won.

"This war with IS, Boko Haram, Al Qaeda, and the Taliban is that kind of war. It's also an ideological war, which is complex. I can't tell you how to win that kind of war. That is the job that needs to be taken on by a unified world. Extremists apparently don't mind dying a 'holy death.' Since we cannot and should not even attempt to kill them all, it seems we need to change their idea of what 'holy' means. Attack the root of the problem: ignorance."

"A dream," came a voice from the far right corner in the Palestinian guest contingent. "A pipe dream."

CHAPTER TWO

"WILLY, WILLY! ANYBODY HOME in there?" Willy twitched to attention to see his World History teacher staring down at him, the room now empty of students. "I have no idea how you get A's and do so well on my tests. I doubt you heard a word of my lecture. Maybe your friend, Peewee, who I saw out in the hall, helps you out? Hmm? Well, you better get going to your next class. Daydream in there as well, do you?"

Willy smiled sheepishly, snatched up his books, and in his odd, high, squeaky voice faked an apology. "Sorry, thir. Your lectures are so . . . um . . . intriguing, I just abthorb sufficient information almotht by osmosis. Bye. See you tomorrow." Willy had trouble with his s's, especially when he was nervous.

Willy peeked around the doorway before he slipped out into the hall, and, sure enough, Bret Piper was standing there flirting with a bunch of freshman girls that always followed him around like flies on shit. They were blocking the doorway, forcing everyone to walk around them. Willy tried to slide unnoticed behind Bret, a brutish senior who was both a washed-up hockey player and linebacker on the football team. But Bret slyly stepped back, pinning Willy between himself and the wall.

"Oh, gee whiz, thorry there, what's-your-name. Yur so puny, I didn't notice you." Bret proceeded to ruffle Willy's hair vigorously, leaving it even more disheveled than it normally was. He then spread his sizable hand around the back of Willy's neck and picked him up until he had him head-high with the girls.

"Thay, girls, ain't he just adorable?" He put Willy's face up nose to nose with one of the freshman girls. "How bout a kiss? C'mon, honey, give the little freak a kiss!" He pressed Willy's face against hers. When she turned away, Bret placed his arm on her back, restraining her, and forcibly rubbed Willy's face against her substantial, for a freshman, breasts.

Bret grinned heinously. The girl's friends laughed nervously; the girl gasped, unable to pull away. Suddenly Willy found himself released. Collapsed on the floor, oddly all he could see were Bret's feet rising as if he were suddenly full of helium. And the scream, remarkably high-pitched for such a brute, also sounded helium-inspired.

Suddenly Bret's squeal was squelched. As Willy regained his footing and equilibrium, he saw that Peewee had come up behind Bret, grabbed his jockeys in the old snuggie-bamboozle and was dangling him by them, his hand now over Bret's lost sneer, snuffing any further screams that might escape him.

Willy looked up at Bret and saw his eyes were rolling back in his head much like his testicles were probably rolling up his rectum. He slugged Peewee in the thigh and yelled, "Let the moron go, you'll drive his nuts up his athhole."

Peewee laughed at this but maintained the pose and addressed the girls. "You're all freshmen, right?"

With mouths poised in silent screams, the girls managed tremulous nods.

"Well, speaking of assholes, listen close, my little misses. Notice there are no senior women following our now ball-less Bret around. They have figured out he is one of the more profound assholes in this school, any school. It's time you learned this now as Bret is proud of bragging about defrocking young freshmen ladies . . . although it appears now you'll be safe for a while. I believe it will be some time before he will be considering even defrocking himself, if you get my drift?"

Willy punched Peewee again, as hard as he could, in the thigh, feeling like he might have broken his hand, but managed to howl, "He's gonna path out. All I can thee are the whites of his eyes!"

Peewee told the gawkers that had assembled to leave and gently laid Bret down prostrate on the floor, cushioning his head. Bret lay there curled, twitching like he had a Mexican jumping bean, not his testicles up his anus. No one was left, except for the awestruck freshmen ladies, as all others had obediently heeded Peewee's directive and headed to hour two.

"Would you," he addressed the freshman with the boobs, "please go to the nurse's office and explain that Bret here must have had a seizure." And, addressing all of them: "If you would all kindly keep this as our little secret?" They all nodded, closed their mouths, and dared one last look at Bret, who was moaning and had placed both his hands between his legs, moving them in circles as if searching for something.

"Go ladies. Please. You've learned a lesson, I hope." To the one with the maligned boobs: "Best encourage the nurse to hurry. If she asks what happened, simply say you don't know. This is how you found him. Which is exactly as you should leave him. O?"

They all had expressions like they'd visited Our Lady of Guadeloupe and seen a vision, but nodded and scampered away.

"Holy crap. You think he's ok?" Will said, watching Bret hunched up on the cream, rubber tile floor.

"He'll probably be fine eventually. Unfortunately," Peewee said, putting his arm on Willy's back and directing him toward his next class. "I thought the government was voting on some mandate to make it easier to punish bullying, much less sexual assault? I imagine they're still arguing about whose idea it was, who's to get credit, and what else to stuff in the bill. Anyway, see ya after second hour."

Willy scampered off, not wondering what his excuse would be for being late to class but wondering if Peewee had scared off Bret, or if Bret would return with a vengeance. He hoped, not for his own sake but Bret's, that he was scared off.

Willy wound his way around the maze of corridors, peaking around each corner to ensure that the coast was clear, but it appeared everyone had found their way to second hour. Willy's second hour was English. Mr. Hahn, the English teacher, was very particular about his students arriving to class on time. He generally locked the door at the bell, thus exhuming many a creative argument from the laggers. Grade-point averages could be damaged, dampening chances of acceptance at colleges of choice.

As Willy turned the final corner, to his dismay he saw two girls milling about the locked door. Fortunately, he noticed as he got closer, one was a dark beauty who intrigued Willy; the other, unfortunately, was Big Betty. Big Betty was more rancorous and embarrassing to him in her various assailments due to her being a quasi-female.

Willy strolled up apprehensively to the two. As he cautiously turned to, as he usually did, knock on the door to gain entrance, Big Betty blocked the way. "What you think yur gunna do, runt? Talk your way into class again?" And she pushed him hard enough that he dropped his books. The dark beauty, Sandy Stickner, bent to help him pick them up. Willy had wondered about Sandy. She was attractive, with long legs and long, straight black hair, but furiously shy. He noticed her frequently floating along the hall, dressed in black like a gorgeous shadow, sliding one hand along the walls, looking down. She appeared to be unaware of who or what was around her, but she always managed to notice Willy and smile in his direction before returning her gaze to the floor. She always smiled and nodded at him in class, but she had never talked to him—of course he had never seen her talk to anybody.

Betty crowed gleefully and actually kicked away one of the books that Sandy was reaching to pick up for Willy. To Willy's amazement, Sandy, as tall as Betty but with maybe half her bulk, stood up and gave Betty a pretty good shove, turning her crow into a cower as she stumbled backward. She looked like she was going to cry.

Willy had wanted to do this several times himself . . . although he knew, first of all, that he would never push, strike, or accost a woman in any fashion, no matter what the provocation, and secondly, he thought Betty could beat the crap out of him. But her acquiescence to shy, slender Sandy made him wonder at her apparent toughness. Was it a guise? Thirdly, he felt sorry for her. She was overweight, unattractive, and not the brightest bulb in the classroom. Although he was aware brutalizing him would not improve her self-esteem in the long run, he could live with it if it brightened her day. She seemed to need it. No serious harm was ever consummated.

Before anything escalated any further, Willy got an idea. As

Sandy handed him his books, he said, pseudo-enthusiastically, "Thay . . . thank you Sandy . . . I've got a suggestion. I'm late becauthe Bret Piper just had a . . . um . . . fit or, I mean, um, theizure I guess, in the hall. If you agree to saying you were there as well, you know, assisting until the nurse came, I think I can talk us all back into class. What ya thay?"

Sandy just smiled. Big Betty, who had recovered and was glaring at him said, "You better, runt, if ya wanna live." But there was not much muster behind her words, and she glanced cautiously at Sandy.

Willy approached the door and knocked on the glass window. Mr. Hahn, who looked like he was having trouble getting the attention of the class, looked over, saw Willy's head peeking up into the glass window, and looked almost relieved for the diversion. Willy was Mr. Hahn's prized pupil, so he was usually able to talk his way into class. Mr. Hahn knew the reason Willy was frequently late and had compassion for him.

Mr. Hahn came to the door and opened it a crack, smiling at Willy but looking warily at the two behind him.

"Mr. Hahn, thir," Willy started, "I'm terribly thorry for being tardy—"

"Again!" Mr. Hahn interrupted.

"Yes, thir. I must admit. But, a student, Bret Piper, had a theizure in the hallway a moment ago, and we all athisted him until the nurse came."

"Assisted? How?" Mr. Hahn seemed a trite suspicious.

"Well," Willy explained, "Sandy here pulled his tongue out . . . you see, he had thwallowed it."

He felt a little jab in his back from Sandy.

"And Betty, here, was ready to give him mouth to mouth." Willy just couldn't help himself. Betty deserved a big jab herself.

"What!" Big Betty blurted out. But she caught herself as Sandy elbowed her inconspicuously in the ribs. "What . . . else could I do? He wasn't breathing." Not a bad switch for a dim bulb.

Mr. Hahn looked at Sandy who just nodded, and then looked at Willy. "Willy, have you ever heard the story of 'The Boy Who Cried Wolf'?"

"Of courth, Mr. Hahn."

"Well, you come to me with all your tales of woe for why you're late to class. This one sounds pretty far-fetched. How do I know when you're telling me the truth? Are all those other excuses fabrications?"

Just then a paper airplane floated errantly into the side of Mr. Hahn's head, alerting him to the chaos going on behind him. "Oh, come in! But no more wild stories. If I find out this kid, Bret, is ok and nothing's wrong with him . . ."

"Oh, don't worry, thir," Willy assured him, "he's not ok and something is, indeed, wrong with him."

As the four of them entered the room, he overheard shy Sandy whisper to Big Betty, "Thank him, you hear?" And surprising him even more, (apparently) shy Sandy gave him a little pat on the butt as she slipped by him. *What was up with that?* he wondered with a smile.

On the way to his seat in the back-row corner as usual, he muttered to himself, "Boy who cried wolf, huh?"

It reminded him of what was going on in in the government. The party that wasn't in power disagreed with everything the president said. Will believed in the checks and balances of a two-party system, but if one party disagreed with *everything* from the other party, who knew when they *should* disagree? Someone needed to spank them. Tell them, "Hey, you lost the frickin' election. Get over it! Let's get on with running the frickin country." Will was going to have to get Peewee to care about the direction that big money and partisanship were taking the government. Not an easy job. But Will had a plan.

CHAPTER THREE

THAT NIGHT AFTER DINNER, Will escaped up to his room when his parents had settled in front of the boob-tube. Since it was getting so difficult for Will to breathe outside with the weather getting cold, he was thankful that Peewee, being the sentient friend he was, had helped him redesign his bedroom, making it a more enjoyable refuge. It had become a sanctuary for Will.

First they'd had to build a desk facing out the big side window. The view looked out on an ancient, gnarled oak that had ever-changing eyes and a medley of features at night, his bedroom lights creating cool images among the branches. They had wallpapered Will's walls in a continuous map of the world, the wallpaper backed by cork. Peewee told Will that, since he may not get to see the world, it'd bring the world to him.

Peewee suggested that Will devise a game where he would stand in the middle of his room, close his eyes, spin until he was dizzy, and randomly throw a dart. Wherever it stuck, Will would google and research the city, state, country, or area it landed on. This became a ritual. Every night, Will traveled the world. When he wearied of travel, he fell asleep to a novel. Of course, before he traveled every night or fell asleep reading, he now added a page to his will.

He pulled out the leather folder containing his will from its hiding place, unlocked the folder (if his mother got wind of it, she would be relentless in trying to discover what he was up to), and sat at his desk. He meditated by focusing on the shadows and dimensions created by the light from his window in the branches of the old oak. Tonight he wrote:

Oct. 1

Item #2: Elected officials have to be reminded that they work for the people, not the other way around. I believe, with all the advantages they've created for themselves, that they've lost sight of this fact. A democratic government has to benefit all of us, not just the already wealthy and powerful. I mean, really! How have they gotten away with this shit for so long? Straighten that out. The benefittin to all of us should get goin soon . . . it's only fair. Start workin on that right away. The wheels of change must be flat. Pump 'em up and get 'em rollin'. Don't look at me to figure out how to do it. You're the one sittin there.

Oh, alright. But if you want some help, you gotta listen. Well, you can't shut me up anymore anyway – what am I thinking? Since I couldn't ramble (yeah, ok, maybe rant or even preach; what can I say?) when I was with you, you're going to get an earful now. So, sit back, grab a beer or have a toke, and listen. I know you abhor politics. Like me, you aren't even convinced of what type of government is actually the best. Even though you never wanted to talk about it, I know you were as skeptical as me that any one form of effective governing is possible. I mean, honestly, a benevolent dictatorship would be the simplest (you'd make a good benevolent dictator when I think about it). But a dictatorship is really too dangerous. It's probably best to diversify power . . . to a point. Past the point that nothing can be accomplished, a lot of time would be wasted with a lot of nothing getting done at an exorbitant expense to the citizens. All those fat cats sittin around arguing. My god, how tedious. I guess if you're getting paid a ton, for life, you live with it. When you see them on TV, or wherever they're sittin, looking bored, like they're not even listening – as if there was anything interesting to listen to. A bunch of self-serving narcissists so involved in their own petty quests for power that the big picture – the future – either gets blurred in the heat of greed or, even worse, is never even considered.

If one part of the government is supposed to check the power of the other part so as to prevent the mistakes a dictator might make, that sounds cool. But if one part opposes every frickin' idea of the other part in order to make them look bad, then the country looks bad. It just doesn't work. Talk about "crying wolf!" And I know you prefer to believe that no politicians are racist, but I think there's too much "bashing the black guy" with this president. Bigoted assholes. And they're our leaders!? Well screw that.

Every brand of government probably has some good points and some bad points. So it makes sense that a good government should probably be a combination of the good points and eliminate the bad points. Look at the Scandinhoovian countries. Their people are the happiest.

Here we are – well, here you are – living life in what is called a democracy, and it's not too bad. People are free to travel, eat fast food, watch bad porn, do whatever their hearts' desire. Yes, there are way too many poor people getting poorer and a few people that are really too rich getting even richer. A great divide that seems to be growing. You always called me a "fairness freak." Well, it's unfair. A few people using their knowledge not to help others but to take advantage of them . . . and grow enormously wealthy through their con. Greedy a-holes. It's ridiculous that while a lot of people are striving to get paid ten bucks an hour, some people are making absurd amounts . . . millions and billions in one year, getting stupid rich! And sometimes by unpunished fraud. Like on Wall Street. What's up with that? The only guy thrown in prison is that Madoff character because he screwed the 1%. None of the Wall Street a-holes get any time because they only screwed the 99%.

You'd like our children to live in a country – heck, a world – that's fair. Right? Democracy is great because a person born poor isn't stuck there because of a caste or unavailability of education or whatever . . . they could advance, even get wealthy, hopefully honestly, if that's what they wanted badly enough. If a democracy claims that all are born equal, then all citizens should have the right to pursue the only thing everyone probably really wants: to be happy. (Which doesn't include burying your head up your ass and chuckling at farts.) So, democracy is cool . . . in theory. But for us all to have a chance at happiness, I'd put it to you that we need a benevolent capitalism, not what we could call our current "casino" capitalism where greed (you know, the ones with the most get 'moster' mostly by taking advantage of us), not fairness, is considered the misguided means to happiness. Agree? It even appears some people are willing to elect a president who got rich screwing people! What's up with that?

And then, speaking of presidents, it's cool that once there was a president who 'presidented' during a pretty crucial time. He was so popular, he actually got something big done that helped everyone, especially poor and older people: social security. He must have been pretty damn popular to get it called "social" because that word seems to strike fear in the cheesy hearts of Americans, due mostly to ignorance – fear and ignorance, a lethal combo.

But I think it's cool. A good dose of socialism and a good dose of democracy combined – a panacea for poor old folks and the infirm – and the prez was even a cripple. In a wheelchair no less . . . yet the public (well, almost all of them) loved him. Cool.

And then to actually have a Catholic president. Wow! Of

course someone shot him. But then a black president! I know you were as excited about that as I was. Maybe all people are born equal in the United States after all. Maybe there could even be a female president. That's maybe the best idea yet. There might be fewer wars if women ran countries.

Anyway, I know you haven't wanted to think about any of this. But someone has to do something. Roads are deteriorating, bridges collapsing, gas lines underground emitting methane gas, possibly exploding. Wouldn't that be cool, sitting there chewing on your tofu taco and BLAM! No more taco Tuesday. Parts of the country are confused: drying up, on fire, flooding, trembling. The Dalai Lama said, "Human use, population, and technology have reached that certain stage where Mother Earth no longer accepts our presence with silence."

I get a kick out of that one. What if it's true? It sure seems like it. But I know you'll say bullshit. You sometimes act like you don't want to believe in global warming either . . . but you'll get a firsthand look at that before I will.

It just blows my mind that all this shit they called infrastructure is falling apart, yet all that's happening with these senator and congressperson dudes is that they're arguing with each other about who is right and who was wrong, whose penis is bigger, and which party sucks and which is going to lead their constituents to the promised land. And while all this childish bickering is going on, we're still sending poor young soldiers all around the world to shoot people. The only thing they apparently agree on is that we have money to kill people in countries of choice but don't have enough money to fix shit at home . . . which is what our "service" men and women could be doing. When you meet with these guys, remember that since light travels faster than sound, some of these politicians might look bright . . . until you hear what they have to say.

Don't look at me like that. I'm not there, you know. You can do it. It has to be done. The Pope, whom I know you admire, as well as the Dalai, has said we have responsibilities to one another and to our planet. You know it. Sorry. If you were some doofus I wouldn't be saying this. But you, my friend, and I apologize for the cliché, can make a difference.

Guess I'm tired. The sermon is over. So it's good night. I fall asleep before I get much read these days. Oh well.

CHAPTER FOUR

AFTER 6TH HOUR WILLY ALWAYS TRIED to lose himself in a crowd of students heading toward the buses so as to be less conspicuous. Not everyone picked on him, but he was always surprised by how many, and sometimes who, felt a need to. What was their motivation? Since he felt no inclination to pick on large people, he wondered what prompted an assault; was it a way to brighten up a rainy day by attempting to be superior? He had learned to live with it knowing that in the long run it would actually make them feel inferior, like drunks who thought they needed another drink or addicts that needed a fix. He felt sorry for them. Anyway, once outside and in view of Peewee waiting for him, he breathed freely, knowing he was safe. Willy had no idea why Peewee skipped sixth hour or what he did instead, but he was always there to pick him up in order to head off to Ed's Hardware and Repair, owned by Peewee's dad, where they both worked.

It was never a problem locating Peewee's vehicle—a Westfalia version of an old Volkswagen camper-van. Peewee had explained to Will, although he had already known, that Westphalia was a town in Prussia where a treaty was signed between Europe and the Roman Empire. Peewee got a kick out of creating little metaphors like this; he said his Westfalia was a symbol that he had a treaty and was at peace with the world.

Too bad, Will had pointed out, that most of the rest of the world today had no knowledge of what had transpired in Westphalia, and they were acting like it.

Peewee had glared at Will. Tough shit, he had firmly stated. He said that *he* was aware of the treaty and that Will should remember that when he went into one of his frickin rants.

Will had just smiled. Too bad.

Will wasn't aware of Peewee ever actually going camping in his Westfalia, but he needed the headroom, and so the top was permanently popped up. Of course he'd had to modify it a bit: he'd removed part of the backseat behind the driver and installed one giant bucket, giving Peewee the legroom he deserved. Above the bucket, he had also raised the roof and installed a giant windshield, connecting it to the raised roof of the camper section, giving him the headroom and view he required. Peewee's favorite author was Ken Kesey, so he had painted the van to look like the psychedelically detailed "Kool-Aid Acid Test" van of Tom Wolfe's and Kesey's vast imaginations. Peewee, who was rather handy, had done all the work himself.

At the hardware store, Peewee was the "Repair" aspect.He could fix or create almost anything. Willy, on the other hand, wheeled a ladder around stocking shelves and assisting customers. It drove Peewee's dad nuts to have such a runt, as he called Willy, stocking shelves he couldn't reach. But Peewee prevailed; Willy was hired, and Peewee had devised an easily wheeled ladder to solve the "runt" problem.

Although the only drug Peewee allowed himself was a little marijuana now and then, as did Willy, he got a kick out of the rumors that drifted like toke around the school and community due to the psychedelic paint job on the Westfalia. The bright, psychedelic colors actually blended in well this time of year.

It was early October, and the color was good, peaking. It was a bit chilly, but both Peewee and Willy had their windows down while on the way to work. Peewee, until the dead of winter when it got well below zero, always wore a T-shirt with the name of some place he'd like to visit printed on it—today it was Hawaii. He always had a long-sleeve shirt thrown over his shoulder, which Willy noticed he always put on in school, at work, or when in restaurants or public places. He didn't have to ask Peewee why; he knew. It was always a large, loose-fitting shirt that masked his biceps and shoulders. They were almost frightening to look at. Willy knew Peewee didn't lift weights or work out. Apparently his genes didn't require him to. He always wore the shirt like a cardigan—unbuttoned.

Today the shirt was a heavier denim and was on the console between them. Peewee and his muscles seemed impervious to cold. Willy wasn't, so he pulled his little jacket tight around himself due to the brisk breeze blowing in through the open windows. Willy liked the breeze, but the cool air hurt his lungs. And he hated that he had to pull his boys'-size-L around himself to stay warm.

Willy was always looking for some way to initiate a serious discussion with Peewee, who wanted nothing to do with anything that upset his content little apple cart. Willy knew he wouldn't want to talk about what was wrong with the way the government had tilted to benefit the wealthy, but Willy knew he was partial to a black person getting elected president, so he thought he'd try this tactic: "You ever think about how cool it is that a black guy was elected president?" Will asked as they pulled away.

Peewee looked over at Will, held his gaze for a second, and

then smiled. "You're a sneaky little shit, you know? You've gotten sneakier lately. I'm not going to talk about politics or what's wrong with the frickin' government. So don't try to weasel me into it."

"But you do realize that we have a black president?"

Peewee again looked over at Will. "You know I enjoy the fact that a black dude was able to become president. He managed to do it without my help. So change the subject, asshole."

Will laughed out loud. "Kinda defensive, aren't we? You don't want to admit that a lot of his problems come from the fact that there are people, even among us, who cannot believe there's a black president?"

"You want a ride, you gotta shut up. I'm pulling over if you talk any more of that shit."

Willy shook his head. "You know Einstein once said, 'Weakness of attitude becomes weakness of character'?"

Peewee looked over at Will with that look that would paralyze most people. "He also said, 'I never think of the future—it comes soon enough.' You want a ride, shut the hell up!"

Will was impressed that his friend who wouldn't graduate from high school could quote Einstein. But Will knew when to shut up. He knew he'd be walking to work if he didn't change the subject. Thinking of earlier events in the day, Willy got that weird tweaking feeling deep in his groin when he thought of Bret Piper. Willy looked over at Peewee who was now whistling to himself. "Hey, Peewee?"

Peewee kept whistling but looked over at Willy and raised his eyebrows.

"Don't get me wrong," Willy said, "I appreciate what you did for me today . . . but messing with a guy's manhood is a little severe, wouldn't you say?"

Peewee smiled down at his little friend, somehow, through

a whistle. "What? You feeling sorry for that frickin' prick?"

"If he ever gets to use it, again," Willy pointed out.

"I think the world'd be a better place without any little Bret bastards running around in it anyway. No?"

"Well maybe a future wife might help mitigate the gene pool?"

"I bet anything if he marries, he beats his wife. That guy is a royal asshole. What he did to you today was cruel to both you and the poor little lady. He demeaned two people he thought he could bully. Hell, if his dad wasn't so rich, we could bring him up on sexual assault . . . but I'm sure the lawyers his father's money can buy would get him out of almost anything. There was that time he slugged that girl because she spit in his mouth when he dragged her into the men's room and forcibly Frenched her . . . remember? Hell, his dad backed Bret, saying it was the girl's fault. 'What was she doing in the men's room?' he'd accused. He's probably as big an asshole as his son. No, sorry kiddo. I know you don't like me running to your rescue, but that guy's balls are a menace. They needed to be tucked away in a safe place . . . appropriately, up his asshole." Peewee snickered nervously at his own little joke. "Ok?"

"I don't know. That doesn't seem in line with your treaty with the world."

"What! What you talkin?" Peewee said, "I think it'd be apropos if the next time he tried to malign one a them poor little freshman ladies again, he thinks of me and 'flup,' his balls get sucked right back up his asshole, where they'll do the least harm." Peewee looked over at Will and grinned.

Willy just shook his head. He guessed that the way Bret had been raised, he'd never had a chance to be normal, to learn how to behave decently toward people. Will settled back in his seat and closed his eyes, drifted off . . .

PEEWEE HAD DECIDED TO DEFEND HIMSELF in the trial. Bret's testicles had needed to be surgically removed from his anus. Due to a surgeon's slight slip of the scapula, Bret had been rendered impotent, his feeble balls now a useless sack. Peewee had been charged with "unpremeditated ballslaughter." He now faced a lineup of the best prosecuting attorneys money could buy.

The trial had seemed not to be going in Peewee's favor. Bret's assault of Willy and the freshman girl had been objected to by Bret's attorneys and ruled inadmissible for being irrelevant. This had gotten a huge roar from Peewee, which Bret's attorneys also objected to and was sustained by the judge who warned Peewee that he would be held in contempt if there were any more outbursts. This got a less uproarious laugh from Peewee, and the judge banged his gavel as if trying to smash an elusive tarantula about to strike.

Bret's testimony, although it involved a lot of crocodile tears and gnashing of teeth, turned out to be both unconvincing and obviously a vain attempt to gain the jury's sympathy. They could totally see right through him and concluded Bret's balls would actually be better left out of play, right where Peewee had fouled them. Words whispered among the jury, although barely audible, could be heard by Bret's gaggle of attorneys, worrying them. Words such as bastard, asshole, prick, entitled. One elderly woman, probably a little hard of hearing, had even referred to him, a little too loudly to a startled younger gentleman next to her, as a "cocksucker!"

This had reached the judge's ears as well and instigated another outbreak of gavel banging. The frazzled gaggle of barristers started to look forlorn. They realized they never should have put Bret on the stand.

When Peewee was asked to cross-examine Bret, he stood and referred to the proceedings as the "Testacalamity Case," which drew laughter from the jury and gallery as well as another gavel exhibition from the judge. When Peewee apologized and said he would simply call it "Ballsgate," the jury and gallery once again broke into laughter, and the old lady even applauded, causing yet another remarkable encore of gavel drumming, after which the judge, obviously trying to choke back a laugh, shouted, "In my chambers! All of you! Now!"

Peewee asked if that could include Mr. and Mrs. Piper. "Why not?" the judge wailed. "Let's include our foul-mouthed little old lady in the jury, as well!" When she stood up, he squawked, "I was just kidding. Sit your skinny little ass down. Now, you big son of a bitch, all you frickin' scumbag attorneys—and fine, the plaintiff's parents as well—all of you except the entitled little cah . . . plaintiff—my chambers!"

They all straggled, single file, into the chambers, Peewee following the judge, then the forlorn attorneys, followed by an indignant Mr. Piper leading his mousey little Mrs. trailing at the rear. Once in the packed room, the judge sat behind an impressive oak desk, told the lawyers to stand in the back, and seated Peewee and the Pipers in front of himself.

"Ok, Mr. and Mrs. Piper, I hope you and your legal entourage realize that the jury can see right through this boy of yours and will likely show no sympathy. I am considering throwing this blasted case right out the window. Mr. Peewee, what do you have to say?"

"Well, Your Honor. I have sympathy for Bret Piper. It's really not his fault he's so screwed up. Do you mind if I ask Mr. and Mrs. Piper the questions in here that I would have asked them in the courtroom . . . saving them from public embarrassment?"

"Go ahead," the judge said, exasperated. "State your case. But no more of your sarcasm, you hear?"

"Yes, sir. Sorry. May I direct a few questions at Mr. Piper first, Your Honor?"

"Yes. Yes. Go ahead. Proceed."

"Ok. Mr. Piper, I recall Bret was kicked off the hockey team because he was considered detrimental to the 'team.' Is that correct?"

Mr. Piper's face got beet red, and he stuck his chin out in indignation. "He was a great player. The coach and other players were just jealous of his ability."

"And then you had the audacity to hire attorneys to sue the coach, the school, the school board, I'm not sure who else, to get him reinstated."

Peewee smiled at Mr. Piper, which infuriated him.

"You're damn right I did! And it worked. He got back on the team!"

"Until he quit."

"Well, he was way too good for that Mickey Mouse team."

"I see," Peewee said calmly, still smiling. "I understand that isn't the only team he has quit. Didn't he play football as well?"

"He shoulda been the starting quarterback. They tried to put him at linebacker," Mr. Piper implored.

"So, you encouraged him to quit the team?" asked Peewee.

"You're damn right, I did. Nobody's going to screw over my kid!"

"He didn't actually quit," Mrs. Piper piped in. "He was kicked off the team."

"Hold your tongue, Loretta!" Mr. Piper warned.

Mrs. Piper looked at her lap, sufficiently castigated.

"Why was he kicked off the team, Mrs. Piper?" the judge asked, apparently taking an interest in the character formation of Bret. "And you keep your mouth shut!" the judge shot at Mr.

Piper, who was scowling at the Mrs.

"I don't recall," she mumbled into her lap.

"Listen," the judge said firmly. "This meeting in here is in lieu of a potentially embarrassing court proceeding. Mrs. Piper, it's best if you answer my questions. Mr. Piper, you will refrain from any admonishing words . . . or glances."

"Hey, I can look at my wife if I want to."

"Fine. Do so and I would be more than happy to find you in contempt." Mr. Piper looked at the judge with contempt. "I believe we're getting an idea here of why Mr. Peewee felt it appropriate to . . . reprimand your son. Although your gaggle of goons managed to twist the law and get what preceded Peewee's reprimand inadmissible. Yes, I am aware of what your son had done to the girl and that little guy. This should be a sexual assault case."

"Reprimand?" Mr. Piper wailed. "He may have ruined my son's manhood."

"Oh, I think you're the one that may have done that," the judge returned calmly. "Now, Mrs. Piper, why did your son get kicked off the football team?"

"Well," she started, obviously afraid to look over at her husband, who was now twitching nervously, trying with considerable difficulty not to look toward his wife, "he was also asked to leave the hockey team again. He told his father he quit . . ."

"What?" the question shot like an arrow from the quivering mouth of Mr. Piper.

"That's a thousand dollars. The next outburst or abusive look will be five thousand, the next, ten. Three strikes and you're out, or I should say 'in.' You follow my drift, Mr. Piper?" The judge almost looked amused.

Mr. Piper glowered at him.

"Continue, please, Mrs. Piper," the judge encouraged.

She looked at Peewee now. "You know, he might have been good at both sports. He lifts weights religiously. His father has an entire gym in the basement. So, the way hockey is played these days, he couldn't score, but he probably could have made a decent defenseman. But he wasn't, or I should say, his father wasn't happy unless he was centering the first line."

"You sound like you know your sports, Mrs. Piper," Peewee interjected.

Mrs. Piper smiled. "Well, yes. I had brothers who were excellent—"

"Excellent?" Mr. Piper, who had been perspiring and twitching almost uncontrollably like he'd had a wallop of wasabi up his ass, couldn't restrain himself. "They stunk!" he almost screamed, his voice becoming high-pitched, eyes piercing his wife like daggers.

The judge shook his head almost sadly. "Since that little scene included *both* an outburst and an intimidating look, we've got strike two and three . . . meaning an additional fifteen thousand dollars. The next incident, short of palpitating and perspiring, and you'll be taken directly to the hoosegow. Is that understood, Mr. Piper?"

Mr. Piper just continued to scowl. An alarming twitch had set upon his eyes, his head nodding with each twitch like a bipolar woodpecker.

Peewee picked up the conversation. "Please continue, Mrs. Piper."

Mrs. Piper, who had been doing a stand-up job of not crying, wiped a tear from her eye and managed a smile at Peewee. "I think he might have made a good linebacker, as well . . . for the same reason. He seemed to have this pent-up anger inside of him. He could make crushing tackles. Of course, you can't throw a touchdown pass from the linebacker position."

"So what happened?" Peewee asked.

"Well, according to my brothers . . . one who was a college football player, the other a college hockey player!" she tossed at Mr. Piper.

"Best not provoke him," Peewee said, and winked at her. "We wouldn't want him behind bars."

"Well," Mrs. Piper started and winked back at Peewee, "not only were they both college players, but . . ."—she looked defiantly at her husband—"they could both score!"

Mr. Piper was unable to control himself. He rose from his chair, his eyes blinking wildly, his head bobbing sharply at each blink, his mouth forming grotesque shapes emitting no more than untranslatable sputter.

The judge hollered, "Sit, you fool!" He stood, himself, and gave the Mrs. a crooked grin as he passed, opened the door to his chambers, and beckoned two guards to come in. After the judge whispered something in one guard's ear, Mr. Piper was cuffed, read his rights, and escorted from the room all the while twitching, bobbing, and muttering unintelligibly. The gaggle of barristers all rolling their eyes.

After things had calmed down and the judge had resumed his position of power behind the massive oak desk, he took a deep breath and nodded to Mrs. Piper, who continued, "My brother said Bret wasn't coachable. Bret was never good at taking direction . . ."

"I wonder why," the judge interjected, spouting a little sarcasm himself.

"When the coach, and even the players, tried to talk to him, he'd tell them to 'F off,' excuse my French."

"Oh, that word's pretty much the same in any language," Peewee said, and all in the room snickered, including the previously mute members of the bar lining the back wall, partially dissipating the pent-up tension in the room caused by Mr. Piper's spasmodic, nearly epileptic tantrum.

"Mrs. Piper, I'm starting to understand Bret's baneful and self-destructive behavior," Peewee said soothingly. "I truly am sorry for the exuberance of the reprimand . . . the snuggie. Although, I was rather appalled at his behavior."

"Someone has to hold him accountable," she responded. "His father has blamed it on your friend, Willy, and the girl. I am a bit concerned about any future grandchildren being in the picture, however."

Peewee grimaced.

"So, apparently, he has not been held accountable for his transgressions in the past?" the judge asked.

"Well, I tried," Mrs. Piper said, once again speaking to her lap. "But, really, I had to give up pretty early. From a young age he learned, for example, that he didn't have to pick up after himself. If I asked him to pick up his room or the mess he had made in the living room, he would just laugh at me. He knew that when his father got home, I would be the one reprimanded for not keeping a clean house. I learned early that my threats or consequences for bad behavior were useless because I couldn't follow through on them. You know, once you say 'do this or else' and there is never an 'or else,' you lose any semblance of control or influence. Maybe if we had had more children, it would have been different. I don't know, but I doubt it." She looked up at Peewee. "I'd like to think the consequences he faced by your hand would make him realize that that kind of cruel, anti-social behavior is not acceptable, and I believe there should be consequences for bullying. I am sorry; I am embarrassed . . . but, well, you can see why a snuggie," she almost managed a smile, "won't help. In his eyes, the way he has been raised . . ." she started now to sniffle, "the way Bret sees it, you're the transgressor. Your little friend is just weak and deserved it, and the girl was asking for it . . . you know—following him around," she left off, now starting to cry.

Peewee handed her a hanky. "Does your husband not see the error of his ways? You seem to be well off, financially. Mr. Piper must be somewhat intelligent, even if he doesn't act like it, to make that kind of money?" Peewee gave her another little grimace.

Everyone in the room gave out a little gasped at the slight. Mrs. Piper wiped her eyes, choking back a sarcastic laugh, and looked forlornly at Peewee. "You're sweet . . . and naïve. My husband has not been very successful in business, even though he puts in long hours trying. Our money comes from his father, who was quite successful and worked himself into his grave at an early age, paying very little attention to his only son but leaving him a tidy inheritance. I never met my mother-in-law. She was long gone before I came into the picture. I'm afraid it's the story of the cat in the cradle and the silver spoon. A pitiful trait passed from father to son."

"Yet, you've stood by your husband all these years?" Peewee asked gently.

"Oh, I've left several times. As you saw, my husband has a temper." Eyes again cast down.

"Yet . . .?"

"I felt guilty about Bret. He's my son. I want to love him. So I always come back." She looked up at Peewee again. "I wish he had a teacher or a friend . . . someone who might have a positive impact on his behavior. But he seems incapable of making or keeping real friends . . . his temper."

Peewee smiled down at Mrs. Piper, realizing that she was the real victim.

WILLY JERKED TO, A LOUD RAP on the passenger window next to his ear alerting him to reality. There was Peewee smiling and shaking his head. Willy quickly opened the door, and they walked side by side into the store, looking like Mutt and Jeff, or in this case, Wee Willy and Podigious Peewee.

Driving Willy home after work, Peewee figured he'd better keep the conversation going before Willy drifted back off to wherever he always went. Peewee thought it might be interesting to go there with him sometime, but Willy would never expose the adventures of his mind, knowing Peewee would not approve of being depicted as a hero, the instrument for change in the world. But Peewee enjoyed talking to Willy and felt guilty about cutting him off before on their way to work. He was the most interesting and, often irritatingly, well-informed person he knew . . . when he was alert and dealing with reality.

"So," Peewee started, "you still upset about my disposition of justice with Bret today?"

"I thought you were going to kill him. His eyes were rolling back into his head."

"He could use a little introspection, anyway."

Willy looked over at Peewee and laughed. "I'm sure his life flashed behind his eyes. Can you see his obituary? 'Here lies Bret, who lost his balls as well as the game.'"

Peewee laughed but said, "Weak, buddy, weak. You can't come up with something better than that?"

"I'll think about it. You ever think about your own obituary?"

It was Peewee's turn to look over at Willy. He figured the little prognosticator had his own all figured out, and Peewee didn't like talking about Willy's questionable future. "Nope."

"You know I think that's why people want to believe in a god, that there's an afterlife."

He didn't want to talk about this either, but he bit anyway.

"Yeah?"

"Well, everyone would like to see who comes to their funeral and hear all the nice things people will say about them. Give their life credence, you know? Validate themselves. If there's no afterlife, where's the validation?"

Peewee smiled, even though he didn't want to. "An interesting concept, you little philosopher. So, you got yours all figured out? I would have assumed you didn't believe in an afterlife? Heaven or hell?"

"Well, who the hell knows about heaven? But I got plans." Willy glanced at Peewee, who was chuckling at his friend's corny sense of humor. "You'll see."

"*I'll* see?" Peewee said.

"'Yip,' as you like to say. So, I want to make sure I've attained heaven before I die."

"What? How the hell you going to do that?"

"I told you, I got it planned. You'll see."

"See what? Never mind. Let's change the subject, H. W."

Peewee's dad always called Willy "H. W." when he was yelling at him. When Peewee had asked his dad why, he told him that on the application the name he had given was H. William Mitty. Every time Peewee had asked Willy about the "H," Willy had cleverly deferred, changing the subject. Peewee tried again today. "Alright little guy. You want a ride home today, you gotta tell me about your 'H.'"

"Look at those two girls over there!" Willy pointed out as they turned down his block. "Man, when they wear those tights as pants, your imagination is only a fraction of an inch away from reality. Can't believe mothers . . . or more like the fathers . . . let 'em out in public like that. It's almost like body paint. Nice legs and butt on that one, but somebody should tell the other to look at herself in the mirror. Ya got a fat, flabby butt, ya gotta mask it, not show it off."

"It's the Kardashian Influence," Peewee said. "Some guys like big women with big booties."

"Well not me, especially mottled, lumpy ones. They scare me. And Kardashian's ass is inflated."

Peewee laughed. "Inflated? What you talkin' about?"

"You know, buttox."

Peewee roared. "That's pretty good if I don't say so myself. Buttox! Pretty good."

"You know who I'd like to see in one of them tights?"

Peewee looked askance at Willy. This wasn't a typical conversation topic for his friend. They rarely talked about girls, sex . . . Peewee wondered what was up. Usually he wanted to discuss or rant about fixing something that was broken with the universe. "Well, I'm guessing it ain't your sister."

"Ahh . . . thanks for that image. It'll probably keep me awake all night. If there's one person in the world who shouldn't wear tights—unless they're under something . . . like a muumuu, which she has an abundance of, thanks to my mother—it'd be her."

"Why in the devil would your sister have an 'abundance' of muumuus? Ain't they Hawaiian?"

"Well, not just Hawaiian, but, yeah, that's where these're from. My parents used to go to Hawaii every year, and my mother recognized that my sister would be a big girl, and that's what the big Hawaiian women wear. I think she must be smart enough to avoid embarrassing herself."

"It is weird your sister's so . . . corpulent." Peewee looked over at Willy and grinned. "Is that a bad word to use?"

Willy laughed. "Well, it's appropriate."

". . . and you're such a small fry. How's 'small fry'?"

"Appropriate."

"Any idea why the discrepancy? Something to do with the 'H'?"

"Aren't you curious about whose rear end I'd like to see silhouetted in form-fitting leggings?"

Peewee squinted at Willy. "Alright. I'll bite."

"Yeah, you'd probably like to. I'd like to."

"Well, who? Spit it out, small fry."

Willy wanted to create suspense, get Peewee really interested. Willy had been interested in Sandy since he first saw her this year . . . a delicious dark shadow floating down the hall. He assumed they would be kindred spirits. He hadn't understood the little pat on his ass today. That would probably keep him awake that night. But he was smart enough to know a beautiful, maybe 5′10″ babe, would not be interested in a 4′7″ small fry. So next best thing would be to play matchmaker. Willy knew Peewee was only interested in being friends with the extra-large ladies. He enjoyed toying with them because it made them and him feel good. But he didn't date them . . . of course he hadn't really dated anybody as far as Willy knew. With the exception of what Peewee did during his first and sixth hours of school, dating was about the only taboo topic between Peewee and Willy. Since Willy wasn't exactly on the dating circuit himself he figured that was fine. If Peewee got involved with a girlfriend, what would Willy do, anyway? But this was going to have to change, eventually, for Peewee, Willy knew. So since he wasn't going to be dating Sandy himself, why not Peewee? But would Peewee clam up with Sandy, like he did with the other dazzling beauties?

"You disappear into that head of yours, again? I wish you'd let me in there sometime. I'm curious to know where you go."

Willy just smiled and said, "Be patient. Thandy Thickner . . . I mean Sandy Stickner."

"Sandy Stickner?" Peewee said, incredulously. "Hey, you lisped saying her name. What's up with that?"

"She makes me nervous, but, of course, her name is not Thandy Thickner. Know who she is?"

"Of course I know who she is. You can suddenly turn that lisp on and off when you want to now? I've never seen that before."

"Maybe now you're going to start seeing a lot of things you've never seen before. Why 'of course'? You've never mentioned her."

"Why would I? She scares the crap out of me. I'd probably lisp or stutter too, trying to talk to her. What you talkin' about? What you mean, 'Seeing things I've never seen before'?"

"You'll see. She 'scares' you, you say?"

"Well, yeah! Shit. She's spooky. What you mean 'I'll see'? See what?"

"Why spooky?"

"Well, mysterious then. Dark . . . not sinister, but—almost spiritual."

"Spiritual? That's an odd take."

"Well, she practically floats down the hallways, dragging her hand against the wall, not lookin' at nobody. She's usually dressed in black, like a wondrous shadow."

"Wondrous, huh?" Willy perked up. He hadn't expected this. They had never mentioned her to each other before.

"Well, yeah. She's gorgeous," Peewee said. "Well, not really gorgeous, she's too unusual to be gorgeous . . . almost exotic."

Willy almost leapt when he heard "exotic." Exactly what he thought. "You ever talk to her?"

"God, no. You kidding? I told you, she scares the crap out of me. I've never seen her talk to anybody."

"Wouldn't you enjoy seeing her long legs and exotic behind

wrapped tightly in leggings?" Willy asked, really surprised Peewee was so aware of Sandy.

"You know . . . I never thought of her that way. She seems almost too . . . ethereal—is that the right word—to think of sexually."

"My, my. Wondrous and now ethereal? Well, I talked to her today. She's also nice."

"YOU talked to her?"

"What?" Willy said, indignant. "*I* ain't afraid of her, you big ox. Maybe in my head, in some ways, I'm bigger than you are!"

Peewee actually believed that. "Sorry. Sorry there, Goliath. "

"Know who else is afraid of her?"

"No, who?"

"Big Betty."

"No way, José!"

"Yup. Since you weren't around, Sandy stood up for me against Betty. Helped me pick up my books when the big B pushed me and I dropped em. And then gave Betty a good shove. Almost made her cry. I don't think Betty is as tough as she pretends to be. You ever had any run-ins with her? She'd certainly qualify as one of your entourage."

"Nah. She ignores me. I don't think I'd like her."

"The other ladies in my 'entourage' don't appear to either. How about Sandy? Would you like to meet her?"

"What? How?"

"I think we're gonna be friends. I can tell. Know what she asked me?" Willy was being as surreptitious as he could, hoping to create the necessary anticipation.

Peewee looked warily at Willy. "What?"

"This will probably keep *you* awake tonight. She asked if I would introduce you."

"What! Christ, whaddya tell her?"

"I said you wouldn't be interested, that you were gay."

"What!" Peewee backhanded Willy on the arm. "You didn't?"

"Ow! Take it easy. Jesus Christ, I think you broke my arm."

"Sorry, Casanova, but I would break more than your arm if you told her that."

"Dammit. My arm hurts. Here's my house . . . why are you driving past my house?"

Peewee slowed but kept on going, looking over at Willy. "So, you didn't tell her that?"

"No, of course not."

"Well, what did you tell her?"

"That I'd introduce you two, but that you were really shy."

"What'd she say?"

"'That makes three of us.'"

"Three?"

"You, me, and her, you fool. Now, turn around and take me home."

"Only after you answer my question," Peewee said, stopping the car at the end of the block.

"What question is that?"

"Thought I'd forget again, didn't ya, Shrimp? After yet another diversion."

"Forget what?"

"Don't play dumb. What's the 'H' for?"

Willy looked away, out the window, conjuring up the courage to talk about it. "I was born premature, as you know. Only weighed three pounds . . . but you know that, too. Why I'm not like my sister I suppose."

"Yeah, of course."

"I wasn't supposed to live through the day. So my parents named me Hau . . . H-a-u, Hau William."

Peewee paused, recognizing how difficult this was for his

friend to talk about. "Hau?"

"Yes, Hau. Hau is a Hawaiian flower that blossoms in the morning light and dies at dark. It only lives one day."

Peewee sat still for a moment then put his hand over on Willy's shoulder, patting it gently before he turned the car around and dropped Willy off. When Willy stepped down out of the gaudy, jacked-up Westfalia, Peewee yelled to his best friend, "Hey, Hau. See you tomorrow."

CHAPTER FIVE

WILL MADE IT TO SCHOOL with only a minor skirmish with some sophomore guys at the bus stop. His trip to his locker and first-hour World History was uneventful except for the usual bumps and smirks as students walked past him. He hadn't seen hide nor hair of Bret. He made English on time, sharing a smile with Sandy on his way by her. Big Betty even managed a smile as he slipped into his seat behind her. He closed his eyes when Hahn's lecture started on grammar, something he's known since fourth grade. Hahn's statement yesterday about crying wolf came back to him. He closed his eyes and drifted off . . .

PEEWEE, AFTER BEING CHIDED by his wise friend, finally agreed that the government was currently run mostly by idiots. There was no incentive for the elected hooligans to fix what had become a comfortable status quo. The voters had to get off their asses and realize that it was up to them to change the dumbass shit that had been going on too long. It seemed so many "citizens" had either given up, resigned to rolling over and playing the victim, or others felt helpless and had become resigned, apathetic, not giving a crap. They hid out in technology. Played fantasy games because they thought they could win there. They needed to be made aware that changing to a new version of their tablet made no significant difference in the real world. Bitching about insignificant trivialities on social media while no one really cared was pathetic. If they were disillusioned with how government was functioning and affecting them, they needed to wake up and realize that the power to actually change things was in their hands. Since the president had pointed out: "Our destiny isn't decided for us, but by us," Peewee figured he ought to acknowledge his agreement. His friend and mentor had suggested he try to convince the public that they actually had control of their destiny and suggested he gave it a shot by talking to the prez. Somebody had to start doing something or nothing would change.

Peewee had acquired a fake Secret Service badge and had it pinned to his dark gray suit coat. Peewee usually carried a smile around, which was genuine as he was usually amused. He was aware his presence intimidated people. The smile often eased their apprehension. But when he glowered, he discouraged interaction. With his size, composure, and confidence, no one was tempted to argue with him when he was pissed. So he looked pissed all the way to the Oval Office. No one, including the cool-looking Secret Service guys, noticed the fake plastic badge, only that there was one. (Maybe if they didn't wear sunglasses all the time they could see better?) All they really saw were Peewee's eyes glaring down at them, and no one was going to confront him.

When Peewee walked into the Oval Office, the main man looked up. "Well, hello," the president said, managing an unsettled little smile. "I am more than a little surprised to see you in here without . . . well, without at least being announced. My, you are an impressive fellow. I doubt anyone in the hallways missed you. And, umm, that Secret Service badge looks like you got it out of a Cracker Jack box."

Peewee laughed. "I apologize for interrupting you, Mr. President. Please don't be alarmed. I am here on account of a friend of mine insisting . . . and he's very insistent. May I say, we are both impressed with the concerts you hold here at the White House for PBS viewers?"

"Well, thank you. My wife and I enjoy them very much ourselves. Listen, I go on in less than fifteen minutes." He looked down at the papers on his desk, which Peewee assumed was his speech to the nation. All of Washington would be there, as well as millions of viewers around the world.

"Sir, I am going to make a rather unusual request."

"Well, that doesn't surprise me. You must be a rather unusual fellow to have gotten in here making any kind of request."

Peewee grimaced and scratched his head. "May I have a few minutes of your time tonight on camera to say something from the point of view of the citizens of the United States . . . well, really, citizens of the world?"

The president leaned back and studied Peewee. "That is an interesting request."

"My friend," Peewee continued, "insists that changes desperately need to be made here in the US and possibly in countries from which your viewers will be watching."

"I won't argue with you there. You think you'll have better luck than me?"

"Well, maybe, since I'm not political and not caught up in the complexity of politics. This little friend of mine is a pretty smart guy. He says to keep it simple. That most complex problems have simple solutions."

"Hmm . . . he doesn't sound like a 'little' guy. Maybe he's only little in stature compared to you? Simple, huh? I like that."

Peewee smiled. "Yes, only little in stature. Yes—simple. He believes 'complexity is the harbor of scoundrels,' sir."

The president laid his head back and laughed quietly. He looked back evenly at Peewee. "A few minutes, huh?"

"Yes. May I say I believe you are an honest, smart man who means well. My friend's only complaint, he wanted me to pass on to you, is that nobody on Wall Street got thrown in jail for the most egregious fraud in history, causing not only the Great Recession here but also causing a global crisis. He can't believe they got away with that without punishment. My friend can be very adamant."

The pres grimaced. "A lot of changes need to be made, which includes in the justice system. Some people just have too much money to get beat in court. I agree with your not-little-friend: some people should have been skinned alive for the harm their greed caused people. Yes, changes have to be made for our world to be fair."

"Maybe after I explain my friend's plan, some of those changes will be easier to accomplish."

"Well, you've got your request. I'm very curious about this plan of your friend's . . . and we better get going."

The president, followed by Peewee, came on stage to vigorous applause from half the audience and vague, half-assed applause from the other half. Rather than approach the podium, the president sat, to everyone's surprise, in a seat alongside the vice president, speaker of the house, and some other pompous assholes holding positions that temporarily required a show of respect.

When Peewee approached the podium the applause quickly

subsided. Everyone's jaw dropped at the vision of such an imposing figure facing them. Rather than smile to the cameras, Peewee glared at the disrespectful half of the audience. Some had little red bow ties. Some had leers like leeches stuck to their faces. Some wore scowls like medals. But all couldn't help shrinking into their seats at Peewee's glare. They knew their lack of welcome for their president was rude and deep down in their genes felt guilty about it. They knew that although historically their predecessors previous had also argued vehemently about issues, they had respected each other and even frequently shared laughter over a brandy Manhattan. But acrimony had replaced camaraderie—one of the primary reasons it was so difficult to get anything accomplished in government. That and the fact that the senators and representatives, although quite sufficiently compensated, for life, were rarely in Washington—like a day and a half each week—like running the country was a part time job that they did when they weren't raising money by kissing asses or out campaigning so that they could get re-elected and campaign some more. Total bullshit. Hardly an efficient way to run a government. Peewee figured this required a snarl, not a smile.

His eyes seemed to burn into the audience and the camera. The figurines in the room and the people of the world held their breath. "I have three questions," he stated with a vigor that gave pause to all. "If a majority answers to the affirmative, I will leave you to your politics and pandering. If you don't answer to the affirmative, I have a suggestion for the citizens of the United States of America to consider and the world to observe . . . to observe that democracy can be a fair-to-all form of government run by honest leaders who have the interests of the citizens foremost in their minds . . . as I hope you agree it should be. Firstly," Peewee paused, "if you feel the elected officials of the US government always act ethically, please raise your hand."

Several hands started to go up but paused as heads turned, and then dropped—hands and heads both.

"Secondly, if you feel the representatives of the Senate and House of Representatives always speak the truth in their official capacity, please raise your hands." This time no hands moved; no heads turned—only dropped once again.

"Lastly, if you feel your compatriots put aside personal gain and always vote for the greater good of all Americans, not their special interests, raise your hands?" All heads stayed bowed.

Peewee smiled at their sanctimoniousness. "Thank you for being, ironically, honest. Ironic, because if I had asked how many of you as individuals act ethically, always tell the truth in an official capacity, and work selflessly for the people of the United States, you would all have adamantly waved your hands . . . thus proving my point. Might you call this hypocrisy? It has always amazed me how you can all bash and dig up dirt on each other, even when you're running for an endorsement from your own party, so that it would appear that none of you are worthy of representing anything or anybody, much less the United States government.

"I'm sorry; I digress. I'm told politics is 'complex' and thus hard to fix when broke. I don't think there's much of an argument that it's broke. The public, your employers, according to the polls, think it's broke. So, even if you fat cats think everything is hunky-dory, your charade should be over. My suggestion is to make it simple: before any official is sworn into office, a lie-detector test, or maybe we should call it a 'Truth Detector,' is to be given centered around the answers to a few fundamental questions regarding the necessary behavior for positions of authority.

"If you believe that this is farcical, as I can see on many of your faces, and that you've got nothing to worry about from this naïve simpleton standing in front of you, let me remind you that the people you work for—yes, you work for them, me, not the other way around—are watching. You should be careful how you treat your assistants, your errand boys, the public—they are your employers. They are watching . . . and waiting. Waiting for change, for things to improve.

"If they happen to agree with my 'reason' for this test, the 'truth' that it will reveal, and the national 'solidarity' it could create and if you want to be reelected or maintain your office, you must submit to the Truth Detector and answer to your employers. Since you're so adamant about 'testing' in schools, I assume you wouldn't object to this little test? Anyone who wants to represent our country must prove they are worthy. If your employers agree with what I have to say, I'm guessing we may not be seeing many of you around here anymore. I apologize for sounding cynical, but in actuality I believe I am just being a realist. If you believe in your oath to serve your country—not yourselves—you would acquiesce to taking the Truth Detector.

"Here are the questions I recommend be presented to you:

"First: Do you see yourself as a: Democrat, Republican, Independent, or American? (Take note there is only one correct answer.)

"Second: Would you vote for a qualified candidate if he/she were Catholic, poor, Muslim, black, female, handicapped, Hispanic, Asian, Republican, homosexual, transsexual, Democrat, short, or all of the above? "Note: To help you out—again, there will be only one correct answer for each question. You've been forewarned. Now you have plenty of time to convince yourself you'll be telling the truth . . . or to change. (Good luck with that.)

"Third: You will attest that you will never: take a bribe, bribe someone, sell your Senate seat, vote 'no' when you believe 'yes,' vote 'yes' when you believe 'no,' vote against something solely because of 'party line,' vote for something solely because of 'party line,' lie intentionally in an official capacity, misrepresent the meaning or intent of an issue intentionally, or create a law or present a bill that benefits only a special interest group, or yourselves, to the detriment of the majority.

"In addition, you will agree to take the Truth Detector test at any time in the future, answering 'I never have . . . '

"Note: The questions do not refer to the past. I'm guessing few if any of you would have passed. Again, I hate to appear cynical, but this gives you a reprieve, a chance to change your ways if necessary. If you are representing fairly the citizens of the United States, you all should be able to pass this test. If you fail, adios. And good riddance."

Peewee stared hard at the employees in the room. "Can you argue that passing this Truth Detector test wouldn't make you a more effective leader of the country, a better representative for your constituents—which, remember, is a poor synonym for 'employers' or 'boss'—and lead to a more effectively-run government?"

Peewee looked directly into the camera. A broad smile lit up the viewers' screens. "So there we have it. Please remember that you out there in TV Land and I are the employers here. We employ and pay these people." Peewee swept the room with his arm, directing the cameras to scan the figurines, some as unmoving and stiff as if made of plastic, others smirking arrogantly.

"In any organization, be it in government or the private sector, it's up to the employers to make decisions that improve the operation of the outfit. If you have untrustworthy, inefficient employees it's your job to get rid of them. I'm sure many of you around the world watching may want to follow suit." Peewee paused, gazing into the camera.

"As simple and obvious as it is that we need honest people running our country, do you feel, unless we demand it, that change is going to happen? We need elected officials to build a fair and sustainable system now—for us and for our children and grandchildren. This bullshit has gone on long enough."

Peewee glared once again at the audience. In spite of many condescending smirks, no one dared look directly at him or say anything.

Peewee turned to the president, who had a sparkling grin on his face, leaned in, and whispered something in his ear. The president looked up at Peewee, shrugged, and then nodded.

Peewee turned back to the cameras. "The president and I will get together and arrange, somehow, a national referendum. If the consensus among the employers of this sheepish lot—you, the citizens of the United States—is that what I have proposed is a good idea, I believe we all, in a vote of solidarity, can affect positive change in our lives and in our country. The president himself has said, 'Our destiny isn't decided for us, but by us.' It's our duty to ourselves and our children. Our duty to set an example for the world. How can we say that the leaders of countries like Iran and North Korea are lying about creating nuclear weapons, that Putin is not being truthful about Ukraine or Syria, when our own employees that we've hired to take care of our own country are full of shit, dishonest . . . lie themselves? Lie to us? Lie to the world? There never will be world peace until we trust one another. The Dalai Lama, a wise man, has told us, 'In our struggle for freedom and peace in the world, truth has to be our only weapon.' So . . . "

"MOON TO RUNT! MOON TO RUNT!" Willy jerked alert to see Big Betty standing over him, arms barely able to fold over her expansive bosom. "Where's your head at, runt? I don't know where you go . . . ?"

"Probably to a happier place where he doesn't get picked on." Softly spoken words interrupting Betty's brashness. The gentle and comely face of Sandy peeked around the broadness of Betty.

"Well?" she said softly and nudged Betty, who pitched forward, frightening Willy. She could do grievous damage landing on him.

"Thanks, uh . . ." She pitched forward a second time and tossed Sandy a look over her shoulder. "Thanks, Willy, for getting us out of that jam with Mr. Hahn. I guess you're not so bad."

Willy could tell it pained her to say this. She made him sad.

"I just feel sorry for you," she added.

Will looked closely at her. He felt she was trying to be sincere. "Why feel sorry for me? I feel sorry for you."

"Oh, how come?" Betty asked, frowning.

Will didn't know how much further he should go with this conversation. He had already insulted her, although she didn't seem to be aware of it. He thought he'd try a little trite moralizing. See if it would make a difference. "People generally feel better about themselves when they help somebody, not put them down."

"Oh, yeah. I suppose. Hmm . . . you're probably right. Well, see ya around," Big Betty said, and turned to leave. Willy bit his tongue and didn't say, "I hope not." Betty left, leaving all of long, tall Sandy in view.

"C'mon Will. Let's head to lunch," Sandy said, and held out her hand, pulling him up.

Neither spoke until they reached the raucous lunchroom, for once without incident. Willy started to thank her, when she interrupted and asked, looking down, suddenly unsure of herself, when he would be introducing her to Peewee. Some food, flung from afar, went flying by their heads. Willy said to come along; Peewee would be saving a place for him at a lunch table now. She said, "No, that's ok. Just sometime. See you around." And she glided away.

Willy wished she hadn't declined as he was less likely to find trouble in the lunchroom with her by his side. But he spotted Peewee's head high above the others, grabbed a tray and food and hurried in his direction. No jerk tripped him, spat on his plate, or stole his dessert. He found Peewee, with a space at his side for Willy, at a table full of larger ladies—some tall, some with big frames, some athletes, some cute, some not—but all confident and, although towering over Willy, always nice to him and, really, quite funny. This crowd was not unusual. They flocked to Peewee, mutually beneficial allies by surrogacy. Willy liked this about Peewee. He flirted with and teased them, and they loved it. Here was the most eligible, sought-after guy in the school, and to them he was theirs for a while. But he seemed to have his heart his heart set on some mysterious woman he wouldn't disclose to Willy

As Willy set his tray down and settled into his spot, Peewee had just finished saying something to them, and they all screamed in delight. The one next to Peewee slapped him on the arm. The big girls certainly loved Peewee. He made them feel good, and, Willy supposed, they didn't feel as big around Peewee. In general Peewee was shy around girls. The popular, pretty ones were always coming up with some excuse to talk to him, but Peewee was constipated by beauty . . . or maybe popularity. He just closed up.

In a lull, Willy told Peewee there was somebody he wanted him to meet, but before he could finish, Celine, a cute, popular cheerleader-type tapped him on the back. Ignoring Peewee's entourage, she stood on her tiptoes and, leaning against him, whispered in his ear.

Peewee's eyes opened wide. He turned to face her, smiled sadly, and shook his head. "Sorry," he said. Celine, pouting, shuffled away. No one could understand or accept Peewee's affinity for the larger girls . . . even harder to understand was his loyalty to Willy the Runt.

The big girl that had slapped Peewee's arm made a big scene of rubbing her breasts against Peewee and whispered something in his ear that got a burst of laughter from him. Willy figured he'd wait until after school when he had Peewee's attention to tell him about Sandy's request. She was much prettier and more striking than Barbies like Celine . . . almost, Willy thought, yes—exotic: dark and lissome—a more quiet beauty. Would Peewee clam up in front of her? Willy hoped not. All Willy knew was that if he were Peewee, he would be on it like dust to a star. He wished he could find a miniature version of Sandy for himself.

CHAPTER SIX

WILLY WOKE A LITTLE LATE and grabbed a couple slices of peanut butter and jelly toast for breakfast. His dad had already left for work, and now that his sister was off at college, his mom slept in. Willy tried to convince himself it didn't really bother him that, if his sister was still at home, his father wouldn't have left yet and his mother would be up making more than toast for breakfast. It wasn't that they loved his sister more, it was that they didn't dare love him too much. Similar to raising a calf to slaughter, you didn't name him. You couldn't allow yourself to get attached. Willy tried to understand.

Although Willy had lived, he was born so immature as well as premature that all of his organs hadn't developed fully . . . and never would. One lung only functioned partially and neither very well. The same with his kidneys, and one chamber of his heart was overdeveloped, too large, from a leaky mitral valve. The doctors wouldn't consider surgery on his heart or lungs—too risky considering his susceptibility to other organ problems—nor put a prognosis on how it affected his life expectancy. But Willy was told it wouldn't be "normal." *Well, who wanted to be normal?* Willy rationalized. But if he wanted to do something to satisfy the responsibility he took seriously, to help make the world a better place, he definitely felt an urgency. He would like to have felt there was no hurry and that the pain in his lungs, his shortness of breath, and weak heartbeat were temporary and he would grow out of them. Every night before he tossed his dart at the world, he would blow into his Voldyne meter, which measured the inspired volume in his lungs. He was determined to beat the meter, but no matter how hard he blew, the pressure dropped gradually over time. He would then distract himself by visiting the almost predestined spot that his dart would locate, google it, and disappear into his errant haven. There, he would imagine an adventure that always incurred risk, but Flash, his secret name for himself since he was a child, would deal with dire villains and escape unscathed, the reprobates remorseful and reconciled to a better life.

SINCE PEEWEE WOULDN'T ARRIVE AT SCHOOL until second hour, Willy had to take the bus in the morning. Most of the upperclassmen drove, so the bus was comprised of mostly sophomores and freshmen. Unfortunately, this had accounted for some of Willy's misadventures. Willy understood the need for underdogs to attempt dominance when they could. So being one of the lone and most accessible seniors on the bus, he accepted that the compulsion to bully was unavoidable. Fortunately, it had been the same bus driver the past two years, and he really liked Willy, so he took pity on him. Although at first Willy thought this was demeaning, he eventually availed of the kindness and sat every morning in the seat behind the driver, saved just for him, and they would chat all the way to school.

When Willy got to school he headed unobtrusively to his

locker and found Sandy waiting for him. He breathed easier. For some reason he felt as safe around Sandy as Peewee. Except this morning, one of the taller freshmen bumped intentionally into Willy, grabbing his books and placing them on top of his locker out of Willy's reach. He smiled maliciously for one second but the next, after Sandy had directed a well-guided punt to his balls, his eyes bugged out. As he attempted to un-hunch, he yelled, "Fuck you, bitch!" loud enough that it attracted the attention of a hall monitor. Fortunately, this monitor was a woman, and she took offense not at the more obvious profanity, which flew around the halls freely, but to the adage "bitch." As she directed a "bitch, eh?" to him, ignoring Sandy's transgression, she half-dragged the hunched and humbled aggressor toward the dean's office . . . or maybe the nurse's.

Sandy reached up and removed Willy's books from the top of his locker, handing them to him and smiling as if this were something she did every morning before school. It appeared a second set of balls was going to need tending to this week. The nurse was going to wonder. Willy smiled at the thought of the nurse asking the freshman kid, "And what is the problem?"

Will's smile grew as he looked up at Sandy.

"Well?" was all she said.

"Well, thanks I guess," Willy said.

"No problem. But I was asking about Peewee?"

"Oh . . . of course. Well, I told him you wanted to meet him."

"Yes?"

Willy could see if this were to be much of a conversation, he would have to provide it. "Well . . . he's shy, like I said. He wants to meet you. But he's . . . afraid of you?"

"Afraid of *me*? The guy's an ape." Willy was surprised at this more dynamic side of her personality previously unrevealed.

"Yes, but I'm afraid beauty renders him impotent."

"I don't want to have sex with him. I just want to be introduced."

She had said that without a smile, so Willy found himself embarrassed.

"God, no," he blurted. "I meant . . ."

"I know what you meant," she said, now smiling. "I was joking. I guessed you'd understand sarcasm? I've seen it get you into a bit `o trouble."

"Gosh. Well, yeah, I guess. Good. Um, until we get to know each other better . . . I mean if we do . . . I mean your . . . um, sense of humor *is* pretty subtle, and you didn't smile, so . . ."

"What! You want me to smile at my own sarcasm? That's just plain wrong. I can tell you, until we get to know each other better, when I'm kidding or not. You know, like all the other girls who follow up everything with 'Just kiddi-n-g,'" she said in a cutesy voice totally incongruous for her.

Willy laughed. Hmm, it seemed there was a bright personality hidden behind those dark, mysterious eyes.

"If it's beauty that tongue-ties Peewee, what's his problem with me?"

Was she serious or just searching for a compliment? "Well, yeah, I suppose. Since you're so fat and funny-lookin' . . ."

"Hey!" she interjected, a big fake smile on her face, "I'm not fat."

Willy broke out laughing. "Look, I may think you're funny-looking, but Peewee thinks you're beautiful."

"Really?" This time the smile was genuine. "He must have unusual tastes."

"Right!" Willy exclaimed. "You gotta know how . . . alluring you are." Now surprising himself.

"Alluring, huh?" She jabbed him gently in the arm. "You

smooth talker, you. Speaking of smooth talk, why aren't you lisping?"

"Not sure, except I hardly can with you. Your name is not Thandy Thickner."

She laughed. "True. True. So . . . can we attempt an introduction? I'll try my best not to scare the brute."

Willy was hooked; he figured Peewee would be, too. "How bout lunch? We always eat lunch together."

"No, he'll have a crowd of admirers around him."

"How about after school then? We could give you a ride home."

"Trying to pick me up, huh?"

Willy looked up at her. He noticed her irises were not just dark but black. Totally opaque. Very hard to see what was in them. "Ok, just kidding again, right?"

"Oh, sorry," and she squeaked, "'just kiddi-n-g.' I have my own ride. How about we meet at Peewee's van?"

Her own ride? Did that mean she already had a boyfriend? Of course she would. Just not a measly high schooler, especially a midget. "So, you know what Peewee drives?"

It was her turn to laugh. It was the softest, most delicate laugh Willy had ever heard. God he wished she'd shrink. "Yeah, it's a little inconspicuous, but I've noticed it."

"Right," Willy said, chuckling. "So, see you at Westphalia—the name of Peewee's van."

She punched him lightly again in the arm, turned, and walked away as the bell rang. Not as good as a pat on the butt, but Willy felt where she had touched him. It felt warm. He headed for class, feeling oddly confident, almost imposing. Nobody hassled him.

Both excited and muddled about the prospect of Peewee and Sandy hitting it off, he managed not to drift off totally into another world during World History class. The drone of Mr. Miller's lecture voice was like white noise as Willy pondered different scenarios for the introduction between Peewee and Sandy. He was sure they would like each other. Although soft-spoken and maybe even a tad withdrawn, Sandy possessed a sense of humor and was witty when so inclined. He just hoped she didn't scare Peewee off.

He made it on time to English without incident. Sandy, as usual, smiled quietly at him as he passed her on his way to the back-corner desk. Willy considered and then decided against wriggling his little butt in her direction. The first pat had been one of the more pleasant surprises in his life so far. Big Betty came in right at the bell. Just before she wedged herself into her desk in front of Willy, she looked down at him and pointed a fat finger in his direction. Willy turned around to see if anyone was behind him but felt foolish as only the wall loomed. When he looked sheepishly back at her, she shook her head and spit out a little burst of laughter. Willy wondered what the pointed finger meant.

The bell rang, and Mr. Hahn went over to the door and locked it, one sad face arriving and peering in through the glass window. "Ok everybody," he yelled above the conversations going on. "Attention, please! Everyone take out your grammar books." A huge groan roamed the room. A little groan escaped Willy, too, as everyone pulled out their books. Hahn must have told them yesterday to bring the grammar books to class.

"Just why this is a surprise to you all is beyond me," Mr. Hahn yelled. "What did you think I told you to bring your grammar books to class for?"

"To burn them!" Big Betty hollered, and the room rattled with laughter.

"Very humorous, Betty. Open up to page eleven, people. Before we get to writing essays, we're going to get through this grammar book." More groans. "Too many of you don't know a noun from a verb. You write like crap . . ." Hahn's voice droned on with a little hysteric tinge to it. Everyone hated grammar, and few saw its relevance to their lives—they thought it was exciting as stewed spinach. Willy figured if they didn't know a noun from a verb now, what were the odds, as seniors with ten years of having it drilled into their heads, that they would miraculously get it now? And know a gerund from a participle? Not a chance. Of course Willy figured most of them could probably do fine even if they thought a gerund was a woodland rodent. Yet Willy, along with three-quarters of the class who had gone through ten years of laboring to stay awake while being told the same shit over and over again, would have to sleep through it all over again . . . unless someone shocked the literary degenerates out of their dismal complacency. No sense in making language more complex than it was. If properly motivated, Willy figured anyone could at least learn to separate a subject from a verb from an object. It would be a good start, anyway. Keep it simple. He slid down in his seat, once again, eclipsed completely behind the broad expanse of Betty.

"Willy!" Mr. Hahn shouted, noticing Betty pointing at Will over her shoulder. "We're all waiting for you to open your book to page eleven."

Willy swallowed and grinned guiltily. "Why don't you give us a mathtery test and exempt those of us who have known this stuff thince third grade, Mr. Hahn?"

"You don't have your book, do you Willy?"

"No, thir."

"Well, see me after class, young man."

"He means 'little man with the lithp.'" Betty's inane attempt at what she must have thought of as humor was barely audible, but out of the corner of his eye he saw Sandy turn and point a dangerous-looking finger at Betty. He smiled to himself. Betty's slight didn't bother him in the least. Why would it? Betty was a moron. But a wave of pleasure washed over him. Sandy Stickner was sticking up for him.

Sandy. How did it take him this long to find Sandy? He wouldn't want *her* feeling anything like pity toward him, though. She changed Willy's theory on nearly everything. Rather than life after death, he would prefer life before death. And loving Sandy would be heaven. Except that she wouldn't fall for somebody his size . . . would she? No, it'd have to be just friends, for now. Nothing wrong with that. He'd have to live his love life vicariously through Peewee. He'd have to convince himself that it was good if Peewee and Sandy hit it off. Frickin' trade-offs!

Willy made it through the rest of the day incident-free. Even Betty had smiled at him, sort of apologetically, as they left English class. He headed out of school in search of Peewee's van, not worrying about slinking or hiding himself in the mass of exiting students. The day was sunny. It felt good today to breathe in the warmer autumn air. Just as he caught sight of Peewee, Willy could feel someone on his heels and turned, oddly without trepidation, to find Sandy looking down at him.

"Trying to ditch me, Shrimp?" He noticed she was glancing cautiously to both sides at the shapes moving around them, and then put her hand on his far shoulder—a sort of hug. "Ready to introduce us, my friend?"

My friend! That's what it would be between them, and it would have to be good enough.

Willy almost peed his pants when, before he knew what he

was doing, he put his arm around her waist. His hand rested on the tender lip of her hip right where it suddenly becomes a waist. The sensation brought on by such an intimate spot startled him. This was the most erotic thing that had ever happened to him. He fell in love with that spot. It felt so sensual that his first thought was to remove his hand quickly . . . but with her hand solidly around his shoulder and his tentatively on her hip they headed toward Peewee. It took Willy a while to get a grip and speak. He had never felt that part of a woman; actually, he'd never felt any part of a woman. Except for one uncontrollable organ suddenly shouting, it had stirred all others to silence—rare for him.

As they headed toward Peewee, Willy felt his hand get sweaty, so he removed it suddenly and found this sentence as well as his voice: "Remember, if he clams up it's probably a compliment," he whispered.

"So, I should assume he likes me if he can't talk?"

Willy smiled. "Something like that."

"So, if he talks, he doesn't like me? This ought to be interesting." She grabbed his sweaty hand and steered him directly to Peewee, who had gotten out of his van. Willy figured since Peewee wasn't hiding—like in the van behind the wheel—and was now leaning casually against the van, arms crossed, smiling, this was a good sign. But he looked nervous, Willy could tell.

Sandy and Willy strode right up to Peewee, who continued to smile while looking at Willy. "Hi, Will," he said, rather untypically formal. "Any trouble today?"

"Is he going to look at me?" Sandy asked Willy, looking up at Peewee.

"Give him time," Willy explained. "He hasn't run away yet. Be happy. Peewee, I'd like you to meet Sandy. Sandy, this is

Peewee."

Peewee remained facing Willy but looked at Sandy out of the corner of his eye. Slowly he held out his hand, inviting a shake. "Nice to finally meet you, Sandy."

Rather than offer a handshake, Sandy tentatively held a couple of his fingers and rolled his palm upwards. "That's the biggest hand I've ever seen," she said, looking at Willy. "Is he going to continue to look at me out of the corner of his eye?"

"Don't know," Willy said. "Why don't you ask him?"

"Will he answer?"

"Don't know." Willy shrugged. "You gonna look at her, Peewee?"

"I am," he answered, to Willy. "This is how I see her looking at me in the hallway. I assumed that's how she does things."

"I'm looking right at you now, you big baboon."

Peewee laughed and slowly turned his head to face her. "So, why do you slide down the hallways looking out of the corner of your eye at the world as it passes?"

"I see ghosts." She said this pretty much like she figured they already knew.

Peewee smiled. "What do they look like?"

"They don't look like much of anything," she answered.

Peewee was still smiling. "Then how do you know they're ghosts?"

"What else would they be? They're like rumors. They don't look like who they really are. If I see them just in the corner of my eye, maybe they aren't really there. Gone. Ghosts."

"But not gone for good. They will always come back." Willy could tell Peewee was enjoying this.

"Maybe, but I prefer avoiding them. They worry me. Even though I imagine they won't be going away permanently, if I only see them out of the corner of my eye, they don't concern me. Why d'ya think I walk near the walls? Think I just got bad balance or something? Think I'm weird or somethin'?"

"Yeah." Peewee's smile was about as broad as Willy had ever seen it.

"I'm weird? What do you mean '*I'm weird*?' And then this little shrimp here. Tell me he's not weird."

"Can't," Peewee said, still smiling.

"Hey you two, my hearing is actually quite un-shrimpish. But, Sandy—is that what you want us to call you?—anyway, you always seem to see me."

"Sandy's my name. It'll do until you know me better. Of course, I see you. You're real, even in color. The ghosts are mostly gray."

"Am I in color?" Peewee asked.

"Gettin' there. You're still kinda pastel-ish."

Willy was pretty happy with the way things were progressing. Not only had Peewee *not* clammed up but he seemed to like Sandy and was even sparring with her.

"But this big fella here," Sandy poked Peewee in his ribs, "he's gonna have to come up with another name for me . . . soon." Although he was happy they were hitting it off, it actually hurt Willy, somewhere in that cheesy heart of his, that she was flirting with Peewee.

"Hey, Will," she retorted, "what you want me to call you?"

He'd like another name as well—he was partial to Flash of course—live forever and do good deeds, fall in love with a beautiful, dark-haired woman, save the world from a bleak future.

"I like Will better than Willy. That ok?" Sandy asked and gave him a gentle hip check.

Of course Will preferred Will . . . if he couldn't have Flash. Although he had always been Willy . . . Wee Willy.

Will and Peewee said they had to head into work. Sandy told them she had to be home for her younger brother, a step-brother, when the governess left. All three, excited about how things went, and since it was a Friday, decided to meet that night at the creek near a place Peewee called hidden falls. It was remote. Not really falls . . . more a ripple. Peewee and Will frequently had campfires there. Usually Peewee brought a little grass to smoke. The campfire always seemed a bit brighter, the ripple a little more like falls. He hadn't let Will smoke until he had turned eighteen. Told him at eighteen he was officially an adult since he could enlist . . . which was probably the furthest thing from either of their minds. But Will understood his point. Will wondered if it would be a good idea to smoke with Sandy before they got to know her . . . assuming she partook, which he figured she did. But was she eighteen? How would it affect her? Although less behavior-altering than alcohol, it still affected everyone differently.

Sandy said she'd probably be able to make it—if she didn't have to babysit her stepbrother. To Will's surprise, Peewee told her if she had to babysit, to call him on his cell and maybe they'd come over . . . if it was alright. Will had never seen Peewee give out his number to anybody. As far as Will knew, he was the only one who had it.

Peewee scratched it down on a scrap of paper and handed it to her. Sandy stuck it down the front of her top, a rather tight black camisole under a loose knit, black sweater. Peewee's eyes looked like they were going to pop out.

"Don't get any ideas, big boy," she said, punching him in the arm.

Peewee swallowed, grabbed his composure. "Well, I feel so close to your heart."

"Weak, big guy. Weak," she said, punching him, again,

something she seemed to get a kick out of.

"She doesn't have any pockets," Will pointed out. "If you were down here on my level, you might have noticed."

Sandy hip-checked him, almost knocking him over. "What you been lookin' at, Shrimp?"

Normally when someone called him Shrimp, it pissed him off. Somehow from Sandy, it was endearing. Although she was not wearing actual leggings, she wore tight black jeans—too tight for pockets he had, indeed, noticed.

"You want us to pick you up?" Peewee asked her.

"Getting a little fresh for just being acquainted, wouldn't you say?" And she poked him in the ribs again.

Peewee actually blushed.

She smiled, apparently enjoying rattling him. "I live a ways out. I'll meet you there. It's off Parklawn, right? What I've heard called Bass Creek? I've never seen any falls there, though."

"They're hidden," Peewee said. "Like your ghosts."

"Well then. We have something in common. See you about eight?"

Peewee nodded and looked at Will. "Yeah, that should work for me," Will said.

"Ok, see ya there," Sandy said, and turned and glided away. As she was walking, she yelled over her shoulder, "Still can't see any pockets?"

They both grinned, caught. "Love those legs," Will said softly.

"Not a bad be-hind, either," Peewee countered, almost inaudibly.

"So, like her?" Will asked as they climbed into the van.

"We'll see," Peewee responded and gunned the motor, popping the clutch, managing to lay a little rubber.

They drove for a couple blocks, Peewee whistling, Will

pensive. Will had read something lately that had upset him and, as usual, wanted to talk about it. This was perhaps the biggest difference between them (besides their rather distinctive spatial disparity): Will wanting to discuss shit that distressed him; Peewee preferring to ignore anything resembling stress. Will tested Peewee anyway. "Can I tell you about those extremists in Africa that kidnapped a bunch of young school girls?" Will asked. "You know Boko Haram—they almost seem worse than ISIS . . . they're Kurds, Sunnis, Shiites or whatever. More like Turds, Sonofabitches, and Shitheads," Will added as he rolled down his window, the warmer air today feeling good, even if it had a little bite.

Peewee smiled, as usual, at his friend's dumb humor and did the same with his window. He always waited for Will to indicate it was ok to let the crisp fall air in. "Nope," he answered. "Why would I want to hear about that?" Peewee as usual seemed to want to ignore the fact that the world was unfair, while Will, on the other hand, was the fairness freak.

"You probably don't. They say they're going to marry some of them off, sell some."

"Sell? For what? Never mind. How old are they?"

"Young, mostly twelve, thirteen."

"What? No, I don't want to hear about shit like that. You know that." Peewee grabbed the steering wheel so hard his fingers turned white.

"The government's done nothing about it. Say they can't find them. Initially refused any outside help. But some tribe-type guys with spears and shit said they'd find the girls . . . and they did."

"Sounds like a movie," Peewee said. "One I wouldn't want to see. Shut up, will ya?"

Will couldn't help but watch Peewee's hands. "A couple

countries including the US want to help. But . . . what the hell is the United Nations all about? I mean, why is it up to the US or any individual country to play cop? Why doesn't the United Nations do something? What the hell do they do, anyway?"

"Probably argue about it. I thought I told you to shut up."

"Ok, but it ain't right," Will prodded. "Somebody needs to fix the UN. If it exists to safeguard world peace . . ."

"Maybe somebody should," Peewee interrupted. "Why don't you? It bothers you so much. Not me. That's why I live here, not in Africa or the frickin Middle East. Now shut the hell up or you'll need the United Nations to protect you. Someone should just blow the Boko-assholes off the face of the earth anyway. I don't think that should be up to the United Nations."

Will was still watching Peewee's fingers getting whiter and whiter as he gripped the wheel.

"Right," Will said, and smiled. Peewee, with his presence, intelligence, uncommon sensibility, and imposing stature could make shit happen . . . if he wanted to. Peewee was special, extraordinary, Will thought—chosen, even. "Want to hear something the Dalai Lama, a wise Eastern phil—"

"I know who the Dalai Lama is," Peewee interrupted.

Will smiled. "'It is not enough to be compassionate, we must act.'"

Will could feel Peewee's eyes boring into him. Will stretched out in his seat, folded his arms around himself, and closed his eyes, a smile on his face as he drifted off . . .

PEEWEE HAD GATHERED ALL THREE together at a clandestine, remote site. It was only Peewee, the Chief Sunni, the Chief

Kurd, and the Chief Shiite. He had thought it unlikely to get all three of these groups' representatives together peacefully. But Peewee's wise little mentor had told him to simply talk to each, explain his intent, and they'd come. No sane human really wants to kill or be killed if they had an option, he had told him. Peewee had still feared the meeting would be to no avail. He arranged it anyway, just to please his mentor.

"Well thank you all for coming," he started after they all were seated in a windblown tent surrounded by arid land and decimated buildings. He attempted a smile, facing them. There had been no handshake, bowing, or any indication of a greeting or show of respect, which reinforced Peewee's apprehension. "A friend of mine," he continued on anyway, "has suggested we sit down and discuss how we might bring peace to the Middle East. Here we are, all together in one room, and nobody's trying to kill anybody. Isn't this how you'd like it to be?"

The chief Shiite spoke, "Your American optimism is imbecilic. You don't understand tribal pride. This is how you can afford your optimism, through ignorance. The only reason I'm not killing this Kurd or Sunni is that you requested we bring no weapons. I'm sure if you asked these other two, they would feel the same . . . envision that in your hallucinations of peace!"

The other two both nodded. Peewee couldn't tell if they were grinning or snarling.

Peewee lost the little smile he had summoned. "I'm curious, do you consider me an infidel, an apostate, destined to die at the hands of Muslim executioners?" he directed at the Sunni.

"Do you believe in Allah?"

"You mean god?" Peewee answered.

"Yes," the Sunni said. "Who is your god's prophet?"

"My god doesn't have a prophet."

"What does that mean?" the Shiite spoke up. "What about Mohammad or your Jesus?"

"Never met either fella." He was trying to remain positive, but it was very difficult to have any sense of optimism when he had the feeling these three would just as soon cut his head off as look at him. "But wasn't it Mohammad something that blew up that school, killing a bunch of children a while ago? Killing children . . . was this done in glorification of your prophet? Nice, real nice." Peewee couldn't help himself.

"They were Christians, not true believers. You do not sound like a true believer," the Shiite replied, anger lying just under his tongue.

"Ok. Sorry I went there. I just needed to confirm what I've heard." He was feeling this meeting was futile, but he had to let them know how he felt. "Let me just say I don't believe you or anybody else has any right to tell me who or what to believe in, how or when or in what way to believe, 'truly' or otherwise. Can't you see to have peace in the world, people need to have freedom to choose for themselves what to believe or whom to believe in? Can't you understand that?"

"Those freedoms have led you westerners astray. You have no moral compass. You let your women control you. Your daughters dress provocatively, your movies and music are scandalous."

Peewee couldn't help himself; he was feeling defensive at their hypocrisy. "Well, I'm guessing you have experienced firsthand our scandalous entertainment, possibly in the arms of one of your conscripted concubines? Ok, sorry I went there also. You're right; I'm wrong, of course—I'm an ignorant, immoral Western infidel who believes in love and freedom."

"Your sarcasm supports our views," the Sunni said.

"I'm surprised you recognize sarcasm . . . or satire, especially.

Oh, that's right, you have asked that people be murdered for creating satire. A little insecure, I'd deem? You believe so falteringly in your faith, you condemn those who think freely and question? I do admit some of our entertainment is tasteless. But we don't kill people because they have no taste."

No one had anything near a smile on their face. Peewee wondered what was in their hearts. He took a deep breath. He knew his little mentor would not be happy at the turn this was taking. "Let's move on. Something I don't understand: you three all seem to be in agreement that I am an 'infidel,' which I can't hide I find tremendously judgmental, I must tell you. It seems to eliminate any chance we have of understanding, much less friendship, you have to realize, if your way is the only way. "

"You must read the Koran. Then you will see the error of your ways."

Peewee sighed and shook his head. "So I am your enemy because I don't believe what you want me to? Would you really like to kill me for that?"

All three shrugged. "Is that why you want us here?" the Sunni asked, a hint of a gleam in his eyes.

"Oh, for sure," Peewee answered smiling . . . a cold smile that gave all three of them a shiver. "If you kill me I get to go to heaven where all the women are naked virgins and subservient. I can sample all the concubines you have 'dispatched.'"

The three stared hard at Peewee . . . but there was fear as well as defiance in their eyes. He definitely got the feeling that if there were rocks in the room, they'd be flying at his head.

"Ok, look," Peewee said. "I am sorry for getting cynical. But how would you feel if I insisted you believe in Jesus and the Bible? That your Koran was wrong and Mohammad a false prophet?

"I am willing, as long as your interpretation of the Koran doesn't require murder, to accept your beliefs. I feel no compulsion to change what you believe. I feel you are free to believe what you like as long as those beliefs don't call for crimes against humanity."

Peewee could feel their desire to leave. "Ok. You all seem to have sided against me and my beliefs. But why don't you three get along? You all believe in Allah and Mohammad. Right? The Koran is your mutual bible?"

The three didn't dare look at each other, much less at Peewee. Peewee's stature seemed to grow as their fear did. Neither of the three spoke.

"You've been fighting since the year 632 AD, I've read. I'm sorry, I just can't understand. The reason I asked you here is that I assumed you're all highly intelligent. Don't you think one thousand three hundred and eighty-two rounds is enough? Shouldn't somebody ring a bell or something?"

"Your attempt at humor shows your ignorance. You blaspheme by your satire," the Shiite spat out bitterly.

"*I* am ignorant? When I leave here I'll go home, have a peaceful dinner with my family, maybe a beer with my best friend who is Catholic, not like me by the way, hopefully get a hug from a beautiful woman who is dark, resembles you mideast folks, and I think is probably Jewish . . . I don't care what her beliefs are. She's a woman who thinks for herself. I just like her. She is free to choose whether she likes me or not. I'll get up in the morning, take a pleasant walk outside without fear. Maybe see someone who I might have a friendly discussion with, maybe even brighten their day. Even the early philosophers deemed happiness to be the thing we all most want. My country even guarantees by law the pursuit of happiness, which does not include beheading those who disagree with me.

Doesn't peace sound like a more satisfying life than worrying about who to butcher, getting killed yourself, or your family getting shot or decapitated? What a great way to begin the day; 'Hmm . . . who should I slaughter today? Men? Women? Or maybe children?

"Or you," he directed at the Kurd, "can maybe convince a beautiful young boy or girl that if they strap on a bomb and blow themselves up along with some infidels, they'll attain nirvana? Of course I've noticed you've spared the suicide bomber tactic for yourselves. No suicide for you? No nirvana?" Peewee's irritation and frustration level was growing. He felt bad but couldn't help himself. "What's the deal you give them? The more they kill, along with themselves, the greater the orgasm? The higher their place in heaven? We Westerners have a saying, 'Faith is no guarantee.'"

"That's because you aren't a true believer. You are an infidel!" The Sunni gnashed his teeth, his anger no longer hidden under his tongue.

Peewee rose. The three went rigid looking up at him. "I believe that if I killed someone—and although you three really piss me off, I don't want to kill you for what you believe—if I did I don't believe I'd deserve to go to heaven or whatever else you call it. It's against the law of life, of humanity. Of course, if I had a god, he or she or it would be forgiving. If I repented, saw the error of my ways. Can't you forgive each other?"

The Kurd suddenly stood and faced the Shiite. "No!" he screamed. "A Shiite killed my wife and son. That is unforgivable! I will never forgive."

The Shiite stood and shouted, spittle flying, "A baby. Yes a baby. My sister's baby—not even a year—hacked to death by Kurds! Killing a baby is unforgivable."

The Sunni now leapt to his feet. "A Shiite planted a roadside bomb that blew up my grandparents on their way to the mosque! If that is not unforgivable, what is? Two old, harmless people!"

Peewee sat back down again, exhausted. All three now stood, rigid and trembling. "So, you can never forgive each other?" Peewee managed to ask, frustration overcoming him.

"No!" all three yelled, venomous, facing Peewee, apparently not able to look at each other. "How can one forgive?" the Sunni shouted, fuming.

"Oh, man," Peewee said, resigned. "My mentor that requested I try to reason with you told me to tell you: 'An eye for an eye . . . we're all blind.'" But you people can continue to massacre each other until there's nobody left. I'm outta here."

CHAPTER SEVEN

"YOU GONNA COME IN AND WORK, you day tripper?"

It first sounded like the question came from across oceans, then Will realized it came from Peewee's lips, inches from his ear. Boy, that daydream took a vicious turn, Will admitted to himself. Not what he had anticipated happening. What was that all about? Did it mean that he must, in reality, believe that the US should not be a presence in the Middle East? Was there really no hope for peace there? Can centuries of hatred and inability to forgive never be erased? He hoped if education at a very early age could be become the norm, even here in our cities at home, compassion and hope could replace the mistrust and violence. Possible?

"I wish you'd let me in on wherever you go," Peewee said, leaning on Will's door. "This one must have been a doozie . . . you actually worked up a sweat."

Will dazedly grinned at the irony of Peewee's wish.

"Or are you going to leave again and go solve some more world problems or whatever you do in there?"

Will broke out of his daze by laughing out loud. "If you only knew, big guy." Will started to open his door, but Peewee was still leaning against it.

"Seriously, Shrimp." Peewee's head almost covered the space of the open window. "One of these times I'm going to sit on you until you let me inside that head of yours. But now let's get our asses in and work fast and get off a little early. I'm pretty excited about tonight, I have to admit . . . on one hand. On the other, I'm petrified. What if she doesn't like me?"

"Have faith, my friend. I know she'll like you."

"Faith, huh? Ever heard 'faith is no guarantee'?"

Will almost split a blood vessel he laughed so abruptly.

Peewee stood back, startled. "What's up with you, buddy? That saying's true but not that funny. Holy shit!"

Will rolled up the window and opened the door. "That's what you think." They walked in side by side, Mutt and Jeff, with Jeff looking down at Mutt like he was one bark short of deranged.

PEEWEE, WHILE DRIVING WILL HOME, was quiet in anticipation of the evening. He knew Will could hardly contain himself, he was so excited. He just sat there, focused totally out the window, as if watching his thoughts go by, almost wringing his hands, unaware of what his body was doing. Sandy was really good for him. This made Peewee nervous. He was not comfortable with two men attracted to the same woman, and that's how it was looking.

They pulled up in front of Will's house, a white colonial with black trim and shutters, tucked neatly between similar homes. The yard was a little too manicured in Peewee's opinion, but now looking unkempt due to the muted scales of dry leaves scattered on the lawn. He liked Will's folks, but Mom was a little uptight, over-protective, Dad a little meek. He didn't like how they coddled Will. Not indulgently but condescendingly, it seemed to him. Will didn't like it either, he knew, although he rarely complained. But their indifference, almost disdain, maybe sprouted from their guilt—why do parents blame themselves for their children's abnormalities?—all contributed to Will's constant fight with worry, initiating his visits, he figured, to his secret life. My God, living constantly aware that he was dying! What could be tougher? Peewee was so proud to have Will as a friend. Being so close to Will all his life, and watching him handle the fate he had been given, gave him a front row view of what it takes to be strong. Mentally, Peewee knew no one stronger . . . including himself. Oddly, that strength is what instigated a lot of the bullying incidents. People were intimidated by Will. The only advantage they had over him was size. Then they lost their advantage by trying to take advantage of it. Peewee knew Will realized it was the bully's weakness, not his. So he could live with it. But he had to lay low when Peewee wasn't around. Best to be invisible. You could only enjoy so much time in your locker. Regardless, nobody was going to ruin his day. As a matter of fact, Peewee was very aware that Sandy was now making his day.

Peewee thought he had noticed a change, somehow, over the last couple days. Normally when he saw Will making his way toward the van, he looked like he was trying to be invisible. The last couple of days, he strode toward the van confidently, more self-assured. Peewee always watched closely to ensure a Bret or Big Betty didn't decide to have some fun at Will's expense. If he saw trouble brewing he would just roar, "Will, over here!" That always did the trick. It bugged Peewee that he was only respected because he was big. Will was big to Peewee. Body size meant nothing in terms of real size. If Will would make it into adulthood, it thrilled Peewee to consider what he might accomplish with the force of his willpower.

He noticed, naturally, that Sandy didn't treat him like

a Wee Willy but as though she respected him, like he was a man to be . . . interested in? Was that possible? This bothered Peewee. Sandy was the first woman that Peewee was not just attracted to but actually interested in himself. He had had his eye on her all year. She was not only beautiful but also intriguing, and he had to admit, more than a little titillating. Now this bothered him. He wondered if Sandy and Will could ever work out romantically. He thought it would be cool . . . really good for Will. She was, obviously, good for Will.

Oct. 3

Tonight is the night of our first sorta double date at your sorta hidden falls. It ought to be interesting. I actually am feeling a little trepidation (sorry – know you think I'm being pretentious when I use words like this . . . but words, except for one rather big deal, will be all I've left behind by the time you're reading this). It's going to be quite a conflict of emotions to watch the relationship between you and Sandy evolve. But by the time you read this, I'm guessing you'll have your own cacophony of emotions to deal with. Ha!

I just want to tell you I realize your bringing about world peace won't be a walk in the park. You're going to have to start in our own town, of course, and then expand around the US. Maybe eventually to places like the Middle East. I guess I'm not sure about that. I don't see the value in trying to militarily impose how we feel they should govern themselves. That is an act of bullying. You know what I think of bullies. Bullies have their heads up their asses, so they get a pretty narrow, shitty view of the world.

Going into Iraq and forcibly removing their leader, even if he was an a-hole, and attempting to impose how we think they should run their country is not only failing but it reinforced to millions of Muslims that we are assholes. I, personally, don't want to be party to assholism. And, big guy, ignoring what's going on doesn't absolve you. Nobody, one example being me and my mother, wants to be controlled, repressed, forced into compliance. If we're not there to help them learn to live in peace, which may only work by helping to educate really young kids, to at least attempt to help them eradicate the hate that has simmered over centuries, we don't belong there. There have been so many atrocities committed that I'm afraid the adults are unable to forgive and too much hatred is already ingrained between the tribes, cultures, religions, and so on. Another of the Dalai's quotes that's right on: "An eye for an eye . . . we are all blind." Those tribes should have realized that hundreds of years ago. I guess that idea exists other places as well . . . like Eastern Europe. Anyway, if you can start when they're young, maybe we can change the hostile culture they're born into to one of forgiveness or, at least, forgetfulness.

As I said, start here in our own cities where, by the number of murders committed, there is almost a war going on. Holy shit! I read that there're more murders in Baltimore in one day than in one year in Canada. Now that's fucked up. I don't think Chicago, New York, or other cities are far behind. You gotta agree? So, maybe even start a model here for how to do it around the world. The US can lead by example, not force.

Item #3: First, people need safe drinking water, as I know you're sick of hearing me say. But there are areas in the US with bad water and countries where kids miss school just to carry and help provide water for their families. As Maslow wisely pointed out, until basic needs are met – water being the most basic – nothing else matters. Then education is the answer. If the enemy of peace is ignorance, which I agree is the problem everywhere, including here in the United States, compassion and understanding must replace hatred and violence. But, don't try to do it all yourself, of course. You're going to have to clone yourself. Maybe get the military involved, ours and in other countries . . . not forces armed with deadly weapons but weapons of peace. Think of the quality of recruits we'd get if they signed up to educate and help, not kill? Get schools going everywhere that there are young, poor children, who'll turn to gangs and into terrorists if they're not educated and given hope. Remember: IGNORANCE is the enemy . . . not these children who will grow up and become their parents. Without this, there is no hope for a peaceful world. Maybe it's a pipe-dream, but a man's gotta try . . . right?

The Dalai says, "I believe all suffering is caused by ignorance. People inflict pain on others in pursuit of happiness or satisfaction. Yet true happiness comes from a sense of inner peace and contentment, which, in turn, must be achieved through the cultivation of love and compassion and elimination of selfishness and greed." A little heavy, maybe, but I know you're *compassionate . . . look what you've done for me? But, if you recall, the Dalai also says, "It is not enough to be compassionate, we must act." I can't remember if I told you this or if it was in one of my dreams? Anyway, I'm trusting you're "acting" now.*

Sorry. Good luck with that minor item – and tonight as well when the Peewee and Sandy saga really begins. I hear Mom yelling up at me. Gotta have hot soup before our "date" tonight, don't ya know. It's a wild, cold world out there. Dangers abound for Wee Willy.

PEEWEE PULLED UP TO WILL'S, wearing his typical T-shirt: Paris, the city of love, appropriately featured for this evening. Peewee would always ask Will where his travels had taken him the previous night. If it were an interesting enough spot, Peewee would try to find a T-shirt related to that place. A couple weeks ago Will had visited Paris and found it very interesting. Over the T-shirt Peewee wore a heavy, tan moleskin shirt, which hung open, framing the Eiffel Tower, making it look like he was wearing the shirt crooked. In the fall, nights in their neck of the woods got chilly. A fire would feel good this evening.

Peewee hunched down, looking through the side window of the van and up the walk to Will's front door. Usually Will was watching, but Peewee, unusual for him, was early tonight. He hated to honk as he knew it irritated Will's mom. Peewee could see Will through the window. His mother was scrunching something on Will's head. Will kept pulling it off. He could see Mr. Mitty standing behind them. He could tell Mrs. Mitty yelled something, and Mr. Mitty turned and walked away.

Dusk was deepening, and the front porch light suddenly flicked on, and finally out walked Will. Peewee rolled his eyes. He could see by how Will's shoulders sagged that he was humiliated, perturbed. He had on a large stocking cap with a tassel, a bulky, childish-looking winter coat, a scarf wrapped around his neck, and heavy boots, all looking enormous with his short legs and small frame. He looked like a troll or leprechaun. His hands hung straight by his sides as if the thick wool mittens were too heavy for his arms.

As he reached the van, he pulled off his mittens, and his mother's voice wafted into the chill, "Willy, you keep your hat and mittens on, you hear?"

Peewee stuck his left arm out his window and waved over the top of the van. "Hello, Mrs. Mitty," he yelled through the open passenger window. "I'll make sure Wee Mitty keeps his mitts on."

"Oh, thank you, Peewee," she yelled back, adding, "but I don't believe you." Peewee was always polite, so Mr. and Mrs. Mitty liked him. But the Mrs. told Will she didn't trust anybody that large, especially in that van. But she lived with it, only because she felt Willy was safe with Peewee.

Will climbed in the van and muttered, "Get the hell out of here so I can take all this shit off. And what's this Wee Mitty crap?"

Peewee chuckled and eased away from the curb. "You look cute enough to cuddle. Maybe you'll get lucky with Sandy tonight."

"Oh, yeah. Just what I want. Maybe I can sit on her lap."

Peewee laughed as Will whipped off his hat and threw it in the back along with his mittens. He then wriggled out of the coat, took something out of the pocket, and tossed the coat in the back as well. This left him with a burgundy merino wool sweater over a silk turtleneck. He leaned back and slipped his boots off, threw them in the back, and pulled on the suede moccasins that had been in his coat pocket.

"Ooh-ee, look at you." Peewee whistled. "Trying to impress someone, are we?"

Will crossed his arms and pouted.

"No, man. You look good," Peewee told him. "Those are cool threads."

Will looked over at Peewee. "Man? Threads?"

Peewee laughed. "Ok, I'm admitting it. I'm nervous. What if I can't even speak tonight? You going to do all my talking for me?"

Will frowned. "You better speak for yourself or the beautiful lady may fall for the ugly yet eloquent guy. Know that story?"

Peewee was well acquainted with the story but knew Cyrano died, so he didn't say anything.

"So, big guy, if you're interested in Sandy, ya better do your own talkin' . . . but I certainly wouldn't mind if you get tongue-tied. Your choice."

"If only it was a choice," Peewee said.

"It is, you fool," Will almost shouted. "You choose to be the person you are, behaviorally at least. You, of all people, can be whoever you want to be. Me, on the other hand . . . what can a leprechaun do?"

Peewee wondered at the mood Will was apparently in tonight.

"You can certainly speak just fine. Pretend you're with your lunchroom entourage. You're just going to have to bone up with Sandy."

Peewee glanced over at Will, who wasn't smiling. He tried to lighten the mood. "'Bone up?' I certainly don't want you speaking for me tonight or neither of us will end up with the girl."

"Would you slow down and ease up on that big foot of yours? My Lord, every part of you is big . . . even your foot . . . "

Peewee looked over at Will again. "Anything else? Since I'm supposed to bone up tonight?"

"That, too, I imagine."

"Think Sandy likes big?" Peewee responded and regretted it immediately.

"Yah, well I got one organ bigger than yours—my heart. And it's still growing." It really was difficult for Will not to get down and feel sorry for himself. Of course his penis wasn't big enough for Sandy when her option was Peewee. It totally sucked. But ya had to play with what you were dealt, even if it was a shit hand. Which was especially frustrating for a guy who would know how to play a good one.

"Sorry, Will." Talking about Will's ailments seemed to depress Peewee more than Will . . . but actually, Peewee couldn't remember a time that Will stayed down. He wasn't ever really depressed for sure. It impressed Peewee. He didn't think he could be as upbeat as Will usually was. Will was short but not small. People were so foolish they couldn't see that. As a matter of fact, maybe it wouldn't matter with Sandy either. It didn't as far as Peewee could tell. If Will had a short amount of time left—nobody would put a timetable on it, but it would be short for sure—Will definitely deserved Sandy in the time he had. Could she like him romantically? Peewee, maybe regrettably, wished so.

They pulled into the narrow lane that led down to the

creek. As they neared the end of the trail, they checked to see if anybody else was there. They could see something glaring through the trees in their headlights.

"It ain't a car, I don't believe," Peewee said, squinting through his massive windshield. "It's too small."

"It's a bike. A motorcycle," Will said. "Who do we know that rides a bike with that much chrome? And that looks like a lot of fringe hanging down on saddlebags or whatever. My Lord."

"No idea. I think I'll park here and let's go . . . let's see now, what word might *you* use? Oh, yeah. Let's go 'stealthily' and see what kind of fellow this might be."

Will just shook his head. "You wanna sneak up on him, you mean?"

"Yeah. You know, spy!" Peewee said, raising his eyebrows. It was unusual for Will to be this prickly. Peewee wanted to get him out of the mood he seemed to be in.

"I can't think of a less conspicuous body than yours," Will said. "Spy? How do you expect to conceal that frame of yours? And what if we get found out?" As soon as Will said it, he realized that with Peewee there was no reason to worry. One guy on a bike? A dozen? No problem.

They crept through the trees. Will became very aware that even though he weighed about a fourth of what Peewee weighed, he was twice as loud walking through the woods. Peewee walked gently . . . the same through the woods as through life. Will almost felt bad about what he was going to do to Peewee. But it had to be done; he had to do it.

"I see him," Peewee whispered. "See his silhouette? He's on the bank, right on the edge of the creek right where we usually sit."

"It looks like a Native American guy," Will whispered. "He has long, straight black hair."

They crept closer—Will, noisy even in his moccasins, Peewee, somehow, barely making a sound. They stopped behind a tree about twenty feet behind the slim shadow. They peeked around the tree, Will's head poking out one side, Peewee's out the other.

"You two stooges wanna come and sit over here by me on the side of this bubbling brook?" the shadow said. "Or are you gonna stay there, trying to hide behind that tree?"

Peewee and Will looked at each other. "Isn't it supposed to be 'babbling' brook?" Will whispered. The guy sounded a lot like Sandy.

"Sandy?" Will half yelled, half whispered.

"What are you whispering for? You sound surprised. Should it be a surprise to hear the voice of the person you're coming to meet?"

"Alright, alright," Will said as he and Peewee walked up to the bank of the creek and Sandy. "We just expected a guy."

"You're meeting me," Sandy said, facing the creek, her back to them, "and you expect a guy? The conversation ought to be just great tonight. You guys on drugs, maybe?"

Will cautiously squatted down, brushing sticks and rocks away, and sat next to Sandy on her left, the downhill side. Peewee sat next to Will farther down. "No," Will answered. "But we have some along, if you're eighteen . . . Peewee's rule."

"Oh?" Sandy said, looking down at Will, then up at Peewee. "What flavor? And why do I have to be eighteen . . . although I am."

"Just grass," Will said to her shoulder. "You know, marijuana."

"Not clover?" Sandy snipped back. Both Will and Peewee were figuring out that there was a rather acerbic side to this previously almost mute shadow. "Why'd ya think I was a guy? Not because you saw a motorcycle?"

Peewee looked away, a smile stuck on his face. He was thoroughly enjoying all of this.

"Yeah, yeah," Will said.

"So, you admit to stereotyping?" she said to the back of Peewee's head, which was still turned, gazing off. She could tell he was smiling; she could see his cheeks move under his beard. "Women don't ride motorcycles?" She was enjoying herself as well.

"You also don't seem like the type to ride a . . . " Will paused.

"Indian Chief Dark Horse," she said, looking over Will's head at Peewee.

"Oh, oh," slipped softly out of Peewee's mouth. "But what else would our Native American ride?"

"Native American?"

"Never mind," Will said.

"And just what 'type' do you think I am, Mr. Underwhelming? And what's the 'oh, oh' for over there, Chief?"

"Alright, sorry," Will said, crooking his neck up to look at her. "I have to admit you're the only one that I believe exists of your 'type.' I think you're in a genre all your own."

Sandy leaned down and kissed the forehead of the face peering up at her. When it didn't leave, she leaned farther down and gave it a surprising, partially-spread-lips-sidewinder right on its little kisser.

Surprised, Will glanced over at Peewee, who was still gazing at the creek. Fortunately there was still a smile on his face, Will could tell.

"Looking for those hidden falls?" Sandy quipped, looking up at Peewee. "Hey, Will, why don't you sit over here on this side of me?" She patted the ground. "It's a little higher and there's a flat rock to give you a little elevation. Then if I get the urge again to give you another little smackeroo, I won't have to break my back bending down."

Will almost leapt up, although he didn't know if it was because he was anxious to be kissed again; anxious about being kissed, quite well at that, sitting right next to his friend; or startled that the kiss immediately sprung him a little hard-on. It occurred to Will that this was now the top sexual encounter in his life so far, better than the previous hand-on-hip affair. Not that he had a plethora of experiences to rate it against nor was it much of an 'affair.' But if his odd heart quit on him tonight, going out with a hard-on by a kiss from Sandy would not be the worst way to go. He could, of course, imagine a better way to go than with a kiss. The potential scenario he had planned played around in his head. Something certainly to look forward to.

When Will had moved over to the other side of Sandy, she said to Peewee, "Why don't you slide over a shade, you big mute? So I can see you better, at least, if you're not going to speak."

Peewee slid smoothly over to Sandy, brushing right up against her shoulder, surprising and pleasing her, and looked down at her much as Sandy had at Will. Sandy looked up at Peewee much as Will had to her. It hit Will that she wanted Peewee next to her in case *he* got the urge.

Peewee bumped her shoulder gently, and then moved away a bit.

"You're an idiot, you know?" Sandy said. "So, slide back, keep your distance. In the dark, so far away, you'll look like a ghost."

"You know," Will said, "kids, little kids, see the people around them almost as ghosts. They're so into their own existences, everything around them fades into an ungenerous, vague blur."

Sandy put her hand over her heart and feigned indignation. "You're calling me self-centered, I'd say, if I didn't know better."

Will realized he was being petty and even a little vindictive because he was pretty sure this Cyrano escapade would end with the good-looking guy getting the girl. "Look," Will said, trying to save himself, "I think they, the mundane, the ordinary, will remain a blur to you. You're special. You're only going to notice special people . . . because you're special yourself."

"You just want another kiss, you little charmer."

"Well, duh, of course." Will surprised himself, but he had noticed that Sandy gave him a surprising sense of confidence, even daring, that he had never felt with a girl before.

She leaned into him, stopped right at his nose, and for a moment peered directly into his eyes. She then gave him a soft but safe little kiss and smiled at him. "You were never a blur, you know?"

"Thank you," Will said. "That's the nicest thing anybody's ever said to me," he half sang to the tune from *Scrooge*.

"I'm serious," she said.

"So am I. How about Peewee? A big blur?"

"He looks like a hulking phantom from here."

Peewee slid closer, stretched his legs down the bank toward the creek, and leaned back on his elbow facing Sandy, now at her level.

"That's better," she said, and Will knew she wanted to kiss him. The sounds of the night descended on them. The gurgling of the running water dominated. The wind, with a little whip to it, rattled the leaves. An owl hooted in the distance. "Well, where's this grass, weed, clover you were talking about?" Sandy asked, breaking the sense of stillness.

Peewee pulled out what looked like a small cell phone made of wood. It was carved so that it looked like it had a screen and keyboard, and printed on the screen was a Bob Dylan quote. "You don't need a weatherman to know which way the wind blows," Peewee read out loud and opened the screen and pulled out a fake cigarette, a one-hitter.

"Oh, man. I like joints. I hate those things. I hate technology," Sandy groused. "Like Dylan, though. He wrote some really cool shit."

"Technology?" Will said. "It's a one-hitter for crying out loud. More efficient is all."

"You've got an iPhone," Peewee snuck in and directed at Sandy.

"He speaks! You hear him, Will? The man spoke. I didn't say I don't use technology. Doesn't mean I like it, though. So, load the thing up and show me how it works."

The three sat silently, serenaded by the babbling of the brook, a firefly hopping back and forth between them as they took turns lighting the one-hitter. All three wondered how it would affect the dynamics of the evening. Will and Peewee pretty much knew how it would affect them—Will would get more talkative. Maybe get on his soapbox, sermonizing . . . sometimes a little too vehemently for Peewee's liking. "If we don't pay attention to water, we're doomed," he'd frequently spout. Will didn't want to be part of a system so stupid that it would allow the human race to dry up. "You can't live without water!" he would expound after inhaling, sometimes leaping to his feet.

Peewee would get pensive and even more subdued than usual, his little friend's tirades more easily tiring him out. He knew Will was right—somebody . . . *somebodies* had to wake up the world to the fact that they were damaging the earth, maybe permanently . . . thus the futures of their children and grandchildren. He believed that. But he felt nothing he could do would affect the kinds of changes that needed to be made. He simply wanted to be happy, enjoy life. Screw all that bad shit. Why should he have to be bothered, irritated? Life *was* too frickin' short to not enjoy.

After Will had let off a little steam, Peewee would eventually tell him to cool it. And Will would . . . not out of fear of his giant of a friend but out of respect. Will understood Peewee's dilemma—trying to not care to care.

Smoking made it a lot easier for Peewee to focus on the positive stuff around him. Grass would frequently make him sentimental. Tonight he would think, *Look at life, my best friend, a beautiful, totally sexy and funny woman—maybe the woman I love—a beautiful autumn night.* Peewee would smile pretty much the entire time he smoked, especially tonight. It got easier to not care . . . with a little fragrant smoke. If his little friend would shut up.

Both wondered how Sandy would be. Both had acquaintances that got weird smoking grass. Some people, even good, great people, shouldn't do *any* drugs, even marijuana, just like some people shouldn't drink. Sandy was a mystery yet to unfold. She certainly wasn't normal. How would marijuana affect her? They both already anticipated that Sandy would be a lifelong friend, regardless. Yet the relationship still felt fragile.

Both were aware of how marijuana, like booze, did indeed alter, even if it enhanced, behavior. Will would also frequently rant about legalizing marijuana after a couple puffs. "Booze stimulates, even in some women, testosterone and stupidity," he would preach. "Grass, on the other hand, mellows." Of course a person prone to paranoia should not use drugs of any kind.

Peewee was concerned about kids under eighteen smoking . . . anything. Too many would abuse it before they were old enough to mature into moderation. Of course, some with addictive personalities never would or could be moderate with anything. But he figured at eighteen you were on your own, ready or not.

Mostly Peewee wished they'd legalize it everywhere so his big-mouthed little friend would shut up. "How can they not see?" Will'd squawk in his high-pitched, squeaky voice. "How much good would come out of legalizing it! All the way around! Everybody would benefit! The economy, police could free up time to chase real criminals. Violence, especially related to the underbelly created by the illegality, would diminish. Prisons would be practically empty! C'mon!" he would expound. As with the water tirades, Peewee would eventually tell Will to cool it . . . even though he agreed.

So, Sandy? Would she get cautious and introspective, like Peewee? Or, like Will, more assertive? If she knew she had less time for life's adventure, Will thought, would *she* be cautious?

"Let's get a fire going," Peewee suggested, after a not uncomfortable silence had settled in. They all wandered for a while, separating, to gather up some firewood. All three came back with not only their load but also birch bark. "Well, we all know how to start a fire," Will pronounced as they set their fuel down.

"Ok, this is weird," Sandy pointed out, sounding uncharacteristically serious . . . rather unusual for the sarcasm queen. "It worked out perfectly—Will has an armful of kindling. Peewee has several big logs, and I have branches. What a team!" Was this her, stoned?

Will laughed. "So, did we all know what the other would do because of our size? Peewee—big, me—small, and you—just right?"

"Sorry to interrupt these fine stoned thoughts, but we need to now build the fire," Peewee said.

"I'll build it," Sandy said, and stripped some birch bark into thin pieces and laid out a base with it. She then added Will's kindling and some of her branches, which Peewee was breaking up for her, waiting on the larger pieces until the fire got going.

"You know what you're doing," Will said to Sandy.

She looked over at him and smirked. "What? Women don't ride motorcycles or build fires?"

"In my family, it's one of the things my mother lets my dad do. Can I at least light it?"

"Oh, please, light my fire," she said, grinning.

Will bit his tongue. Several comebacks popped into his mind . . . all dangerous when smoke was strolling around his brain.

After Will got the birch bark started, Sandy blew on it to get the flames ignited, igniting some more inappropriate thoughts in Will's pleasantly altered state. Peewee laughed to himself, aware of what his usually jump-at-every-chance-to-poke-fun—which was one of the reasons he was a target for the morons of the world—but suddenly cautious little friend was thinking. Will, when not stoned, generally tried to shush his sarcastic tendencies as they had provoked considerable punishment from some of his insecure targets. But after a couple puffs of the magic weed, he usually couldn't restrain himself, especially with Peewee around for protection. But tonight, Peewee could see his friend was more circumspect than usual, in spite of one smoky and one sexy catalyst.

When they had the fire going, they huddled around it, Will positioned again on higher ground, Sandy in between, and

Peewee, although still towering above them, on the lower side. Sandy looked back and forth between Peewee and Will. "So," she started, settling on Will, "your father would build the fire? He the dominant one? A traditional marriage is it?"

Will mulled over the question for a while. Frequently, growing up, he had resented his parents' coddling and yet oddly remote affection. Like how they distanced themselves from him as he got older. When he thought about it, his mother treated his father much the same as she treated him . . . with a certain amount of disdain. Disdain for having what she felt was a weak husband and disdain for having an unhealthy child . . . which drove both, ironically, he had realized, to live part of their lives in fantasy-land.

"They're a pretty pragmatic couple," he started, "not really warm toward each other. I can't see there's much intimacy. Disdain rather destroys any chance at intimacy I'd assume. Certainly not the 'fulfilling each other' type we all anticipate going in. No, they're calmly settled into their roles. Dad is a business analyst but has trouble analyzing my mother. He would build the fire to assert himself. He's not what she considers a 'success.' It's one of the few things he could do without my mother chastising him."

"Really? That's not cool. So, your mother is the dominant one?"

"You have no idea," Peewee interjected. It really bugged him that Will's father didn't stick up for himself more often . . . or for Will.

"Mother saw her job as nourishing my sister. When you meet her you'll see she did a pretty good job. She blossomed daily . . . and blossomed and blossomed. But this has created a little bit of a monster. She has a difficult time relating to men. She's smart but not very attractive. Guys might accept, at least initially, being controlled by a beautiful woman . . . not saying that's healthy, by the way." He smiled cautiously at Sandy. "But my sister has not had much luck with men."

"Well, shit," Sandy said, and looked over at Peewee. "He always analyze shit this deep?"

"You'll see. A little dope does the trick. Don't encourage him or you'll be sorry."

"Of course, Hau William tested her complacency." Will was on a roll. "I gather she saw nourishing her Hau as an effort in futility, as Hau may not blossom tomorrow. So, she kind of panicked; she felt she needed to control something that she couldn't by trying to keep little Hau incubated, to protect him from the inevitable. My dad didn't agree but would only challenge her if I encouraged him. If he sensed that I was suffering under her bridling me, he would try to intercede. I admit, when I was young, to fabricating much of my suffering. Now my father's response is usually to smile insipidly and drift off into his happy place. This incenses my mother and at first made me angry. I finally just decided to be happy for him because he seemed to find contentment in his secret life."

Peewee laughed. He admired the way Will could subdue his mother when he wanted to and encourage his father to stand up for himself. Peewee had exactly the opposite problem in his family.

"'Hau' William? Really?" Sandy said, the smoke apparently taking the edge off her sarcasm. "Why Hau? What's with that?"

"Hau is a Hawaiian flower that blossoms in the morning and dies at night. It only lives one day," Peewee told her.

"Screw that!" Sandy shouted angrily.

"Ditto," Peewee said, almost under his breath.

"They didn't mean any harm," Will explained. "Peewee gets

pissed because he thinks they favor my sister, but, really, why not?"

"What do you mean 'why not?'" Sandy said, still riled. "You mean they act like you're not going to live?"

Will didn't answer.

Sandy turned and kneeled, staring at him. "Well?" she demanded.

"Why wouldn't they feel that way? I was premature, not fully developed—not everything by the way," he slipped in, "—and wasn't supposed to ever live a long life, if at all." He bit his tongue.

"But you did live, for Christ's sake! And you'll continue to live if I have anything to do with it." She looked over at Peewee who was staring into the fire. "Doesn't that bother you?"

"Yip," Peewee whispered.

"No, not really," Will answered. "The thing that bothers me is when I'm treated like a schwa." He didn't know why he was saying shit like this. He never did in front of Peewee. Typically, the last thing he felt he needed, or wanted, was sympathy.

"A what?"

"A schwa. An unstressed vowel in an unstressed syllable."

Sandy pushed Will hard enough that he fell back. She straddled him, placing her hands on either side of his head while he lay there, confronting him inches from his nose. "You talk like that again, I'll beat the shit out of you. You hear? You think Big Betty is trouble? You haven't seen nothin'. You hear?"

Will became possessed by quite the concoction of emotions: the most exciting woman in his life was straddling him, which was something he could get used to, but was threatening to beat the shit out of him. He certainly didn't feel like a schwa at the moment.

Peewee continued to stare into the fire, slowly shaking his head.

THEY TALKED INTO THE EVENING until they ran out of wood. The boys asking Sandy why it had taken her so long to approach them. She arguing that it's traditionally up to the guy to approach the woman, that if girls approach guys or even act friendly, guys take it the wrong way. Will said bullshit, that Sandy was about as traditional as Christmas in July, and she had come on to him. "See," she yelled and smacked him in his arm. "Helping pick your books up off the floor was not 'coming on' to you."

Will said, "Oh, right," and got smacked, again.

After they doused the fire, Sandy asked Will if he'd rather ride home on the back of her Indian rather than in Peewee's bland, boring van. The vision of him with his arms around Sandy's waist made this an easy decision. Peewee told Will he wouldn't be seeing him tomorrow at work. Will said that Peewee'd not been working a lot of Saturdays lately; what's up? Peewee told him it was none of his business and held his fist out for Sandy to "knuckle." She took a look at it and slapped it away, hard.

"Ah, shit!" she yelled, clutching her hand. "Your frickin' hand is hard as a rock."

"You're not supposed to . . ." Will started.

"I know what I'm supposed to do, you little shit. It's been such a romantic evening, what with all the kissin and all, I didn't think knuckles were apropos. I'd rather depart feeling all warm and fuzzy inside, probably without a broken hand."

"Well you slapped an iron fist; whaddya think would happen?" Will said.

Sandy rolled her eyes and looked up at Peewee who was just standing there, arms at his sides like he had no idea what to do with them, with the same glum grin he'd had on his face most of the night. "How about a high five? Is that the ticket?"

Peewee clasped both his hands around her hips, below the waist, and lifted her up to his face. Sandy didn't bend; she stayed ridged like a mannequin. He gave her a gentle peck . . . on the lips at least . . . and set her down.

Sandy's turn to not know what to do with her hands, or anything else. She finally crossed her arms. "Well that was very interesting. Never been kissed like that before."

"Wow, was that cool," Will said, grinning. "It was like he was kissing a wooden Indian."

"No, not much different," Sandy said, "this time!"

"No," Will interjected, "I mean you stayed totally rigid. That was cool. It was almost like you were levitating."

"I think you're levitating, buddy. You've smoked enough tonight," Peewee said.

"Levitate—ha! Like 'high?' Pretty lame," Will said, realizing he was acting stoned.

Sandy wrapped her arm through Will's and propelled him in the direction of her bike. "Night Baron . . . That's the pretty fellow Cyrano was talking for . . . "

"I know the story," Peewee shouted as he headed for his van.

Peewee disappeared into the dark. They heard his van start.

"I got an extra helmet for ya," Sandy told Will as they approached the motorcycle.

"No way," Will protested, excited and feeling it. "I want the wind in my hair. Throw caution to the night."

"Yeah, well, if you get thrown into the night, you best have a helmet on that little noggin of yours."

"You gonna wear one?"

“Yup. One of the few rules my stepdad enforces.” She bent and handed him a helmet. He looked up at the most beautiful face he'd ever seen, anywhere. Her eyes were, indeed, black as the night. Her lips glowed a little. Her hair, loose tonight, slowly slid down over her face, until it was hidden.

"You're right," Will said. “If I had a face like that, I'd wear a helmet.”

“If you're looking for a kiss, you've had all you're going to get tonight.” She looked up, shaking her hair back to watch Peewee drive away, pulled on a black leather jacket, turned and swung her luscious limb over her bike, spread her long legs wide and pushed the bike forward off the stand, and settled on the seat.

“Tonight?” Will kidded, jumping on behind her, settling a hand deliciously on her hip. "So, how about tomorrow ni—”

“Don't get fresh,” she said, cutting him off. “And watch those little paws of yours. Now, let's put on these helmets and . . .”

Just then a dozen headlights from the opposite direction that Peewee had gone turned into the trees and all came directly at them, motors revving, the lights bouncing over the rough terrain.

“What do you want to do?” Will whispered.

“Why are you whispering?”

“Well?” Will pressed.

“I'm thinking. Maybe we should just get the hell out of here . . . quickly.” She got the bike started right away and started backing it up to get clear of the tree in front of them. As she started to pull forward, a dozen bikes surrounded them.

“Hey! What's your hurry?” A voice Will knew well.

Will thought he recognized several of the riders as they were not wearing helmets, but with the headlights glaring in his eyes, the faces blended into the shadows, like ghosts.

Mostly jocks, Will guessed, and if they were hanging around with Bret, most likely assholes. And probably drunk. All but Bret were silent, menacing, like a pack of wolves, the Alpha doing their growling.

"Well, look who we have here," Bret snarled when he recognized them. Will and Sandy hadn't, unfortunately, had the time to put their helmets on.

Bret shut off his bike and the others followed. He staggered over to Sandy and Will and straddled her front tire.

For a moment Will felt Sandy stiffen. She revved the engine. If she accelerated she would have left Bret worse off than Peewee had. Will wondered if Sandy thought that with the alpha down, the pack would be rendered harmless. Bret was definitely a horse's ass, but . . . running him over? Will knew Sandy would not appreciate Bret straddling anything of hers, even her bike. She didn't seem like a woman who would accept restraint of any kind. "Don't," Will whispered in her ear. "He ain't worth it."

Bret smiled cunningly and made a signal with his hand for Sandy to turn off her motorcycle. She revved it again and let out the clutch, leaping forward enough to send Bret sprawling.

"Go!" Will whispered hoarsely in Sandy's ear, but several of the ghosts shifted over in front of them to Bret who was curled, once again on his side, cussing, blocking Sandy and Will's escape completely.

When they got Bret up, they turned back to Sandy and Will. Will was starting to sweat. He knew Bret was going to have to save face. Will couldn't see Sandy's face, but he knew she was probably smiling, pissing them off even more.

"Think that's funny, huh?" Bret growled at Sandy after brushing himself off and limping around. He grabbed her handlebars and leaned over, turning the ignition off. He stood back, grasping the handlebars, a cruel grin on his face.

"Grab this bitch and hold her to that tree," he ordered.

There was a little hesitation, and then two of the subordinate pack members grabbed Sandy and pulled her off the bike. Someone grabbed Will from behind, pulling him off as well.

"I want no part of this shit," said one of the guys Will recognized as a football player. He started his bike, and most of the pack followed him as he left. This left the two holding Sandy, the guy with his arm around Will, and Bret.

"Well, guys. What should we do with the bitch?" He turned to Will. "Just what were *you* doing with the bitch? Huh? You get any? A mercy screw, you miserable little prick?" He laughed drunkenly.

Bret turned back to Sandy. "I bet you didn't give him anything, did you? How cruel, teasing this little pecker." He poked Will hard in the chest with his finger. "You got a pecker at all? Huh? Let's take a look."

"Screw you, you asshole," Sandy hollered and wrenched, trying to get loose from the two holding her. Will could tell they were club monkeys. Weights had bulked them up, but he didn't recognize them as any of the athletes. They pulled her back against the tree, one on each arm, exposing her like a sacrifice.

Bret walked over to Will, told the guy to hold him tight, and he pulled Will's pants down. "Oh, look how cute. Smokey the Bear undies."

Shit, Will thought in spite of his panic. Why had he worn these tonight? His mother always got him underwear in the boys' department.

"Well, let's see what you're packin'?" And he ripped Will's underpants off. "Whoa! I can barely see it. Let's see if we can help with that. Bring him over to the bitch. That interest you?

Huh, bitch? Or would you like to see a real pecker," he drunkenly jeered at Sandy. "A man's?"

He started to unbuckle his belt and turned to face her, thrusting toward her. Her foot shot out, aiming for Bret's much maligned crotch. His hands caught most of the brunt, but it still bent him over, a muffled curse escaping along with a huge belch. He immediately struck out, slapping Sandy hard across her face, Will screaming incoherent warnings at him to stop.

A trickle of blood dripped from the corner of her mouth. Right then, Will decided he was going to kill Bret. They couldn't hold him forever. Tonight, tomorrow . . . whenever. He was going to kill Bret. At the moment, he also hated himself . . . who he was. He was harmless. Bret had hit Sandy and there was nothing he could do. He couldn't protect Sandy. Squirm as he might, he could not free himself from the jerk holding on to him. Peewee would have killed all four of them.

Bret pulled out a switchblade and menacingly snapped the blade out and grabbed Will, hooking him around his neck. He dragged Will over to Sandy, pointing the blade at her chest. "Hold her tight against the tree," he ordered. The two blokes pulled her arms behind her, and her breasts pushed forward. "Well, don't those just look inviting." He poked the blade lightly against each breast.

Will struggled hopelessly to break Bret's neck lock.

Bret pushed the lapels of Sandy's leather jacket apart with the knife. She was wearing a white blouse with a light blue camisole underneath. One at a time he flicked each button off the blouse until her camisole was exposed. He then separated the blouse with the tip of his blade. "Well, lookie, lookie." he sneered. "No bra. Look at those nips. Suppose they bleed?" He poked the tip of the blade at Sandy's right nipple.

Will had trouble seeing exactly what Bret was doing, buried in his armpit. He summoned all his strength and tried to jerk himself free. He saw a spot of blood start to soak through her camisole. Will struggled, but Bret tightened his grip, choking Will.

"Hey, Bret," one of the goons said, "no cutting."

"Just a little nick of the nipple. Suck some red milk from the whore's nipple? What ya think?" he asked Will, holding his head up. He stuck the blade up under Sandy's camisole and, from the inside, cut the thin fabric from the neck down to the hem and used the tip of his knife to slide the material apart, exposing her bleeding breast. All Will saw was a drop of blood before he closed his eyes.

"That's enough, Bret," the other goon said.

Bret was transfixed by Sandy's exposed breast and started to breathe heavily, burping up beer. "Hey. Drew, get a pic of this."

Sandy had said nothing the entire time, a cold grin frozen on her face. She would not give Bret the satisfaction of seeing her frightened. She knew he wanted her to beg. She had quit struggling and bored into Bret's eyes with a burning black stare, her lips grinning hatred.

"C'mon you little pecker, lap up that blood," and Bret pushed Will's face to Sandy's breast and pressed his face against it. Will twisted his head away as best he could. "You getting hard or are you a fag?" he goaded. Although Will was choking, he held his breath and sent his mind somewhere else. Now neither Sandy nor Will moved a muscle.

"Suck her tit, you little shit!" he screamed, agitated and breathing hard, burping. "Strip her and lay her out on the ground!" he yelled. "Let's see if this pathetic little asshole's pecker is big enough to screw her."

Everyone froze. Sandy continued to stare hate into Bret's eyes.

"Move it!" Bret screamed at the two holding her. "I'll teach the bitch a lesson!"

"I ain't having no part of rape, man," one of the two said.

"Me either," the other guy holding her said.

"You frickin' wimps," Bret yelled, impassioned and totally out of control. "I wouldn't screw this slut; I'll make this little midget do it."

Suddenly it hit Will. There was no way Peewee wasn't going to find out about this. Bret *was* dead. Although Bret was choking him, Will managed to gargle out, "Peewee."

"What? Peewee? Your big baboon isn't here to protect you."

Bret let up a bit, and Will looked up at the two guys still holding Sandy, who was still not struggling but rigid, a part of her spirit summoned from hell emanating from her eyes. "You know this is Peewee'th girlfriend?" Will was able to squeak out. "You have any idea what Peewee ith going to do to you when he finds out?"

Bret squeezed Will harder in his chokehold. "Thut up!" he mocked.

"Hey, man," one of the goons said, and looked at the other, who looked back wide-eyed. "I didn't know nothing about that big dude being with this chick."

Sandy turned her face back and forth between the two guys holding her. "You idiots don't know this is Peewee's best friend?" Sandy heard Will gagging and screamed at Bret, "You're choking him! Let him go."

"Hey, we're outta here, man," they both said.

Bret lurched at Sandy, grabbing her breast roughly and engulfing her mouth with his.

A terrifying, gurgling scream suddenly filled the night.

When Bret stood back, blood was gushing from his mouth. Sandy smiled, held the piece of tongue she had just bitten off between her teeth, pulled the chunk into her mouth, and swallowed.

Bret let go of Will, who slumped to the ground. The three other guys looked at Will crumpled on the ground, and then at Bret, who was emitting a continuous guttural howl. The two guys released Sandy, grabbed Bret, and hauled him away howling like a castrated dog.

Sandy knelt down to Will and found him unconscious but breathing, although it was labored. "Fuck you all! You're totally screwed," she yelled as they all started their bikes, throwing Bret on the back of one, blood splattering over the driver's back, leaving Bret's bike behind.

CHAPTER EIGHT

WILL WOKE TO FIND TUBES stuck up his nostrils and his parents' backs poised near the side of the bed he found himself in, looking out what could only be a hospital window. Tubes were pumping oxygen into his nasal passage, he could tell. When he looked around the room there were monitors everywhere. What the hell? He could see his parents' reflection in the window. They both looked grim. He wondered who would be the first to realize he was conscious.

It took a moment to tally the events that had led him to this bed. The memory, suddenly vivid, smacked into his head, almost exploding it. His face flushed, and his head started to pound. Bile rose into his mouth, and he turned and spit it out into his sheets.

"Oh look Martha! He's awake," his dad, Walter, gasped. Will realized his father had been watching him through the reflection in the window, his mother looking out at lights in the night.

They both turned and hovered over the bed. "You're lucky to be alive, young man," his mother immediately scolded. "What were you doing with that punky woman out there in the woods? What were you two doing?"

"What's wrong with me?" Will asked, ignoring her question. "What happened?" His head felt like it would burst.

"That's what I'd like to know," his mother again admonished. "Just what were you doing?"

"Dad," Will started, trying to take deep breaths to relax, but he began to hyperventilate. He couldn't get enough air in.

His mother reached down by the side of his bed, and suddenly three nurses bolted into the room. He forced himself to breathe slower, as easy as his temper would allow. The recollection of the events came at him fast, with Sandy howling odiously in his memory. He wanted to get up, right now, and go kill Bret.

The nurses each checked various monitors, and then the oldest of the three, a pudgy maybe fifty-year-old with puffy blonde hair came over to him. She didn't look at Will but said to one of the monitors, "All the vitals are good." To his mother, "What happened?"

Will's mother started to stammer an answer.

"Mom, I can talk." He looked up at the nurse who had now grasped his wrist and was concentrating on his pulse. What the hell were all the monitors for, he wondered. "I started breathing hard and then couldn't catch my breath."

The nurse finally looked at him and smiled down condescendingly. "Oh, you poor little fella. I s'pose yur wondering how you ended up in our little hotel here?"

Hotel! What the hell was she talking about? "What happened to me?" Will asked, wheezing a little.

"You must just take slow, small breaths. Poor little fella," she said, looking at his mother.

Will wanted to scream. He was not enjoying being dismissed as a poor little fella. He wanted to punch her in her pudgy nose. "Would you pleath explain what happened to me?"

She looked at his parents. "The doctor will be by any time. Try to keep the little guy calm."

Calm! He wanted to take his oxygen hoses and wrap them around her fat, flabby neck until she needed oxygen. Before he thought he actually might do it, she turned and left, the other two nurses scurrying after her.

"Dad," Will said, trying to be calm, "would you please explain what happened to me?" All he could remember was seeing Bret cut away Sandy's undershirt, a drop of blood that in his imagination now appeared the size of a balloon, Bret's grasp around his neck tightening . . . and that was the last thing he recalled. When he thought about it, he was more concerned about Sandy than himself. "And what about the girl—Sandy?"

"You threw up or something and swallowed your vomit," his mother said, still sounding like she was scolding him. "You're lucky to be alive. What we want to know is what you were doing there. The police came and everything. But they won't tell us what happened. What was going on, young man? Where was Peewee? Who was that girl?"

"Is she ok for Christ's sake?"

"Watch your language. And don't yell at me," she said, conjuring up one of her counterfeit pouts.

"Dad, will you please tell me what you know," Will said, trying, again, to calm himself, but he felt like he couldn't catch his breath or stop the blood boomeranging around in his head.

"Never mind . . ." his mother started.

"Will you shut up for a second?" Will's father said, startling both Willy and his mother. Walter rarely bucked the Mrs.

"We don't know much," Walter started. "Apparently you passed out, like your mother said, swallowed some vomit. The police didn't say much, but apparently this girl called 911 and got the ambulance and the police there. She's ok. I guess she rode in the ambulance to the hospital, and, as you can see, you were put in this ICU room. She was in here when we arrived. She had told them she was your sister, but your mother threw a hissy fit, and they made her leave. She seemed very concerned about you."

Will's mother's mouth was still open in indignation as Will threw her a dart of a look. It must have hit the target as for once in her life she did shut up.

"Dad, how long have I been out?"

Walter tossed a sideways look at his wife, who stood rigid, arms folded defiantly, and mouth now tightly shut. "About an hour, I suppose, more or less." Walter was back to his indecisive, hesitant self.

Just then a surprisingly young-looking male doctor with tortoise-shell reading glasses strode into the room, clipboard in hand, and like in every hospital show on TV, flipped it open and smiled. "Well. Good to see you've come around. How's the breathing going? You comfortable?"

"He . . ." his mother started.

"Mom!" Will cut her off, his voice high-pitched and raspy. "I believe he's asking me, the one with these blathted tubes up his nose."

The young doctor laughed. "I think we'll leave them there for a while until we know more about your lungs."

"My lungs? Whath's wrong with my lungs?"

The doc went back to his clipboard. "Well, looking at your history, it appears you were born quite prematurely. Your lungs will be sensitive to any sort of trauma. Something caused you to vomit, and instead of a disemboguing reaction, you ingested it and aspirated on the vomit."

"I'm not as thmart as you, Doc," Will said, miffed. Why did doctors always talk in medical jargon and terminology? Like mechanics about cars: the ultra laser seared the opt-drive and the rotary twat was tweaked. "Could you condescend to the language of uth peons so I understand, please?"

The young doctor laughed again, seeming pleased by Will's insolence and not put off by his lisp or unusual voice. "Something tells me you're no peon. Sorry. Yes I can be more direct. You barfed and rather than emitting it, you swallowed it. Your lungs filled with fluid, causing a rather dangerous form of pneumonia, especially dangerous for you. Your neck was quite red and bruised. Were you being choked? That could have caused this reaction."

Will glanced up at the ceiling. He now understood what happened.

"Answer the nice doctor," his mother interjected. She looked at the doctor. "We haven't gotten to the bottom of this yet. He needs to do some explaining."

Will looked at his mother. Although he felt a bit of guilt being short with her, he still felt she was more concerned with what he had done rather than how he was. He shook his head disdainfully and turned back to the doctor. "I've been told there was a girl with me when they brought me in?"

"Yes, apparently she insisted on riding in the ambulance with you. Wouldn't take no for an answer. The authorities came along a little later and are also interested in what transpired," Doc explained. "She was very, very concerned. A rather interesting young lady."

"Is she ok?"

"Oh, yes. She looked more angry than anything. A big fella showed up as well. She had said she was your sister, but when your parents showed up and we found out she wasn't, we had to ask her to leave. She and the big fella are in the waiting room down the hall. Shall I send them in? According to the nurses, your signs are all good, and you seem to be breathing fine."

"Oh no you don't!" Martha exhorted. "Nothing happens until you tell us what happened." She turned back toward the window, and Will could see from her reflection that she was starting to cry. Walter shuffled up next to her, but Will could see he was still looking at him in the reflection. His mother wiped her eyes, crossed her arms, and once again peered out into the night.

"Can I go home?" Will asked the doctor.

"Oh, heavens no. You were on a ventilator for a while until you started breathing more normally. I think we'll keep the oxygen tubes in for a bit and monitor your lungs. Your heart rate was frighteningly rapid when they brought you in. It's still quite accelerated. Your face is flushed as well. No, you'll be under observation for a few days."

"A few days?" Will almost shouted, which increased the pounding in his head.

"As a matter of fact," the doctor said, closing his file, "I think it's a good idea for you to get some rest. Mr. and Mrs. Mitty, can I talk to you outside the room, please?"

Walter turned immediately and followed the doctor. Martha, who had composed herself, looked at Will and stood her ground for a moment. He assumed she was worried about him, but she always made him feel like he was a burden. A hau that hadn't yet but soon would wilt.

After they left, his door was pushed almost shut. Will could hear the doctor's and his mother's voices, barely audible, outside the door, and then, silence. He couldn't think straight. He knew he had to do something. He wanted out of the hotel. He really felt like he could kill Bret. Then a realization slapped him; he remembered Bret telling the guy that had been holding him to take photos. Shit. Then another realization suddenly made him shudder—although he, Will, would like to kill Bret, he knew he probably wouldn't, or couldn't, but . . . what about Peewee? Would Sandy have told him *everything*? Will guessed she'd feel like he did, afraid that Peewee could and would kill Bret. That it would be way too risky to tell Peewee the whole story. But Peewee would get to the bottom of it eventually anyway. And Will wouldn't be up to lying to him. He doubted Sandy would either when he thought about it.

The door opened quietly and the two friends slipped into the room. Peewee strode directly over to the bed, Sandy in tow. "Are you ok, Will?" he demanded. Will couldn't tell if he was pissed, concerned, or both.

Sandy peeked around him and caught Will's eyes. He raised his eyebrows, and she shrugged and nodded her head, indicating Peewee probably knew the whole story.

"Will, what exactly is wrong?" Peewee asked.

"So, you know what happened?" Will asked.

Peewee looked down at Sandy, who had pulled up bedside next to Peewee. "I'm not sure I got the entire story. Something tells me she's holding some details back. I can tell she's embarrassed. So, you tell me the whole story . . . after you tell me what's up with you."

"You scared the shit out of me, you know?" Sandy said. "They had an oxygen mask over your face in the ambulance. I was afraid you were dying. Then in here they had you on a ventilator. Does this have anything to do with you being . . . um . . ."

"Being prematurely born and underdeveloped?" Will said, helping her out.

"So, does it?" she said.

A door opened, and the head of one of the younger nurses popped around it. She raised her eyebrows at the two friends but looked at Will and smiled. "Some people are here for the miss." She then directed at Sandy, "I kinda thought you might be in here. They said they're your ride."

"Ok. Thank you, ma'am. I'll be right there." She walked to the bed and leaned over Will. "Look, you better be alright. You hear?" She leaned down farther, pushed the tubes aside and gave Will a good smack on the lips. "I gotta go get my bike. See ya."

She looked at Peewee. "I think Bret's is still there, too."

Peewee smiled. "Not anymore. He'll never see that bike again. I called someone who'll know what to do with it. Just one of his consequences. I could have taken you to pick up your bike, you know?"

"Yeah, I know. You stay here with Shrimp." Peewee nodded. Sandy looked at Will and tried a smile. Nobody was feeling terribly joyous. There was a huge, menacing elephant in the room. "I want to be kept informed on any plan. Right?"

Both Will and Peewee nodded.

"So, see ya." She poked Peewee gently in the arm and slipped out of the room, holding her jacket tightly closed.

Neither said anything for a while. They both stared at the door. Finally Will looked at Peewee. "So, what are we gonna do? Kill him?"

Peewee sat on the bed. "Tell me the story. And don't leave anything out."

When Will was done explaining what he remembered, Peewee shook his head slowly and said, "There's part of the story you don't know. You may have been out."

Will perked up. "Oh, what?"

"Bret grabbed Sandy's breast and stuck his tongue in her mouth."

Will's eyes grew hard at the thought.

Peewee smiled. "She bit it off, stuck it out at him, and then swallowed it."

"No shit? Like the whole tongue?"

Peewee smiled a little wider. "It sounded like a good chunk of it. She said blood was gushing out of his mouth."

They sat there, grinning at each other. "No shit," Will repeated. "It went down? She didn't choke?"

Peewee shrugged. "I guess. Sandy said he, like, went into shock. The other guys hauled him away. You must have been out because she said you dropped, limp, to the ground. And here we are."

"Should we kill the asshole? You hold him, I'll do it."

Peewee laughed lightly. "Good thing you aren't my size. You've got too much testosterone. No, he's not worth killing."

"What then? He can't get away with this. I'll read up on lobotomies and sterilization."

Peewee laughed louder.

"Well, even though the odds are against any woman in her right mind marrying that sucker, I could see him forcing himself on someone," Will said. "You want any little Bret Bastards running around? If he hasn't already, he's gonna rape somebody."

"Actually," Peewee said, "I bet he's impotent."

Will flinched and looked wide-eyed at Peewee. "How the hell do you know that? I thought he liked to defrock freshman girls."

"From what I've heard a lot of groping goes on but not much else. That's why the girls following him around are all freshmen. The older ladies know better. They talk, you know. And then, twice with you, he used you as a, I don't know what, maybe a prop . . . with the freshman girl and Sandy."

"Goddamn it!" Will screamed and pounded his fists into the mattress as the memory he was trying to repress resurfaced. "I hate that prickless ass."

Peewee shook his head and smiled vaguely. "Exceptional use of the language there, Shakespeare. He's reprehensible, but I feel sorry for him. Especially after what Sandy did to him."

"Sorry for him?" Will's voice pierced the air like the high-pitched screech of an eagle.

Then he started wheezing. "Well, he's gonna be shitting about what you might do to him," he got out between breaths. "The other guys, too. When I reminded them that Sandy was your girlfriend, they about shit their pants. That's when it ended, as far as I remember. They're all afraid to death of you, you know? They're not going to have any idea what you're gonna do."

Peewee smiled sadly and shook his head. "They're all afraid of me, huh?"

"Ya think? I'm surprised you're not afraid of yourself." Will took a slow, deep breath to settle down. They were both quiet for a while, lost in their thoughts.

"So, what exactly is wrong with you? Why are you having trouble breathing?" Peewee asked.

Will told him what the young doctor had said. Then, to change the subject said, "So, what *are* you afraid of, Peewee? Anything?"

"Noise," he answered without hesitation.

"Noise?" Will repeated. "You're afraid of noise?"

"Yip."

"What kind of noise?" Will said, a smile creeping onto his face. He never knew what Peewee would come up with.

Peewee walked over and looked out the window. "There's all kinds of noise," he said.

"So," Will said, figuring already this was going to be one of Peewee's metaphors, "you mean like you're afraid of people because they make noise? Say hurtful, evil things?"

"I'm not afraid of people. But I am afraid of their noise. Like a howler monkey, I'm scared shitless of their noise. Google it sometime. I'm not afraid of *them*, though. There's all kinds of noise that scares me. Especially the noise of the unseen."

Will noticed that Peewee said this looking at Will's reflection, in order to see his reaction. Peewee always created these little allegories. He said Will was about the only one who got them.

"So, like Sandy's ghosts you mean?" Will asked playing along. "Echoes? Eclipses? Reflections?" He looked cross-eyed at Peewee's reflection in the glass.

Peewee tried to smile. "Never mind."

"No, I'm interested," Will said. "Seriously, I really can't imagine you afraid of anything. Do you mean you're afraid of things and people you don't understand?"

"I suppose," Peewee answered. "I don't understand most people, but I guess I don't need to. I'm not going to judge or try to change anybody. I can protect myself from them, physically, of course, if I have to. But I can't protect myself against their noise."

Will lost the grin. He knew where Peewee was going with this. "I can't, being four foot seven and unimposing, and running out of time, make a difference, an impression in the world, you know?"

"You make a difference," Peewee said, turning around from the window.

"Yeah, sure, with you—we're friends."

"Nah, you make a difference, just who you are. You're definitely, as Sandy said—'real.'"

"That's not what I mean," Will implored. "I mean change things. Things have to change. You know that. Fix things that have to be fixed . . . before it's too late. Make a frickin' difference. Somebody has to do it. There's just way too much shit, serious shit, going on."

"See, now you're scaring me. Way too much noise. I think you know not to expect me to knock my head against the wall."

"It's so big and hard, you'd knock the wall down. You're capable of breaking down barriers. You could change things if you try."

"Hey you little shithead. If I'm scared, and you're scaring me, I'm leaving. Change the subject."

"Alright," Will said. "I'll drop it. But I'm just warning you. Some rather momentous event in our lives will change your mind. It will."

"Oh, and what might this momentous event be?" Peewee said, raising his eyebrows.

"Never mind."

"So, there is no *event*?" Peewee pressed, turning and standing over Will.

"Oh, yes. There will be."

Peewee laughed. "I love your weirdness, you little shit. When is this event to happen?"

"Don't know."

"But you know it's going to happen?" Suddenly a shiver overtook Peewee. Some internal noise shook him to his soul.

Will stared at the tiles on the ceiling. "Was there an event in your life, something traumatic that gave you this surprising fear of noise?"

Peewee sat on the bed again but peered out the window. From this perspective, Will couldn't see Peewee's reflection but his profile. God he was imposing. The bald head. The cropped but thick beard, which couldn't mask his strong jaw. All his features were profound yet proportionate. He carried himself effortlessly. Spoke calmly and self-assuredly . . . until he was angry, and then the earth trembled. Will could not imagine him being afraid of anything.

"Yes," he finally answered. "There was an event that frightened me so severely it changed my life."

"So let's hear about it, you big sissy."

Peewee was quiet again, obviously pondering. "Well, it may not seem like a big deal to you, really."

Will clasped his hands behind his head, breathing easy for the first time. "Try me."

"Well, ok. I was up at my uncle's place on Burntside Lake, you know—by Ely. It's on this big open bay. I've told you about it. My parents and I were up for New Year's. I was just a kid. The lake had frozen over early, and then it had gotten warmer and thawed a bit. But this night it was cold again. Really cold. Frigid. I walked down to the point and stood at the edge of the ice, looking out, listening to all the noise the ice was making. Some groans, like souls in agony. Some like spirits that had frozen and were splintering. One sounded excruciating, like lightning shattering, acute but deep, shooting out as if it had come out of the bowels of a beast."

Will was mesmerized, wondering where this was going, Peewee being more lyrical than usual.

"I can't think of any other way to describe it. The noise was menacing, an intense shriek of noise, sharp, like an arrow, not as sudden as lightning, though no less frightening. Like it was emitted from the gut of some monster, something evil. Then there was a huge boom. I mean HUGE. Like something big imploded under the ice. It made me jump. I mean the ground shook. That big. And suddenly this loud cracking, threatening noise came screaming at me, building up speed and momentum, like a screeching horde of hallucinations. Without thinking I just turned and fled. I stopped when the noise ended, abruptly. The sudden silence made me feel foolish. It was only noise. Just noise. What had frightened me so bad? I looked up. The stars shone like a thousand eyes mocking me."

Will wrinkled his eyebrows. "Did this really . . . or is it a . . . ?"

"Oh, yeah, buddy. It really happened."

"So?"

"So, what's noise? I don't know. Intention? Unknown consequences? Anyway when I dared retreat back to where I had been standing, there was a two foot crack, a jagged fissure as far out as I could see. Like a streak of lightning burned into the ice. It had stopped at the edge, where the ice met the shore. I could see my footprints . . . and right between where my feet had been was this fissure that ended just shy of me. If I had been *on* the ice, it seemed at the time that it might have killed me . . . Rendered me in half. It was coming for me."

"No shit?" Will said.

"Yes, shit. I almost did. But, man, it seemed a warning; as long as I kept my distance, the noise wouldn't hurt me."

Will shook his head slowly, and it dawned on him that his friend, who hadn't graduated from high school, *had* just laid another parable on him. Will didn't argue. He did understand. It was too bad. He almost felt sorry for what he was going to do to Peewee.

"Ok, you're smarter than you look, you big oaf. I don't agree, but I do understand. You and now Sandy keep telling me how weird I am, that I disappear inside my fear, a fear that I may not have lived enough to die happy . . . but you, Sandy and her ghosts, you're fractured spirits . . . both of you . . . I am more afraid I will die leaving you thinking that you're content fleeing, then ending up unsatisfied, unfulfilled. That's just as weird to me."

"Well, what can I say? That's what I've learned: Be content with what you have. Don't go looking for trouble; keep a safe distance."

"You're not trying to imply there'll be no avenging Sandy?"

Peewee stood and walked over to the window again, looking out.

"We have to do something," Will implored. "Impotent or not, Bret's a menace and needs to be taught one big frickin' lesson. He's out of control. The police actually should be involved."

"What about his tongue? Sandy seems to think that may be a lifelong punishment."

"Although it appears I might have died from his choking me, it's retribution for Sandy I need. You weren't there. What he and those guys did was reprehensible. I couldn't bear seeing him hit Sandy . . . any of it. He can't get away with it, tongue or no tongue. They have to pay, or they'll keep doing it."

Peewee turned from the window and sat on the sill.

Will sat up and pulled the oxygen tubes from his nose. "Goddamn it. What are we going to do?"

"Settle down. Your blood pressure is already off the charts." Peewee laid Will back down and put the air hose clip back on his nostrils. "No one should ever act when angry. They usually regret it."

"Well, I'm gonna stay angry. Why aren't you pissed? What about the photo?"

"Who says I'm not angry? I've learned not to make decisions when I'm pissed. Nothing good can come out of it."

"So, Mr. Cool, what we gonna do?"

"Don't know," Peewee said, and headed toward the door. "I'll be taking care of the photo, by the way."

"What about making a police report?" Will suggested again. "That's really what should happen."

"She's not going to do that."

"Why the hell not?"

"She's heard what happens. A woman, even if in Sandy's case it's just offering up a nipple as evidence, goes through a bunch of embarrassing, demeaning interviews and exams or whatever. She said her mother had a friend who was actually raped. The cops put together a rape kit, she said they called it, and even though there was proof of a rape, the rape kit never even got looked at. She said hundreds get done and rarely are any ever followed up on."

"That's total bullshit!"

Peewee knew his friend would be googling "rape kits." Will always got indignant and all worked up when an underdog got the short end of the stick or was not treated fairly. Apparently women were treated as underdogs in the world of sexual crimes. "It's more like her to take care of this herself, anyway. I agree the appropriate thing would be to file a police report. Bret deserves to be arrested. She feels the missing tongue was bitter justice for Bret. A life-long sentence."

Will shuddered. "If she swallowed it, will she shit it out?"

Peewee laughed. "I pointed that out and she slugged me. Said she'll watch for it and if she finds it, mail it to him all shriveled and full of shit. I think she was the wrong woman for Bret to mess with. She wants us to leave him alone."

"She's probably worried about what you'd do to him," Will said.

"She sounded more worried about what you would do," Peewee said as he headed for the door. "Said she could tell you were a smart, devious little fart."

Will smiled. "I'll have to think about that; come up with

something. A challenge."

"Peewee turned as he opened the door. "You settle down. Take it easy. We'll figure something out."

Peewee walked down the hall, mostly worried about his friend but also knowing he'd have to defend Sandy's honor somehow. He'd never felt like this toward anybody before . . . besides Will. Although he didn't look like it, his blood was close to boiling. The look on his face, the glare in his eyes, scattered the nurses as he passed.

Will realized how pooped out he was after Peewee left and felt slow and sleepy. The strange silence of a hospital at night settled around him. It was as if there was a distant, vague buzzing of machines, only broken by rubber-soled shoes squeaking menacingly down the hallway. At midnight he woke up, his head feeling better but his bladder not. He fumbled under the sheets until he found the bedpan urinal. He dozed off almost before he was done. Then, at one a.m., he was woken by a cheerful nurse checking his vitals. Couldn't she have just looked at the monitors he was hooked up to?

And an hour later, he was awoken by another nurse. This one was kind of cute, a dishwater blonde. "Do you have to micturate?" she asked. "Micturate" sounded a little like something he was sure she wasn't asking about. Seeing a blank stare, she said, "Go to the bathroom, pee?"

Why do they use those damn medical words, especially nurses? Then "pee"? Urinate would have sufficed. Something told him she must be a real blonde. "I did a while ago. I had trouble finding it," he mumbled, barely awake.

"Oh," she said, sounding sympathetic, concerned.

"Ith ok," Will said, yawning. "I finally did."

"Oh," she cooed again, dripping with sympathy. What the hell was her problem? "Is it really small?" she asked. "Do you need help?"

Is 'it' really small? Do I need help? What the hell was she talking about? Weren't all the bedpans and urinals the same size? Now awake, it hit him what she thought he'd meant. He considered having some fun with this, having her help him find 'it' but decided against it or he could probably get arrested.

Will had a little trouble getting back to sleep. It seemed he had just dropped off when at three a.m. he found a different nurse, a redhead this time, sticking a thermometer in his mouth. "Sorry, hate to wake you, but I gotta check your temp." At four a.m. he awoke to another nurse needing to stick a needle in his arm.

"How can a guy get any thleep around here? Couldn't this wait until morning?"

"Sorry," she said, sounding like she meant it. "We have to get the blood to the lab so the doc has the results when he makes his morning rounds."

"Don't tell me. He'll be in at 5:00?"

"No, 6:00. But I happen to know that at 5:00 they'll be taking you in for X-rays."

"X-rays of what?" Will asked, tired and getting crabby.

"Your lungs."

"I know, so the doc can have them when he makes his rounds an hour later."

She smiled understandingly. "I know. Hard to get much sleep around here."

It seemed he had just closed his eyes when he felt several nurses disconnecting him from his monitors. "Don't tell me: X-rays?" No apologies; this group was all business. Although it was dark, the day had begun.

CHAPTER NINE

At 6:15, THE SAME DOCTOR he had seen yesterday came in and told him that it appeared his lungs were clearing. He warned him that because of his premature birth, his lungs were not fully developed, which Will already knew, and explained that as he got older, an infection in his lungs or a severe pneumonia could actually be fatal, which he didn't know. He guessed his mother knew but was embarrassed by this. Protecting him by not telling him, she would rationalize.

The doc also told Will that the police would be in as soon as he gave them the ok, and that they had asked the lab to check for alcohol or drugs in his blood samples. They would be aware that he had ingested marijuana recently. He was told to expect that a psychiatric nurse would also be in to talk to him soon, before the police.

The news about his lungs alarmed him. The cold air had been bothering them lately. He knew since he was very young that his lungs weren't up to par, but he had learned to live with it. But he wasn't ready to admit that the events of last night could have killed him.

They had hooked him back up to all the monitors. He was beginning to feel restrained, claustrophobic, which put him in a foul mood. He was just beginning to feel like he could fall back to sleep when the door swung open and in walked a woman striding undauntedly into the room, not acknowledging Will but apparently strobing the room for a comfortable chair. She looked like she should be attractive: lean . . . but mean. Slim but boney. Everything about her was jagged, long skinny fingers with knobby knuckles. She wore a suit, so Will didn't think she was a nurse. Was she the police? Her suit looked expensive but looked like it was covering a bunch of broken twigs or hanging on a scarecrow. She scared Will. He wasn't sure why, but besides being crabby and stuck in this bed, something about her attitude just pissed him off.

When "Ms. Stealth" turned her back to him to slide the chair she had settled on over to the bed, he noticed, being an ass-man, that there wasn't one.

Finally seated, she looked at him. "My name is Ms. Headley. Let's see, your name is . . . " She looked at her folder. "Hau William Mitty?"

"Who are you?" Will asked. The way she talked sounded so . . . clinical. It was insulting.

"I told you, I'm Ms. . . ."

"Ok," Will cut her off, "*what* are you?"

She stared at him for a moment, before speaking again. "I'm a psychiatric nurse."

"You don't look like a nurth."

She once again stared, expressionless.

Will stared back. She didn't blink, and neither did Will. Finally she looked down at her file.

"We have some issues to discuss," Ms. Headley said flatly and cleared her throat.

Will maintained his stare.

"It says here you were born prematurely. There were no

brain bleeds, and, with the exception of a valve problem, lung underdevelopment, and being diminutive, you survived your time in the hospital . . ."

"That's nithe to know," Will interjected.

She sighed, then continued, "But there was a suspicion of necrotizing enterocolitis . . ."

"Necro-what?" Will again interrupted. "Makes it thound like I didn't thurvive."

Ms. Headley slapped her file down into her lap. "Would you kindly not interrupt me," she said.

"Thpeak English then." He couldn't quite put his finger on why she was pissing him off so much, but he had no desire to be respectful. She clearly did not respect him. She made him feel like an in animate specimen to be evaluated.

"You had an intestinal infection at birth, but no surgery was done to remove any part of the intestine. But the infection obviously had an adverse effect, as you are so underdeveloped."

"Well thank you. That's nice of you to say."

She ignored this and trudged on. "Often with premature births, there are neurocognitive problems . . ."

"There you go again. But I think you're calling me thtupid."

She actually rolled her eyes but continued. "The prevalent problems often include learning disabilities, like a lisp," and she looked up at him with an I-told-you-so smirk, "and various behavioral disorders."

Will figured if she wanted behavioral disorders, he'd happily oblige.

"Premature babies," she continued, "tend to do worse in school."

"Besides my lithp, I have dythlexthia and I am failing my thenior year." He was getting on a roll.

"Oh?" This got her attention. "Also, often patients that

have a lot of health problems tend to have a lot of thych—" she cringed, "psychiatric problems," she corrected, "substance abuse problems, tend to be immature, and are over-dependent on their parents even as adults. It says here there was marijuana found in your system. Do you abuse drugs often?"

"Oh, you won't tell my mommy? Pleath? I abuthe drugs because my parents do. So why can't I? Oh, please don't tell my mommy and daddy that I told you."

Ms. Headley really perked up now. "Oh, no. Don't worry. This is all confidential. What drugs do you use, and how often do you use them?" She prepared to take notes.

Willy had to bury his face in his hands to stifle a laugh. Of course this only titillated Ms. Headley more, probably assuming Will felt ashamed. "You can tell me. I can be your friend," she said, totally unreassuringly.

Right, Will thought. What an outright lie—she could maybe be a friend to a snake. "Well," Will said, sniffing, "I only use pot in the morning. I can't go to thchool drunk, you know—my breath—you do underthtand?"

Ms. Headley nodded.

"Then, at lunch, I snort a little coke, you know, to keep me going? How would you like to sit in a clath where you don't underthtand a thing the teacher is thaying." He was laying the lisps on her as heavily as he could. "I mean, it's all tho dithheartening. I feel like a total loother. They all make fun of me. Call me thrimp and other hurtful things. Tho coke keeps me going."

She was scribbling like crazy in her notebook. If this was all so confidential, why was she writing it down? "Umhum. I understand," she encouraged.

"Then, after thchool, I have a group . . . we're all outcaths. One guy, well girl, I mean she . . . he's . . . transgender. One girl is really fat, I mean O-beethe, you know? Another has bulimia. Anyway, we all meet behind the bleachers and get drunk. It's the only fun we have all day. We drink, have sex . . . you know, pretend we're normal."

She had quit scribbling.

"When I get home mommy can smell my breath. Of course hers reeks ath well. But she sends me to my room, and there I ethcape . . . usually L-ETH-D so I can really tranthend mythelf. I'm no longer tiny, underdeveloped, emotionally dithturbed. I can fly, like an eagle, thoar like an albatroth."

Ms. Headley stood abruptly, slapped her folder shut, and stomped toward the door. "You can now deal with the cops, buddy."

"Oh, aren't you my friend?"

"Thuck off, kid," she snapped and slammed the door shut. Rather unprofessional, Will thought, but he liked her spunk when she had lisped, even if incorrectly, on purpose.

But now what was he going to tell the cops? He wasn't wild about lying to the police, but he didn't want to get Sandy into an uncomfortable, compromising situation. He wanted to see Bret accused and get what he deserved, but there was no way to do this without involving Sandy. He'd need to talk it over with her and Peewee before he was questioned. He figured they all needed to have the same story.

The door swung open and two men walked into the room. Obviously these guys were detectives. Like he had seen the crooks say on TV, they had "cops" written on their foreheads. What to do? What to do?

One guy was big, with an intimidating scowl on his face. The other guy was short, smiling. The old good-guy, bad-guy routine? When the good guy asked Will if he was who he was, he pretended to be unable to breathe. He started gasping and thrashing around on the bed. Maybe a little overkill, but the officers retreated and in came the doc after they had left.

He looked at Will for a while, not acting alarmed at all with this thrashing. "So, you don't want to talk to the cops, huh?"

Will discontinued his charade and smiled sheepishly. "I need to talk to my friends, first," Will explained. "Is that possible?"

"What? To corroborate your stories? I don't think it's a good idea to lie to the police." The doc was sincere. Will liked him.

"I have to," Will told him. "Not for me; to protect somebody else from humiliation. Can you hold them off until I see my friends, especially the girl?"

"I don't know if I should do that."

The reason Will liked this doctor was that he felt he saw Will as a person, not just a body. "If someone would bite off a good part of a tongue and swallow it," Will asked. "What would happen to it?"

The doctor wrinkled his eyebrows but looked interested. "To the part that's left or gone?"

"Uh, both I guess."

"Interesting question," Doc said, and sat down in the chair vacated by the dour Ms. Headley. "Depending on how much is left, there would definitely be problems with speaking, eating, swallowing, producing saliva . . . kissing."

Will smiled. This doc was no dummy. "Like, what could have been done, you know, with the part that got bit off?"

"Well, if they had the piece that was bit off, and it had been put on ice immediately, they could have attempted to reattach it, but there would still always be speech and other problems."

"What if someone . . . swallowed the bit-off piece?"

The doctor leaned forward in his chair. "Two issues: one, the person who swallowed the piece could choke on it. That would be dangerous. The person whose tongue was bit off—there would be a lot of blood—could aspirate on the blood, much like you did last night on your vomit." The doc cleared his throat. "A young fella was brought into the emergency room last night about the same time you were. His blood-alcohol level was off the charts. He was missing a good chunk of his tongue and had choked on his blood . . . and vomit. He aspirated like you did on this combo." Doc paused. "This sounds like too much of a coincidence."

Well, that was copasetic, Will thought. "He alright?"

"You know this fella? The cops need to talk to him, too."

"Have they?" Will asked.

"No, he can't talk yet. What's left of the tongue is quite swollen, and he is heavily sedated. A few sensitive nerves in those tongues."

"If a person . . . you know—the one who bit it off—were able to get the piece down, what would happen to it?"

"It would get worked on pretty good by her—I assume this is a her—digestive system and then passed. It would have taken quite a lot of fortitude to swallow it." The doc stood, started toward the door, and turned. "I think that's already more than I should know. I can tell the cops they need to wait until tomorrow to question you." He lowered his head, raised his eyebrows, and looked at Will over his glasses. "Pretty smart move with the cops. Didn't look like you and Ms. Bone . . . um, Headley . . . hit it off." He smiled and left.

Will considered trying to go back to sleep, but he knew his parents would be back in, and he hoped Peewee and Sandy would show up. So he took his leather notebook out from under his mattress, spun the combination, and opened it. When his mother had brought it to him she had grilled him on what the dickens he had in there that it had to be "under lock and key?" She'd asked if Will wanted to tell her the combination in case he forgot it. Nice try, Mom.

Oct. 4

Ok, I don't want you sittin' there thinking you can be all righteous and smug and dismiss my instructions in the will just because I said I wanted to kill Bret. I admit to having gotten a little insight into how people around the world develop hatreds. I admit, I'll have a hard time forgiving Bret. The Dalai Lama would probably be laughing his ass off if he knew the peace shit I've been spewing. Maybe those Kurds, Shiites, and whatever the hell the rest of them are have got it right. Maybe there can't be peace in the world. But don't you think we have to try? The Dalai says, "You must not hate those who do wrong or harmful things; but with compassion you must do what you can to stop them – for they are harming themselves as well as those who suffer from their actions." Easier said than done. But of course he's right. If not, retribution and killing will never end. Remember what he said, "An eye for an eye . . . we are all blind."

So it sounds like a comfortable, simple lobotomy and sterilization for Bret is the ticket . . . just like I told you.

Right? Painless – so compassionate. I mean it'd be easier to just poke his eyes out and cut his pecker off, but that might hurt a little. Probably not compassionate . . . hmm . . . makes me think of something though. I wonder if you know the Edgar Allan Poe story "The Pit and the Pendulum"? Hmm . . . that would be fun. Anyway, I'm not you. You're probably straightened Bret out by now anyway? Of course that'll be after I've had a little fun with him.

JUST THEN THE DOOR OPENED, and in walked his friends. He stashed his will quickly back under his covers.

They came right over, pulled chairs up on either side of the bed, and the three of them went right to work. Peewee told them he had already discovered who the assholes were that had been with Bret last night and had a little powwow with each of them, persuading them that they were all dead, painfully, if a photo got out. Willy doubted Peewee's persuasion involved much compassion.

Peewee reiterated that he was handling the cell photos, not to worry. Then explained that they all, everyone involved in the "incident," had to have the same, basically true, story for the police. Except, unfortunately, anything sexual, for Sandy's sake . . . not counting the kiss, of course, would be left out of the story . . . everybody's story.

"You alright with that, Sandy? You sure you don't want to make a sexual assault accusation? And how will Bret even know what to say to corroborate our stories?"

"Of course I'm alright with it. I don't intend to submit to all those . . . I don't know—it's just too embarrassing and humiliating. If I thought it would make a difference somehow, like for other women who face this dilemma, I might consider it . . . but no, I'm not going to humiliate myself."

"Ok, I understand I guess," Will said. "Although I've convinced myself I no longer wish to kill him, it's only fair we come up with some way to punish the asshole then, ourselves." He looked at Sandy. "I'm afraid I can't forgive him for what he did to you."

"I understand," Sandy said. "But he has a lifelong sentence already. Thank you, though, for wanting vengeance for my sake." She leaned over and kissed him lightly on the lips; Will didn't kiss her back. "But," she said, nose to nose with him, "I'd simply rather not go through the whole thing. I'm ok. I'd rather just move on. It won't be as traumatic for me as for women who have been actually raped and have to fight to get their lives back."

Will's parents showed up then, before Will could fully process this last tidbit of information. Will's mother led the charge into the room. And nothing, ab-so-lute-ly nothing was going to happen until Mother got to the bottom of this. She asked Peewee nicely if he and the little lady would stay since she now knew they had both been there. Then suddenly she directed at Peewee, "Where the hell were you, anyway? You're supposed to protect little Willy here . . ."

"Ma!" Will groaned.

"Martha, just sit down and shut up for a minute, will you?" Walter said. "Then maybe we'll find out what happened."

Will gave his dad a sly fist-shake under his covers. *Way to go, Dad. She needs that . . .* And he told them the story—the story as agreed upon—which did include smoking grass. No sense lying about it when the police knew.

It didn't go over well.

CHAPTER TEN

EVERYBODY, IT TURNED OUT, corroborated each other's story. Bret's buddies had gotten to Bret before the police did. The stories were close enough that the cops bought it. Warned them all not to drink or take drugs. The judge they all appeared in front of said if he saw any of them—excluding Bret who was not out and about yet—again, he'd throw the book at them.

The doctor reluctantly released Will from the hospital, at Will's insistence, in three days. While lying in bed, bored, Will had googled 'rape kits' and discovered that 3,449 unanalyzed rape kits sat in storage, in Minnesota alone. He had a hard time believing this. It was almost incomprehensible. Was the justice system that broken?

He wanted to go back to school the same day he was released, but on the way to their house from the hospital his mother had one of her hissy fits and insisted he stay home. Will told her, fine, he'd stay home the rest of that day, but he was going to school after that. His mother wouldn't be able to argue, anyway; he'd be gone before she woke up. Will's mother's diatribe continued to rattle the windows on the way home. Will, in the back by himself, stared out the window, seeing nothing. The whole incident just wouldn't leave him. Bret had to pay somehow. He couldn't get away with what he'd done, even if he was tongue-less. That it was Sandy's fear of the legal process itself that prevented actual justice from being inflicted was just not right. It really pissed Will off. Fear of justice should be an oxymoron. He closed his eyes, the drone of his mother's voice dissipating as he drifted off . . .

Peewee sauntered into the closed meeting with the city council and police department. He had his reporter girlfriend, Sondra, at his side. Sondra was well known by the political figures around town. She somehow dug dirt from under the toenails of the city's leaders and badged protectors. Any news outlet, all under Sondra's spell, would gladly publish her digs. The officials didn't dare to bar her presence. Everyone loved a beautiful woman who could wield power. The fact that she was a tenacious researcher and marvelous scribe was second only to her beauty and allure. Long and lean, she showed off her legs with daringly short but tasteful skirts and wore tight tops to highlight her other attributes. Her jet-black hair against her soft, lightly bronzed skin a contrast so striking the men in the room were momentarily speechless and helpless. The women, including the mayor and head of police, didn't want to appear insecure if they acted petty and revealed their jealous sides. Anyway, nobody wanted to rile Sondra. And the imposing gentleman with her didn't appear to welcome any shit, either.

Sondra addressed the city council, "This is my associate, Mr. Peewee. He has some questions for you, regarding my next exposé."

All the Adam's apples in the room bobbed.

"Good evening," Peewee's voice boomed and reverberated in the room, even without a microphone. "I have just one question to ask," Peewee started as all eyes turned back to him. "It's a bit sensitive, but so is the issue . . . as well as your answer, right Sondra?"

"Indeed," she said, taking out a pad and sitting on the edge of a table off to the side, one leg bent, the other long, luscious limb exposed to the thigh.

"So, ladies . . . your attention again, please," Peewee resumed.

Sondra's finger directed their eyes back to Peewee.

His voice powerful, the men's heads snapped back to him. "Ladies and gentlement, last year a reported four hundred rape kits were filed in the city, but none, not a single one, was followed up on or even looked at. And 3,449 sit in storage, drawing dust. Not that it should make a difference, but as a woman and head of the police department, how can you live with that?" he directed at the frowning official. "Honestly, now. You shouldn't have to be a woman to know how humiliating and potentially damaging, psychologically, it is to report a rape to your authorities. What if you two, our Ms. Mayor and you, Ms. Police Chief, were raped? Would those kits get lost, stashed away somewhere? Never mind. It's a rhetorical question. The real question is, why does this happen? Ms. Police Chief?"

She looked at the other members, then at Sondra, who smiled expectantly. "We do what we can with the funds we're provided," she answered calculatingly.

"So, it would appear the buck is passed to you, Ms. Mayor?" Peewee had softened his tone a bit. He was becoming aware of how intimidating he could be.

"We have a huge budget for the police department. What they do with the funds is up to them," the mayor said, passing the buck back.

Peewee laughed. "Excuse me if this is sexist, but you ladies do an exceptional job covering your aah . . . excuse me—rear ends."

The two women grimaced.

"So, Ms. Police Chief, how much money would you estimate was spent last year hunting down, arresting, and prosecuting marijuana users?"

"I couldn't tell you off the top of my head."

"Off the top of your head?" Peewee was getting a bit petulant. "Would you say the number-one reason for incarceration last year was for marijuana use?"

"And sales!" she said, defensively.

"Well, yes. You're right. Everything that costs money must be sold. Now, if it were sold legally in stores, could that raise some precious tax dollars, free up some time for the police force to investigate real crime?"

Peewee held up a hand at each side of himself like scales. "In this hand a medicinal herb already legal in some states; in this hand rape, brutality, even murder. Where should we spend the money and time? C'mon. Really? The stats say 94% of rapists are never incarcerated! Rapists run free and a mother, who offers her son an epileptic, a natural opiate that relieves him of pain and paralyzing seizures could get a prison sentence? Tell me you don't think that's absurd."

No one said anything.

"An older gentleman who has a degenerating eye disease smokes a harmless natural herb to be able to see clearly and stave off blindness. But nope—that's illegal, we can't allow that. We gotta find these felons smoking that illegal weed and arrest them, put them away for a few years. Those black kids on the corner, let's put them in prison and make real criminals out of them. Maybe even arrest that woman that's easing her pain from cancer. It's illegal! So what if a few rapists go on raping, we've got to stop this drug abuse. It's illegal to smoke marijuana. That pot makes you dangerous . . . oh, that's right—it's booze that makes you dangerous. Oh well . . ."

"WILLY, WE'RE HOME," MOTHER MITTY CHIDED over her shoulder, interrupting his reverie. "I hope you've been listening. If you don't straighten out you'll be restricted to your room. No more going out at night when you abuse those dangerous drugs. You get that marijuana from that girl?"

"Good God, woman. Leave the boy alone for a moment. He just got out of the hospital."

"Well, he wouldn't have been in the hospital if he had been behaving himself. He can't do those things. He could have died," she pronounced and punctuated with the slamming of the car door as she stomped off toward the house.

Will and Walter sat silently for a moment. "Thanks, Dad," Will said dejectedly. It was hard to be mad at her when she thought she was just trying to protect him.

Walter sighed. "She's right, you know. You've got to be careful with what you do. You're not like Peewee. Just so you know, she's talking about hampering a lot of your activities . . . especially with Peewee. She doesn't think much of that little lady, either."

"What?" Will shouted. "What does she plan on doing, following me around with a leash and a whip?"

Walter grimaced at him in the rearview mirror. "She also says she wants you to quit working at the hardware store. Says she can homeschool you the rest of the year."

Will met his gaze in the mirror. All he could see were his

eyes. They looked pathetic, sorrowful.

"Not gonna happen," Will said, sliding out and slamming the door himself. He walked into the house, up to his room, fell on the bed and, he couldn't help himself, started to cry.

CHAPTER ELEVEN

Oct. 5

Item #4: EVERY rape kit that gets put together now gets analyzed and followed up on. I can't imagine you arguing against this one . . . a good one for you and Sandy to work on together? This is one of the most absurd, noxious things I've ever heard. Over three thousand rape kits . . . a stupid name to begin with. A kit! It sounds like a hobby for Christ's sake. But over three thousand sitting somewhere drawing dust! What the hell? First a woman is violated, violently, probably beaten, then put through the humiliation and personal invasion of having to prove it . . . and nobody follows up! Inexcusable. I can't fuckin' believe it. Take care of it.

If I'm beginning to sound a trifle adamant, excuse me, but . . . I am getting worried. I know you don't like to hear this, but if you're reading this, I've taken my last brief breath into these god-blasted lungs. This last stint in the hospital has me scared. And that I almost died at the hands of that asshole confirms my cynicism about fairness in who deserves the afterlife. I guess I've probably never come right out and said it, but you're my afterlife. Sorry buddy, but that's the way it is.

I do want to tell you how much you have meant to me. My life probably would have been miserable without you in it. The massive snuggie reprisal with Bret was probably the highlight. He's such a big asshole, regardless of how he was raised, I'm surprised his balls didn't get lost in there. There is no other person anywhere in this perplexing universe I would have wanted as my best friend. Actually, not to get too sentimental, but you're more like a brother. A big brother. Sandy entering the picture is a godsend. Rounds off our world. I hope, no – know you won't be blaming Sandy for the state of affairs you're finding yourself in, but I still want to say, because of who she is, she really had no choice. If there's any blame, blame me. It was my plan.

You can even agree with her that I'm a devious little fart.

Thank you. I've never said this . . . probably didn't really need to . . . but: I loved you.

WILL ABSENTMINDEDLY TOSSED HIS DART at the world. When he pulled it out he didn't know what to think. It was too weird of a coincidence; the dart had stuck directly in the middle of Burntside Lake. They had been talking about going to Peewee's uncle's cabin on Burntside. Had the Twilight Zone taken over his sanctuary?

CHAPTER TWELVE

THE MORNING WAS OVERCAST, cool, and humid. When Will went downstairs he found the kitchen empty, his dad already gone to his office. He finished his toast, slipped on his jacket, grabbed his backpack, and hoped to be out of the house and gone before his mother got up. As he opened the front door he heard her padding down the stairs.

"Willy," she started.

"No, Mom!" Will cut her off.

"Where . . ."

"No!" he repeated and shut the door shut behind him.

He heard it open. "Young man . . ." she started.

"No! No! No! No!" Will hollered as he trudged off toward the bus stop. When he got there a couple sophomores were pushing each other around. A freshman who always kept his distance was watching. They quit wrestling and stared at Will as he walked up. The one Will had never liked smirked at him and said, "Nice jacket, Shrimp."

Will slowly slipped off his backpack and, suddenly, lost it. He swung the backpack into the kid's face. The kid went down like a lump. The other sophomore stood there with his mouth hanging open. The lump got to his knees and looked up at Will, crying. Will could see blood running freely from his nose. His lip had also been split, spewing blood.

Will looked at the freshman, who was smiling brightly, holding up his cell, and then to the startled upright kid and calmly asked if he had a cell phone. He managed a nod. "Then call this guy's mother. It appears he may need a stitch or two." Will threw his backpack over his shoulder and walked off toward school. He actually felt terrible . . . so much for peace in the world. The Dalai Lama would not have approved.

As Will strolled up to the front entrance of Oak Grove Senior High, he found Peewee and Sandy sitting on the steps. He wondered what was up. An ominous shudder shook him, robbing him of breath, as he stopped in front of them. The chilly, damp morning air felt thick and heavy as it entered his lungs.

He had a hard time looking up. He had never felt bitter before. In spite of being the brunt of a lot of bullying, what he usually felt for the poor perpetrators was sympathy. He thought them sad. But the asshole sophomore, the almost daily maligned little freshmen standing off to the side, his mother, and the fresh memory of Bret slapping Sandy was too much for one morning. He couldn't even get himself to look up at her. Bret's had simply been too flagrant a transgression. He hated Bret for it. He hated himself. He finally looked up. They were both just sitting there staring quietly at him with shit-eating grins on their faces. "What's up?" Will asked.

"Had an interesting morning already, have we?" Sandy said.

"What?" Will wondered if word of the morning's backpack episode had already hit the grapevine.

"Whaddya mean 'what,' tough guy?" Sandy said, still smiling.

"You know what happened already? How?"

"You've gone viral, my man," Peewee said, also still smiling.

"A kid observing took a photo with his cell of you dogging it out of there and one of your poor victim. Now you're famous, you brute," Sandy said.

The freshman who had gleefully held up his phone, Will realized.

"What the devil did you hit him with?" Peewee asked. "There was major damage. The kid was bleeding quite profusely."

"Is he alright?" Will asked. On his trek to school he had tried to put the entire escapade out of his mind, focusing on the reason Peewee and Sandy were probably waiting for him: Bret, the four assholes, and now, foremost, the photos of Sandy getting out—just like his assault of the sophomore bully had.

"He'll live. So what did—"

"My backpack."

"Wha'd'he do to deserve such a bashing, Shrimp?" Peewee asked.

Will smiled. "Called me 'Shrimp.'"

All three broke out into laughter.

"I wonder if the kid will report it," Will said. "Wouldn't that be an ironic twist . . . me being the bully?"

Peewee and Sandy laughed again. Peewee stood and offered Sandy his hand. "The world will know eventually. But that's not the biggest concern right now. Bret, proving what an idiot he is, is threatening to put the images from the other night out on the internet if we try any sort of retaliation."

"So?" Will asked.

"Well, apparently there's got to be some kind of retribution to satisfy your bloodlust. So Bret will have to pay somehow. But we can't let him keep those photos."

"It really isn't that big a deal . . ." Sandy started.

"Oh, yes it is," both Peewee and Will responded

simultaneously.

"We've got to get his phone before he does something really stupid," Peewee said. "He's just too big a dumbass. Let's head out, now. Sandy, you sure you want to come?"

"Absolutely. I'm not going to act like I'm backing down or afraid to face the assholes."

"Where we going?" Will asked, walking with Peewee and Sandy toward the Westfalia.

"We're meeting with Derek, Scott, and Roscoe."

"The other four guys?" Will asked.

"Yip," Peewee said as they climbed into the van, Will riding shotgun, Sandy in the only other seat behind Will. "You don't know them?"

"I've seen em around," Will said. "Didn't know their names."

"Any of them ever give you shit?" Peewee asked Willy as he pulled away from the school.

"Mostly just hanging around Bret, guffawing as he tortures me." Although several of them had pulled various antics in the past, Will was worried what Peewee might do to them, especially now. As far as Bret was concerned, Will had no compassion. Previously he had looked at Bret—like his cohorts—as weak and insecure kids. Lately his idealism had been failing him. He no longer hoped that they would eventually mature. Like the kid he bopped with his backpack—did Will teach him a lesson? Or do little assholes just grow up to be big assholes?

It struck Will that just like the Middle East, any hope of straightening them out had to be when they were very young, before they got filled with hatred or whatever and became assholes.

Regardless, he had decided that with a smattering of penitence, the world was better off without Bret. He had spent recent nights lying awake, first devising ways to torture Bret, and then feeling like a hypocrite.

Every night after traveling the world and closing his book, he'd think about Sandy. She was a mystery. On top of the fact that she was gorgeous, although she might be playing with him, she seemed to imply that she thought of him sexually. Even if she was just "playing," he didn't care. Unless he found a four-foot-seven-inch version of Sandy, he'd accept what he could while he could. He felt like he could love her, did love her, but wouldn't allow himself to believe she loved him. How could she?

He'd have to be happy that he had introduced her to Peewee. He felt she was worthy of his friend. But part of her mystery was just what she was capable of . . . like regarding Bret for instance. Would she really be satisfied with the tongue maiming? Or did she have something more planned? Hard to tell. Even if *she* might be satisfied, he wasn't. The thought of Bret outliving him irritated the hell out of him. Edgar Allan Poe's dark side shaded his mind, again.

"You sure none of those guys have given you shit?" Peewee asked again before they got to McDonald's. "They've only watched, not participated?" When Will didn't answer, he said, "Well, these guys, especially the two that held Sandy, are totally complicit in what happened that night. They can't think they got away with it, either. And then the idiot, Scott, although he wasn't in on restraining Sandy, was holding you and took the photo and sent it to Bret. If Bret shares it with anybody, Scott's just as much to blame. If they've been bugging you, I want to know."

"Just look at them as collaborators," Will tried. "Maybe we can just consider discouraging them? Maybe encouraging them to find better friends." Will peeked back at Sandy, who had been pretty quiet.

Sandy just smiled. "You're a better person than I am, Shrimp."

Once again Will wondered what she was capable of; she was perplexing yet thrilling to him . . . much like Peewee. He had decided, as the recent realization of a probable shorter life was laid on him, that life was about relationships and adventures. These two were the relationships that made his life worth living . . . and the adventures, especially what he hoped to be the ultimate adventure if things worked out, he knew would be worth dying for. He almost could look forward to his dying because of the good he knew Peewee, maybe with Sandy at his side, would do after Hau wilted and willed over his spirit. But, while he still had it, he wouldn't be content until Bret was held accountable. Will looked out the side window. It was a bleak, dim, Edgar Allan Poe kind of day. The world became a blur as it passed by his window. Will settled back, closed his eyes, drifted. The thought that Bret would lose his sense of taste had aroused his imagination. He closed his eyes. A sinister smile slowly inched onto his face . . .

WILL HAD DISCOVERED AN ABANDONED mental asylum in an old part of town. In one of the rooms there was a table previously used to strap down and restrain violent patients. Peewee agreed to snatch Bret, bring him, and strap him, naked, to the table. Peewee was leery of doing this, but Will told him Bret would be alive when he was done with his little adventure, that Will was going to give Bret a little of his own medicine. Peewee left reluctantly, leaving a squirming, sputtering Bret lashed to the table.

After Peewee left, Will attached a large wooden frame to the table that draped a razor-sharp pendulum over Bret's midsection. Smiling devilishly at a wide-eyed, terrified Bret, Will started the pendulum, back and forth, back and forth, inches from Bret's groin. To stifle Bret's incoherent guttural sputtering, Will smacked a wide strip of duct tape over his maligned mouth.

"Now listen," Will began, "I'm going to tell you what I'm going to do and why. Every time you cry out, scream, or arch in pain, I'll lower the pendulum. Cut you like you did to Sandy. It's up to you: nobly accept this punishment for your transgressions, or die a painful death. The pendulum will sever you inch by inch with each swish . . . swish, finally slicing your body in half. I'm inflicting this punishment on you not because you've been a bastard to me but because of what you did to my fiancé, Sandy.

"Now quit squirming, you big baby. Every time you move, I'm going to lower the pendulum. Got it?" Bret's eyes opened wide at Will's hysterical laughter. Bret's entire body was trembling, his eyes pleading, beseeching.

"Sandy," Will continued, "has already taken care of your sense of taste and of 'speaking no evil.' I'm going to complete the task, so you are no longer able to get any pleasure out of tormenting people. I'm going to leave you 'senseless.'" Will's high-pitched, shrieking laugh shattered against the walls like broken glass. "I'm sure you've heard of 'hear no evil?' Well first I'm going to take away your sense of hearing by drilling into your eardrums." Will held up a cordless drill, smiling gleefully, pulling the trigger for effect. Bret's eyes bugged out in terror at the sound of the drill bit spinning menacingly, inches from his ear. "Look at it as a mercy. You won't be able to hear your own screams when I remove your hands with this chainsaw."

Will started the chainsaw; the clashing whirr of sharp metal blades spinning drowned out Will's crazed cackle. Tears of remorse dripped down Bret's ghostly white face. "You know, the less commonly used 'feel no evil.' You'll no longer be grabbing anyone's breast," Will yelled over the screeching whirr of the razor-sharp blades gyrating now inches from Bret's eyes. Will then cut into the table, inches from Bret's fingers, splinters flying like pieces of bone.

Will shut off the saw. Silence, save for the sound of Bret's terrified, muffled, tongue-less beseeching. "Then, I'm going to pluck out your eyes. 'See no evil,'" Will shrieked in a maniacal howl. "No more porn for you."

Will then held up a blowtorch, smiling demonically. Lit it. Held the flame close to Bret's nose and blew the flame into his nostrils, singeing the hair. The pungent smell permeated the chamber. "I plan on using this to take away your sense of smell . . . you know, 'smell no evil.' Ah, yes, yes . . . but wait. Even better." Will's high-pitched voice pierced the putrid air. "As long as I went to the trouble of igniting the blowtorch, I might as well burn your eyes out. Yes, yes! Less blood that way. Although the way your eyes are bugging out, maybe I'll just pluck them out with this." Will held up a set of pliers. He pinched Bret's thick, brutish eyebrows in the pliers and pulled out a few hairs. Bret twisted, his horrified, deep, guttural grunts escaping the duct tape.

"Oh, no, now look what you've done. You've got a thin slice just above you know what. You must control yourself, or *shlip* . . . off with your malignant penis. OFF, OFF. HA!

"Not much blood yet, though," Will whispered menacingly in his ear. "Like with Sandy." Just the thought incensed Will. "I know—that gives me an idea. I can't see you procreating any little Bret bastards. One of you is way more than enough. So let's leave your beady eyes, pug nose, and cauliflower ears for last, so you can hear your screams, smell your blood, if . . . you cannot control yourself." Will smirked gleefully. "Think you're capable of suddenly developing some self-control? Now, quit squirming, you've got another little nick down there awfully close. I'm afraid I'm going to have to lower the blade again. There it goes: swish, swish. Back and forth. Swish, swish.

"Peewee says you're impotent. That'd actually be good news for the women of the world, but especially for you, today, if you get my drift. Well, let's see. Let me show you some interesting pictures in this *Playboy*. C'mon take a good look. Now don't get excited or zip, zip, your malignant little thing will be flopping on the floor. How about this one? Ain't she something? No? I don't see any reaction down there. Either you suddenly have remarkable fortitude or . . . well, we know that's not true. Maybe it's men beating women that turns you on? Does that do the trick? Oh, I see a flicker down there. I know, how about this ? Two guys restraining this pretty dark-haired young lady, while this asshole threatens her with a knife.

"Oh, oh . . . it looks like that's the ticket. You better control yourself. Ohoh!"

Bret's muffled screams escaped through the duct . . .

"WILL!" PEEWEE KNOCKED WILL OUT of his malicious but delicious reverie by punching his arm. "We're here. You were gone again, weren't you? And you had the weirdest smile on your face. Almost scary. I've never seen it before. What the hell were you thinking?" Peewee turned to look at Sandy. "You ever seen him disappear into his head before?"

"Yes," Sandy said, "in English class, although I can hardly blame him."

"Where's here?" Will asked as he shook himself alert. He felt on odd sense of release, satisfaction almost. He had never had a dream so . . . on one hand depraved, on the other hand appeasing. It was almost like he had satisfied his vengeance for Bret. He definitely felt different. Could that be?

"Yeah, McDonald's. Remember? We're meeting our assholes here," Peewee said.

Right, Will thought. Witnesses, just in case Peewee got pissed.

Peewee, Sandy, and Will walked calmly into the fast-food joint and located the three stooges silently waiting, attempting to look penitent. The place was mostly empty as it was late for breakfast, early for lunch. They were in a large corner booth, and Peewee slid in first, then Will and Sandy, facing the stooges. Peewee glared across the table. The three of them were unable to return the look and stared down, playing with their cups of Mountain Dew.

"What! No food or pop for us?" Peewee asked. "That's not very hospitable."

"Oh, uh, you want something? I can go get it," Drew said, starting to slide out of the booth.

"Just sit down and shut the hell up, you moron," Peewee reproached, something resembling carnage in his tone. "First off," Peewee began, "you're to apologize to my friends here for your participation in what better be the last time you degrade another living thing—male, female, or animal."

They didn't look up but all three muttered, "I'm sorry," into the table.

"Look at them!" Peewee warned, firmly.

"No!" Sandy said immediately. "I don't want them looking at me. Just keep your hideous eyes on the table."

Derek, the biggest, dumbest one of the group, looked up

anyway. Smiled at Sandy. Instantaneously Peewee's hand shot out and smacked Derek's face, knocking his head into Scott's head. They both dropped their heads, blood starting to drip into Derek's lap.

"Dammit," Derek muttered under his breath and froze, immediately regretting that he'd said it. Peewee slapped the back of his head, bouncing it off the table.

"That's no way to talk around a lady," Peewee reprimanded.

Derek groaned and held his head in both hands.

"Now listen up, you dumb shits," Peewee continued. "You're on probation. You dimwits understand 'probation'?"

None of them dared say anything or even nod. They just continued to stare at the gray Formica.

"First condition of your probation: you're respectful to all people. I'd like to say kind and compassionate, but I don't want any unrealistic expectations. The word will get out if you break your probation. There are a lot of people out there who would love to see your asses kicked. This does not only include my two friends here but probably every man, woman, child, and animal you come into contact with. You're going to reform yourselves from royal assholes to respectful assholes. If I hear of anything you've done, anywhere, that's degrading to another living thing, your ass-kicking will involve broken bones. Bones—plural. If there is a second offense, well let's just say there won't be a third. Nod your heads if you understand."

All three heads nodded immediately.

"Second condition: you make sure those photos are gone. If it or they get out, it will haunt you for the rest of your lives. I will hunt you down, and, I'm dead serious, it'll be the last image you ever see. Nod if you understand what I mean."

Roscoe nodded.

Derek said, "You can't do that."

Scott said, "What about Bret?"

Peewee said, "You wanna try me? How did Bret get the photo, Scott?"

Scott squirmed in his seat. "He made me."

"You're pathetic. 'He made me,'" Will repeated in a whiney, cry-baby voice.

Scott started to look up at Will but stopped himself.

"I repeat," Peewee said to Scott, "if it gets out, ever, the first one I come after is you, for taking it. Next will be Bret, and then the rest of you."

Peewee glanced at Will. "I know my kind and astute friend here would rather you become decent people than be maimed and become a burden on society."

Will grimaced.

"He's much more idealistic than I am and probably than Sandy is now that she's met your sorry asses. What you did to her is close to unforgivable."

Sandy, who had been quiet the entire time, finally spoke, "What you did to me was not only degrading and demeaning but perverted. Do you really want to be perverts? And Will almost died. He ended up in the hospital for days."

"Bret did it all," Derek said, still to the beige Formica.

"Wrong," Peewee interjected. "You all participated, and by doing nothing, you are just as much to blame. You could have stopped it."

"What about Bret?" Scott asked.

"What about Bret?" Peewee said.

"He says," Scott said hesitantly, "that if you do anything, he'll release the photos on the internet."

"Well," Peewee said, "I don't suggest you do nothing this time."

"But . . ." Derek started.

"I've told you how it is. And I hope you realize that I'm dead serious. The key word being 'dead.'" He paused for effect, his eyes cold. "It or they don't get out. Nod if you agree."

Their heads all bobbed.

"Let's blow this pop stand," Peewee said to Will and Sandy.

As they walked out, Will looked back, and the four of them were still staring down, afraid to look up. Will shook his head; just think of the things Peewee could accomplish if he put his mind to it. He honestly thought Peewee had scared these guys straight. He liked to believe in people. Why would someone *want* to be an asshole? Maybe, if even out of fear, they could reform and see the error of their ways. Will certainly hoped so, for their sakes. Bret on the other hand . . .

Will turned back for one parting look as Peewee and Sandy exited. He saw Derek look up, smile, and . . . give Will the finger. Oh, shit, Will thought as he followed Sandy out the door, leaving his faith in people behind in McDonald's.

When the three of them climbed back into the van, they decided they needed to talk everything over, and Will and Peewee lobbied to get together that evening. Will said someone's house is probably a good idea but not his. He had to get out of the house because his mother was being relentless. Peewee said absolutely not his place. Sandy said her house was fine. When she told them the address, Peewee, familiar with the area, looked up at her, saying that was rolling and rocky and woodsy countryside . . . beautiful but rather expensive. After he finished writing it down, Peewee said that he knew the property. That he'd wondered about who or what was on it, only having seen lights, what looked like a lot of lights, visible through the trees, with impressive stone gates guarding the place.

Oct. 6

I have to admit to being a little confused. Am I a hypocrite for professing a desire for peace in the world, and yet wanting to torture and maim Bret? Yeah, I've given up on wanting to kill the bastard. Too easy on him. I wanted to believe that a little maiming wouldn't bother me, but actually I have repented. I'll leave any retribution or redemption up to you. I only hope he's not stupid enough to let those photos out. I'll probably end up telling you about the idiot, Derek. He's probably dead by now; a fatalistic, tragic cloud seems to follow him around. I just hope it wasn't by your hand. Anyhoo, he gave me the finger when we were leaving McDonald's that day. I'm guessing that didn't bode well? I'm sure you took care of it. Probably broke off the nasty finger. Ahh . . . I can just hear it snap.

Well, we'll probably be meeting your future in-laws tonight on our first visit to Sandy's. I have a plan I hope you can live with. By the time you read this, you'll know what I'm talking about. I believe you'll understand. Just remember, I love her, too. And, in case you don't live up to my expectations, this plan is my backup. I know you. I know you don't want to interfere in my friendship, or whatever you want to call it, with Sandy. I also admit to being conflicted there as well. I can tell you two should be together . . . yet, yes, I love her attention. Who wouldn't? BUT, I fully realize, unfortunately, a 4'7" damaged shrimp and a 5'8" perfect mermaid ain't gonna happen. So she's yours. You hear, right? She's yours. Take care of her and any baggage she may be lugging along.

CHAPTER THIRTEEN

PEEWEE PICKED UP WILL AT 6:15. Will had come out from the back of the house, rather than the usual front. Peewee assumed he was sneaking out. They soon were out of traffic and the transition was palpable—from anemic blacktop streets with crowded little 'boxes' to rolling countryside in every shade of green, gold, and red imaginable and 'estates.' They mostly made small talk in the van. Finally Will asked how Peewee knew Sandy's folks' property so well. Did it have something to do with first and sixth hours? Peewee smiled at his intuitive little friend. Told Will that he was not the only person capable of forecasting surreptitious events. Warned Will that he'd better stay alive to find out just why he was familiar with the property. That he would be pleasantly surprised.

When Will asked why not surprise him now, Peewee asked him what magnanimous, surprising event was it that he had been forecasting.

"Ok, be that way," Will said. "Bet mine is the bigger surprise."

Peewee looked over at his friend; raised his eyebrows. "I guess we'll just have to live with the suspense, you weird little fart-head."

When they came to the mailbox of the address Peewee had written down, they found the stone pillars Peewee had mentioned, bookending two cast-iron gates. Serious gates fortunately open. They followed the driveway as it wound through a mix of birch, red, and white pine—all giants—and the smaller spruce and fir. The view of the house never really opened up due to the dense tree cover. They could tell it was long and low-slung with a lot of glass. In the fading twilight, yellowish light illuminated the trunks and branches around the house. The cobbled drive ended at an open area surrounded by trees, which left them facing a large gabled garage that had the look of a carriage house. They pulled between two trees that obviously designated a parking spot.

They followed a stone paver walkway, edged by evergreen shrubs and withering hostas that led them through trees to the side entrance of the house. The roof's overhang was seven to eight feet wide with vertical log supports, but the walls they could see were mostly expansive windows separated by steel. They arrived at a side door, a massive wooden French door that managed to look like it belonged on a lodge.

Sandy surprised them by opening the door before they knocked and let them in.

"Holy shit," Will shot out. "Quite the place. What the hell does your dad do?"

"Makes money," she answered matter-of-factly. "So does Mom."

"Great house," Peewee said. "We get a tour?"

"Not tonight. My parents are home."

"We get to meet them?" Will asked. "I'd like to meet your parents."

"Not tonight. Let's head down to my apartment."

Will and Peewee followed her through a knotty pine

mudroom with antler horns for hooks where Will hung his coat. "We're going to go down the back way," Sandy explained, pointing to a staircase of wooden steps with a Navajo blanket runner. The walls here were also knotty pine with a smooth, twisting piece of pine log for a handrail. They walked down and into a room with a wall of glass overlooking water visible through the dusk in the distance. They passed a kitchen on the right and followed her into a living room facing the water. A very real-looking gas fireplace illuminated the room with an amber light. A hallway next to the fireplace led off into darkness. Chips, salsa, and fruit juice were laid out on a coffee table in front of a large leather couch.

"You look like you're used to entertaining," Peewee said. "Obviously not guests from our school, considering your apparently limited social life."

They sat down, Peewee and Sandy on the couch, Will next to Sandy on an adjoining Indian-blanketed chair, all nestled around the very unique coffee table made from a thick slice of burl set on the back of a carved wooden bear. "I've been trained by my mother—the hostess with the mostess," Sandy explained. "And you're correct. You're my only guests so far from our illustrious school . . . and probably will be. But you know I've only been going to Oak Grove this year."

"Oh?" Will said. "I always wondered why I hadn't seen you till this year. Thank God for Big Betty."

Sandy laughed, leaned over, and punched him lightly in the arm. "I had decided already I was going to meet you. You didn't have a chance."

"Me?" Peewee asked.

"Yeah, you, too. You didn't have a chance either. Figured you and me would make good babies."

Peewee recoiled. There was no beating around the bush

with this lady. He raised his eyebrows at Will and recovered by whistling the tune to "You must have been a beautiful baby . . ."

"Quick there, big guy." She looked over at Will and smiled. "Our babies, you and me, would . . . I don't know. I'd love to see what kind of babies we could make, too."

Peewee and Will shifted in their seats and glanced at each other, Will crossing his eyes. Both reached for a handful of chips.

"Umm . . . just how many babies you plan on having?" Peewee asked, sitting back and looking over at Will who again crossed his eyes, which was something he did when somebody said something goofy.

"Whose?" she said.

"Mine and Will's, the way it's sounding."

"A dozen or so. Can't you imagine all your kids, you two—dozens, playing together, growing up together, taking care of each other. What ya think?" And she sat there smiling, looking back and forth at each of them.

Peewee again looked at Will. "Ah . . . when do you plan on us getting going?" Peewee asked and reached down, grabbing another handful of chips.

"Don't know," she answered and pushed the bowl of salsa toward him. "If I'm the one to supply this hoard, I decide when. Who knows? Maybe tonight?"

Peewee and Will looked at each other and shrugged. "Naturally," Peewee said, laughing. "Might as well get started if we're going to have dozens. Who you plan on starting with?"

Will loved it. You could never tell if she was serious or being sarcastic. It frightened him a bit that he almost thought she was serious. He was surprised at Peewee's nonchalantly going along with it.

Peewee's phone rang. It surprised Will he had it with him. He looked at whom the call was from; listened without saying a word; ended it without saying a word. "Gotta go. Sorry, Will."

"What? You gotta go already?" Sandy said.

Peewee stood up. "Ah, yeah. Sorry. Will, let's go."

"You can stay," Sandy said to Will. "If you have to go," she finished, frowning at Peewee. "I'll drive Will home."

It drove Will nuts that his parents wouldn't let him drive. Their excuse being they couldn't afford to alter a car for his four-foot-seven-inch frame. Will knew that wasn't the real reason. Mom had to protect her little guy. She would think it was her fault if something happened to poor, helpless Wee Willy. "Aw, I'd hate to make you have to go out and . . ."

"Nonsense," Sandy cut him off. "How about we get that ride on my Indian?"

That shut everyone up for a second.

"I've got to go," Peewee said abruptly. They followed him up the stairs to the back door. "After while," he said as he left. "Crocodile," to himself after the door closed behind him.

"Want to watch a Janis Joplin concert?" Sandy asked as they retreated back down to her apartment. "Got some good clover."

Will smiled. He loved *her* making fun of him.

For an hour and a half they watched Janis sing her heart out. Sandy took a couple puffs, but Will declined. He wasn't sure what was going to happen the rest of the evening, but he had learned that with smoking, he would be more inclined to fall to certain temptations and say, "What the hell. Why not?" He had an inkling she was up to something, especially with the crazy "baby" talk.

While they watched, Sandy became rather animated . . . dancing to some songs, leaping around, expounding on certain lyrics, bopping into Will, grabbing him, hugging him. Will not protesting.

When the concert was over, she flopped back on the couch, patted her lap, and said, "Head, here." Will didn't argue. She had on what he'd call lounging clothes. The top was a soft, loose button-up sweater. Will couldn't help but notice that there was some quite noticeable shifting and swaying going on behind the flimsy fabric, what with her bouncing around and bopping against him. The pants were a silky fabric, flowing, not tight but . . . flimsy like the top. A lot like pajamas, Will realized. But—his head in her lap? In a heartbeat.

She ran her fingers gently around his skull, lightly massaging his scalp. It was nearly heaven, and Will focused on her fingers rather than the flimsy fabric separating his head from . . . he couldn't think about what. Suddenly she told him to stand up. He did, curious, and so did she. "I want to show you my breasts."

Will's mouth opened but nothing came out.

"Ok?" she asked.

"Uh, well, I don't know." This was as flummoxed as Will had ever been. "Sure, I suppose . . . but why?"

"Well, you could have already seen them, but, since you were a gentleman and didn't look, I just feel like I want you to see them."

"So, you want me to . . . Why? Or why now?"

She slowly unbuttoned her top. Will kept his eyes on her eyes, but he could tell in his peripheral vision that he had been correct; there was no bra, or chemise, or anything but flesh under the delicate fabric.

"You can look," she whispered and held her top apart.

Will continued to look only at her eyes. "I still can't." Will couldn't believe what he was saying, or—what she was doing.

She sat down on the couch and patted her cushion next to him, without rebuttoning her sweater. He sat awkwardly, not taking his eyes off hers. "Why not?" she asked.

"I do want to look. I think you're the loveliest thing on this planet or any other. I'm sure your breasts are totally lovely."

"But?" she said, softly.

"I love you," Will spurted out, surprising himself.

"I love you, too," Sandy said. "Look, I was obviously exaggerating about dozens of your and the big oaf's kids, but if my crystal ball is right, I see myself settling in for the long run with the big guy."

"He have any choice in the matter?"

"No."

Will laughed. "Well, then, they're his to look at."

"No way. They're mine to do with as I wish." She still hadn't rebuttoned; it didn't appear she was going to. It was starting to drive Will crazy. He felt like he was getting a stiff neck holding his eyes up. "Look. Tell me straight up," she asked. "How long are you supposed to live?"

Will swallowed hard. This was not his favorite subject. Yet he figured if he was Sandy and he really did love himself, which at the moment made him probably the most conflicted individual alive, he figured he'd want to know this rather important detail.

"All I know . . . is . . . my life will be shortened. And as we just discovered, I am more susceptible to things that could kill me."

"Like with your lungs, you mean?"

"Yeah, I guess. The heart's a little iffy, too."

"Well, listen. I've never had really good friends before. People I could trust. I really do love both of you weirdos." She sat back, her top flopping open, he could tell.

She's calling us weirdos? He was going nuts. He wouldn't believe himself if he told himself the story; he just tells the most beautiful woman in the world he loves her, and she tells him she loves him, and her tits are in full view, and it just didn't seem right to look. Damn!

"The reason I asked is I'd like to make love to you."

"What?" Will sat straight up, ready to bolt.

She sat up, too, and put her hand on his thigh, either to stop him from taking flight or to turn him on . . . both of which were working.

"Are you a virgin?" she asked and grimaced. "Sorry to be so direct, but who knows how much time we've got, right?"

"I don't plan on dying tonight," he said, thinking he just might.

"But, who knows? Right? So . . . ?"

"No. Yes. No, I've never slept with a woman."

"Everything works, right?"

"Take a look." He leaned back and there was a rather impressive bulge in his jeans.

"Yikes," she cried. "Why are you hard now? You haven't even looked at my boobs."

"You kiddin'? It's worse not looking, and I've never had a woman's hand on my thigh, except for probably my mother's, and especially not the hand of a woman . . . a woman . . . well the sexiest woman I know."

"How sweet," she said.

"Sweet?" Will said. "I'm not sweet. I'm . . ."

"Yeah, what?"

"I'm a four-foot-seven midget. A shrimp. Shrimps aren't sweet."

She leaned into him, the hand on the thigh sliding precariously close, cupping her other hand on his cheek, holding it as she gently kissed him on the lips. He could feel the energy from her bare breasts, inches from him, causing his skin to prickle under his shirt, every tiny hair standing on end. "Let's go into my bedroom."

"What! Now?" He couldn't relax. His entire body felt like a static electric magnet, every nerve and hair follicle twitching.

"Why not?" she said.

"What about your parents?" Will scanned the room as if they might be holed up behind a chair, ready to pounce.

She smiled. "My parents are nothing like your parents are, having met them. They're very sophisticated. They respect my space. They would never just walk down to my apartment, much less into my bedroom, without getting permission."

No, nothing like his mother for sure, Willy thought. "Permission? How would they even get permission?"

"The intercom, silly." She touched his cheek and kissed him lightly again. Will only partially responding. He was going nuts.

"What about Peewee?" Will argued.

"What about Peewee? This is not about Peewee."

"What do you mean!" he almost shouted. "You plan on having Peewee's babies, and making love to me has nothing . . . oh, I don't even know what I'm saying."

"Will," she was back to whispering, "I hope Peewee and I make it. It just seems right. I've never met anyone like him . . . or you, either. You're my men. But you and I just wouldn't get married. Doesn't mean we can't have babies. It'd be fun, like I said, to see what we could create. Heck, if it could work, I'd marry both of you fools, have your babies, and watch em all grow, like I said."

"You don't really, I mean really, think that would work?" Will asked, shaking his head. "You can't be serious?"

"Oh, I'm serious. You want to make love to me, right?"

Will looked out the window, but it had gotten dark, and all he could see was the reflection of the flames in the fireplace.

"Well?"

"Of course," he finally said, exasperated. "But not now."

"Why not?" She kissed him again, and this time with a flick of the tongue, doubling the size of his erection. He imagined her breasts lingering, luxurious, lyrical, singing sweetly to him. Still, he refused to take even a glimpse.

"Does Peewee want to make love to me?" she whispered.

"How do I know?" Will said, knowing but not wanting to know.

"What you think?" This time he couldn't help himself; when she leaned into him her right breast . . . the injured breast—the breast that had been bleeding . . . touched his shoulder. He met her tongue with his.

"No. Yes. Why wouldn't he want to?" he managed as she sat back. Why was she asking him this? Why was she torturing him? How could he think of Peewee when his penis was now doing his thinking?

"Well, can't all three of us be happy and get what we want?" she whispered.

This was scaring Will. Was it starting to make sense to him? If three people loved each other, why not share the love? There were "open" relationships. The Mormons seemed to manage the multiple-wife bit, and in the Middle East the sheiks had harems. But he had always thought of this as debauchery, the women subjected to the sexual whims and servicing of the man. He had thought about children. Why not? Just because he was a little underdeveloped? His sperm could swim with the best of them, he was sure. Of course he'd like to have babies with Sandy. There was nothing he'd rather do in his diminished time on earth than make love to Sandy. But not tonight.

"You think Peewee'd think this was a good idea?" Will asked.

"Don't know. But he doesn't push it with me. He's very careful not to be romantic."

"Why?" Will asked.

"I imagine because of you."

"What do you mean?" Will asked, knowing exactly what she meant.

"I think you know," she said. "I'm stuck in the middle, anyway. I can't imagine having only one of you. Why not both? The alternative is neither."

"Because . . ." he started. Because societal norms would . . . but why would he give shit about norms? After all, he wasn't normal. Of course his mother would have a massive hissy fit . . . but what if she had nothing to say about it?

"Look," she said, holding his hand. "I don't want you to die without experiencing what it's like to make love."

"You know what it's like?" Will asked her.

"Yes and no."

"What do you mean?"

"Well, before I came to Oak Grove, I was at Highcroft."

Will knew of Highcroft, an extremely posh private high school.

"My 'friends' were the kids of my parents' country-club set. Rich, entitled, wealthy kids . . . with dangerous drugs. Drugs that trick you. You do things that, well, damage you."

"Sorry. I don't want to pry," Will said.

"Pry? God, no, I want to know everything about how you see life, and I want no secrets from either one of us. I'm not a virgin. Booze and coke were my downfall for a while. I thought I was having fun, but I was being used. I didn't really have a breakdown, but I lost faith in the human race. Until I saw you, an interesting little oddball, I preferred to think of *everybody* as ghosts—vague. I really didn't trust anyone. I've got a psychiatrist, but she's a ghost, too. They make me see her."

"Make you? How can they make you?"

"They thought I was suicidal."

"What made them think that?"

"I withdrew. I stopped talking. Wouldn't go to school. I crashed my car one night, almost hurt somebody. So I quit drinking, snorting . . . everything. Quit the fake friends as well. Just pretty much quit."

"What about tonight?"

"You're different. You're real. She cupped his cheek in her hand again and gave him a not-so-gentle, open-mouth kiss. When her tongue found his, he quickly withdrew it. He wasn't sure about reciprocating. If he stuck his tongue in her mouth, what would that imply?

"I . . . I don't really know how to kiss," he said.

"Know how to kiss? You're doing just fine. You just let your feelings take over . . . you know? Let's go into the bedroom, slide under the sheets, take our clothes off and . . . and we'll practice. I want to be the one to make love to you, even if I am damaged goods."

CHAPTER FOURTEEN

Oct. 7

If I was confused yesterday, I'm . . . flummoxed, I guess I'd say, tonight. Flummoxed doesn't do it. No: baffled, befuddled, bewildered, discombobulated, unzipped . . . there – unzipped does the trick. Am I the stupidest man alive? Noble? Trustworthy or un? I doubt I'm going to get any sleep tonight trying to figure out just what the hell happened tonight. I imagine by the time you're reading this you'll know what transpired after you had to leave. Although I don't know . . . I don't think I can tell you. If I haven't:

Item #5: You cannot ASK Sandy about it. I'm sure she'll tell you, anyway. Nothing we did would deter you from *fulfilling the terms of my will. That's all you need to know. You may be unzipped yourself by the time you're reading this, I suspect, and what happened or didn't happen that night will no longer make any difference. Just be the man I know you to be.*

Speaking of that, your destiny in life no longer includes having a smoke and contemplating your naval. Sorry. There'll be serious shit to deal with . . . so don't sweat this "small" stuff.

Guess I'll toss the dart and see where my destiny takes me.

PEEWEE PICKED WILL UP THE NEXT MORNING, which he rarely did, saying they couldn't have another bus-stop incident again this morning. On the way to school, Will decided he'd better tell Peewee about Derek.

"You know," Will started, "yesterday when I looked back at the assholes when we were leaving?"

Peewee looked over at Will but didn't say anything.

"Well, Derek . . ."

"Don't tell me he gave you the finger."

"Well, yeah. How the hell did you know? You were already outside."

"It just doesn't surprise me. It's why I whacked him a couple times. Some guys only understand fear and intimidation."

"So you don't think it'd be cooler to sit down with him, get him on our side? Try a little diplomacy rather than violence and intimidation? Why would he want to be an asshole? Maybe he could come to realize that what they did with me and Sandy wasn't right, and . . . and . . . really, why would anyone want to be an asshole?"

Peewee smiled down at his eternally optimistic, sanguine friend. "He can't help himself. If he gave you the finger, he's gonna be trouble." They pulled up in front of school, Peewee wishing Will good luck with his newfound notoriety.

"What if the principal knows about it? And we skipped yesterday. My mom will kill me."

"I suggest you quit worrying about what your mother thinks. I'd ok'd it with the principal yesterday, anyway. You're in the clear."

Peewee said he'd see him after first hour. They'd talk to Sandy about a trip to Burntside over the three-day break—which was coming up the next week.

Will perked up. "Really? We *can* go to your uncle's place?" Will wondered if he dared tell Peewee about the dart. He probably wouldn't believe him. It was like the Twilight Zone. All he could say was:"That's really weird."

Peewee smiled at Will's exuberance. "Yip. I talked to him a couple days ago. What's really weird?"

"And it's cool with him if we bring Sandy?" Will decided he wasn't going to tell Peewee about the dart. It almost seemed like predestination, fate, or destiny . . . something Peewee would not want to talk about.

"Yip. He won't be there anyway. See ya later."

Will made it through homeroom and first hour without any incidents with bored bullies or tongue-less tormentors. Was this because he had gone viral? Of course Big Betty was in his second hour. As Peewee said, Will heard nothing from the principal. He assumed the sophomore kid might be too embarrassed to make a big deal out of it: "Yes Mr. Principal, the four-foot-seven-inch midget attacked me without any provocation and totally whipped my ass." He also wondered who knew about Bret and the incident? He hadn't seen any of the four stooges. Nobody had mentioned anything about anything, which was probably good because it meant the pic of Sandy was not circulating.

When Peewee stopped by before second-hour English they waited for Sandy to show up. Big Betty walked by, nodding at Will, ignoring Peewee. As the bell rang, Will slipped in before getting locked out—but there was still no Sandy.

At lunch they tried her on her cell but got no answer. Will texted her that they needed to talk, explaining that it was about heading up to Ely over the long MEA weekend, not about last night. By the end of the day, he had had no response. They tried calling her again, but it went right to voicemail. Will left another message: they could have a fun long weekend, if she would be able to go.

On the drive to the hardware store, both were quiet, both wondering what might be going on. "What happened after I left last night?" Peewee finally asked.

It took Will a while to answer.

"Well?" Peewee urged, looking over at Will.

"We watched a Janis Joplin concert, and then she drove me home. Why'd you have to leave?"

Peewee recognized Will's strategy to avoid answering. Something he had become very adept at. Peewee paused a moment.

"It was my mom who called. Dad had too much to drink."

It was Will's turn to look at Peewee. Will had guessed it

was a problem at home. Peewee's dad, although a little ornery around the hardware store, was a decent boss most of the time and could even be funny. He actually deferred a lot to Peewee at work. But, at home, he ruled the roost with the Mrs., and when he got drunk, the rooster in him was aroused. It was not unusual for Peewee to have to intercede. Will knew this upset and embarrassed Peewee. "Anything bad happen?" Will asked gingerly.

"I probably should warn you before we get into work. I'm not sure what kind of mood he might be in. He's going to have a hangover. Hopefully it's worn off by now. But I had to get a little firm with him to settle him down last night. I don't know how he's going to be."

"Sorry," Will said. "He didn't hurt your mom?"

"I don't want to talk about it. Was Sandy getting sick last night or something? Why isn't she in school?"

Will hesitated.

"It appears something is up. What happened?"

"Nothing, nothing. She was fine when she drove me home."

Peewee peered over at Will, one eye closed, the other boring into him.

They rode the rest of the way silently. When they walked into the store, except for the bell that tinkled when the door opened, it was quiet. No customers. They walked back to the repair-shop counter in the back and found Peewee's dad working on a lamp, trying to fix it. Before he noticed them, he threw the lamp behind him on the floor, smashing it. When he looked up and saw them, he glared.

"H. W. or whatever the hell your name is, you're fired. Your old lady called, doesn't want you workin' here no more. You're worth shit anyway. Too damn puny."

Will didn't like "puny." He abruptly turned and headed

back out. He heard Peewee say calmly, "Dad . . . " and heard Mr. Kovak yell, "Go drive your puny friend home. We've gotta talk before you come back to work anyway. Both of you, get the hell outta here!"

Peewee followed Will out. "Sorry Will. I think he's been drinking today, too."

"I've never seen him lose his temper like that," Will said.

"Yeah, well, like I said, he's been drinking. Don't worry. He can't run the store without us. What's that about your mom not wanting you to work here?"

"Never mind," Will said. "You might as well take me home. I've got to have it out with her. I especially need to get an understanding with her about how things are going to change. What was with the lamp?"

Peewee laughed and scratched the back of his head. "It got broken last night. Looked like he was trying to repair it."

"So he's mad at you about last night?"

"No," Peewee replied, sighing. "He's mad at himself. When he drinks he just takes it out on other people. Let's go out to Sandy's. See if we can rouse her."

"Really?" Will asked. "I don't know if we should."

"Why not?"

"Well, we don't know her parents, and . . ."

"And what? This isn't like you. What's up?"

Will walked toward the van. "Nothing. I just think it would be respectful to talk to her and even her parents before barging in there. Let's go."

"Where? To face your mother or Sandy?"

Will groaned. "Quite the choice. No, Mom and I need a talk."

Oct. 8

I hope that, before you're reading this, I've figured out some way to get me a place to live or at least out of this house. Mother won't talk about college. I've been accepted, of course, at the U, but Mother says they can't afford a dorm for me and both my sister's and my tuition. I've been saving up but was hoping to buy and modify a car. I've got my own account. Mother doesn't know about it. And now that I'm eighteen, I've even put some in a mutual fund. Short term of course.

So, what should I have done? Just gone out and bought a car on my own? I haven't wanted to ask you. You know how popular that would make you with Mother Nazi. I feel bad about my father, but I almost blame him. He's allowed her to control everything for so long, she thinks that's the way it's gotta be. He gives in, and she expects poor little Wee Willy to follow suit. I guess refusing homeschooling and not quitting the job is something. I'd refused to even talk to her about it. She tried earlier today. Not much luck. She's just beside herself. She can make life miserable, as you know. How ironic, huh? Maybe that's the way it's supposed to be. The more you're repressed, the more you want to break free. And how ironic that the repression is the result of love. I really do feel sorry for her. I know she loves me . . . she just doesn't know how. But who would?

I'm worried about Sandy. Hopefully you're sitting somewhere nice with a pregnant Sandy reading this. But she's so, I don't know . . . an enigma. A contradiction: tough, strong . . . yet so fragile. Be careful, you hear? Yeah, I know you will be.

Item #6: Protect Sandy . . . even from herself. Be a good father, no matter what. I think we're way more influenced by our parents than we want to admit. Look at me. I'm stubborn like my mother, and I hide like my dad. You seem to be strong enough to counter any of those errant genes in your father . . . although when sober, he can be great. He's got some good, strong ones in there, too. It's remarkable how drinking can mess you up. Maybe he should try smokin' a little dope, instead? And your mom's cool. I've always really liked her. She never treated me like a Wee Willy. Anyway, I know you'll be a great father.

That's the big reason why I wanted to meet Sandy's mom, to see what genes she comes from. I imagine you know the man in the house is her stepfather. It'd be interesting to know what his expectations for Sandy are. She won't talk about her real father. She will always remain an enigma, I'm sure. A dark, delicate one.

Speaking of delicate, it's rather how I'm feeling lately. "Delicate" . . . not the way a man wants to feel. I am worried, Peewee. This may be weird, but at night in my room, I talk to my organs, cheering them on (No, wise guy, not just that one!). I can hardly hear my lung's response . . . but it's not encouragement. My heart feels old. It doesn't listen. It just resolutely pounds away, without time to answer. Like a long-distance runner at the end of a race. Actually more like a gimpy marathoner – working hard with no hope of finishing the race.

Sorry. I gotta get better at not bitching. There's no sense in it. It is what it is. I can smell food. I'd better go check. I could starve. She's so mad, she doesn't even scream or holler for me anymore.

The next day Peewee talked Will, who was still acting reticent, into driving out to Sandy's after school before going into work. Nobody answered the door. They ventured back into work not knowing what to expect, and Mr. Kovak yelled at them for being late . . . as if yesterday hadn't happened. Will had had it out with his mother. He told her he wasn't going to be homeschooled and he wasn't going to quit his job. His dad had, surprisingly, supported him, standing his ground against a full-blown barrage of threats by Mother. Will left them fighting and exited to his sanctuary, feeling bad about his dad who would now get the worst of it.

Two days went by. Both Will and Peewee called, texted, and emailed Sandy to no avail. They didn't know whether to be concerned or irritated. Peewee knew something had happened at Sandy's, but Will continued denying that anything had happened, starting to get defensive. Peewee, knowing his friend well, couldn't figure out why Will wasn't being forthcoming with him. It was one of the first times their relationship had been strained. They would eat lunch, ride into work, work, and ride home not talking. Sandy's mysterious absence caused and worsened the strain. Both of them were going nuts.

Peewee, not used to letting things slide, needed a resolution, needed to fix whatever was wrong. So, finally, Friday evening after dropping Will off after work, he called Sandy's parents' landline. A voice much like Sandy's answered. Her mother had been cautiously friendly, telling Peewee that Sandy was not doing well, did not want to see anybody, and was considering dropping out of school and might go visit her aunt in Florida for a while. She mentioned that she and her husband were going to be out of town that weekend. Peewee took that as an invitation to come and see what was going on with Sandy.

After work on Saturday Peewee, rather than argue with Will, drove, alone, out to Sandy's. He found the gate closed, climbed it, but found no lights on, and nobody answered the doors again. He decided to venture down to the lower level, concerned about setting off an alarm. He felt guilty, but he looked into Sandy's apartment, which was dark. He felt like he could see a shadow on the couch, but it didn't move when he knocked, and he wasn't sure.

Sunday evening, Peewee called again. Mr. Stickner answered this time and said Sandy didn't want to see him or Will and that they should not bother Sandy, or them, again. If Sandy wanted to see them, she would let them know.

Monday, Peewee told Will about his Saturday night visit and what Mr. Stickner had said. Will was upset that Peewee had acted on his own, leaving him out. But he understood and even felt guilty, leaving Peewee in the dark about what had happened that night. But this was something Pewee had to hear from Sandy. This discord was something they had never experienced before. They both dazedly went through their day at the store, not knowing what to say to each other. Will was actually surprised at Peewee's lack of success in discovering what was going on with Sandy. Will felt guilty about this as well, since he was pretty sure he knew. It was the first time Will could remember Peewee not accomplishing something on his own that he badly wanted.

Oct. 9

Funny; it hit me today that nobody has picked on me in quite a while. Big Betty even smiles and nods to me in English class. Even asked me where Sandy was. What's up with that?

Ok, I'm avoiding the big issue; what the devil is up with Sandy? Why won't she respond? When her parents told us to leave her alone, I almost panicked – I imagine you did as well – and that she might move to Florida! Holy shit. Then I realized you'd take care of it. No need to worry. I will have tried a little guise tonight anyway when I call. Play on her sympathies. Make her feel guilty if she doesn't respond. BUT, if she doesn't, I suspect we will have done something proactive . . . before she might have gone to Florida. I guess we would have had to track her down down there. Mother would have loved that. I know, I know, gotta stop worrying about what my mother thinks. It's hard to break away from her control. I keep telling myself she's only doing what she believes a mother should do. Of course, by the time you read this, I hope to hell I have broken away. I apologize for having resisted being proactive about figuring out what's up with Sandy. Of course now I'm sure you understand why, and you two are laughing about it. How about that: "proactive?" Pretty good, huh? Get used to it.

Item #7: I'm willing to you my newly discovered skill – PROACTIVITY. But not only regarding a mislaid, dark, exotic lady. Sorry big fella. But there's stuff here in the U.S, and around the world that needs attention, needs taking care of. By someone like you who can make a difference. Hiding is not a consideration. Remember what both the Pope and the Dalai said: you have that responsibility to your fellow man and your planet. The Pope, the other day, speaking to a large group in Europe, implored that the youth, today, not be 'couch potatoes,' not hide in computer games, social media, or wherever. To have a social conscience and try to have an impact against social injustices in the community and around the world. This is the Pope talkin, not just some shrimp. Again, sorry . . . but it is what it is and you are who you are.

That evening Will tried Sandy several times, resorting to sympathy, embarrassingly, to get her to call him back. He said things like, "What if I die and you had refused to see me?" But no luck. Finally, he called Peewee to tell him he had not been successful. Did they dare just wait it out? Let her get over whatever it was? Except, what if she decided to get over it in Florida?

Will, of course, understood better what might be going on. It must have something to do with that night. He worried but found it hard to believe that she might place Peewee and him in the same category as those other insensitive a-holes she used to hang around with. They didn't really know her all that well. She had told Will that she was "damaged." Just how severely had she been hurt? He considered talking with Peewee about what had happened but decided, again, that that would be up to Sandy. He didn't think Peewee would hold it against her, but it was personal, and he felt that what she had told him and what had, or hadn't, happened was in confidence.

Peewee had told Will that he was going out to Sandy's after work the next day and asked if he wanted to go. Will vehemently agreed this time, proactivity being a newly admired trait. He would be a hypocrite to expect it of Peewee if he did not expect it of himself.

THERE WAS A YELLOWISH LATE-AFTERNOON LIGHT filtering through the trees as they headed out. The sun was slipping, but the wind picked up. As they got out of town and near Sandy's, the tops of the big red and white pines were whipping wildly back and forth. They could hear, through the always-open windows, the creaking of the trunks as they swayed. It was chilly, but it felt good to both of them in spite of Will's lungs, as if they needed to suffer. Will had his size-twelve boys' jacket on, Peewee his plaid shirt open as usual over a T-shirt that read "Hope Town," with a red-and-white-striped lighthouse below the letters. Will's dart a few days ago had stuck on a little village—Hope Town—on a tiny island in the Bahamas called Elbow Cay. Will had suggested it would be a cool place to go. Peewee had ordered the shirt the next day. When Will noticed, he managed a smile. "Nice T-shirt."

Peewee just winked at him. It was not like Peewee to wink. Things were definitely uncomfortable.

When they pulled through the stone pillars, the gate

fortunately open this time, wound down the drive through the swaying trees, and arrived at the garage, there were no cars. "Lookth like nobody's home," Will said. "Leth go."

"What? This is not like you. And why the hell are you lisping?"

Will took a deep breath, forcing himself not to lisp. "So, what are we going to do?" He was still uneasy about facing what he assumed was the cause of Sandy being AWOL.

"Well, I know this is extreme, but we could try knocking on the door."

"Yeah, yeah, you've had a lot of luck with that." They looked at each other for a minute. Will overcame his reticence with his new sense of proactivity. "Ok. Let's go," Will said, and slid out of the van. "What do you think her parents will think of this thing? They'll think we're druggies."

"What? Where in the devil does that come from? Now you're embarrassed by my van?"

"No, well yeah, I mean no, I don't care."

"Looking at this place, I'd say they're sophisticated, apparently unlike you. I doubt the van will be a problem, if they ever even get to see it."

Will ignored the deserved slight, and they walked up to the side entrance. They knocked several times at the side entrance, but no answer. There were no lights visible on the main floor of the house, but it was barely twilight so they weren't really necessary. "Well, looks like nobody's home, should we go?" Will said.

"Normally you'd be the one to be sneaking around, checking the place out, insisting we try a different door. Why don't you just tell me what's going on? Something had to have happened that night." Peewee was confused. As far as he knew, Will had never been deceitful with him. Was it something

Sandy had done?

"I . . . told . . . you . . . a thousand times—nothing happened!" Will answered irritably.

They followed the stone walkway around the corner of the side entrance, Peewee leading the way, and found the main entrance. The entire house was dry-stack stone, steel, and glass. It sprawled off into the trees past the recessed main entrance, which was enclosed on both sides and overhead. Although the exterior of the entrance here was stone, the door was massive, made out of a dark-gray steel, with the outline of stark birch trees imprinted on it. There was a doorbell next to the door and an intercom screen with a tiny lens above it. Both of them were uneasy with what they were doing, especially after what Mr. Stickner had said, so they looked at each other and hesitated. Finally both shrugged, and Peewee rang the bell, Will pushing the button on the intercom and saying into it, "Sandy?" Neither got a response.

"Let's walk around to the lower level to Sandy's door," Peewee suggested. "If she is down there she may not have heard us. I thought I saw her in there in the dark Saturday night."

"I think she can see us through a camera or something. Remember last time, she met us before we even knocked."

Peewee countered, "Maybe she's not looking."

"You sure about this?" His discomfort was starting to even irritate himself. They had to get to the bottom of this. He realized, a bit startled, that this thought was much like something his mother would say.

Peewee gave Will another questioning look, shook his head, and walked back by the side entrance and down the stone steps toward the lake. Will followed, brooding. The back of the house faced the southeast, and the setting sun illuminated the still-blazing colors of the far shore. Will followed Peewee as he turned the corner and walked along the wall of glass, respectfully not peeking into Sandy's apartment this time, to the sliding-glass-door entrance. When Peewee was about to knock, they both jumped back, startled. Sandy was standing at the door looking out at them. She was barefoot, wearing a robe, her hair mostly covering her face. The three of them stood there staring at each other, not moving, for what seemed like hours. Peewee and Will's message: they were not leaving. Sandy's apparently that she wasn't going to let them in.

The house blocked the setting sun, and Peewee and Will soon found themselves in shadows that were cooling rapidly. No lights were on in Sandy's apartment, and she was fading into the dark, although she hadn't moved. Just before it got dark enough that Sandy would disappear in shadow, Will finally shivered and hugged himself. Sandy slipped the door partly open and said, "Yes?"

"You sick?" Peewee asked.

"Don't know how to answer that," she responded.

"Can we talk?" Peewee was doing the speaking for a change. Will atypically quiet. "Inside might be a good idea or we're going to have frozen shrimp pretty soon."

A smile almost broke out on Sandy's face. Will shivered again. "I'm not dressed," Sandy said. "Just go away."

"No," Peewee answered, surprising Will.

She slid the door shut but stayed there looking out at them.

Will rubbed his arms to get warm.

Sandy slid the door open again. "Go away," she said, and slid it closed.

Both Peewee and Will shook their heads, standing their ground.

She slid the door open. "God you two are stubborn. Alright. Come in."

She flipped on the gas fireplace and retreated to the dark couch. Peewee and Will followed, Peewee sitting next to her on the couch. Will sat on the edge of the coffee table, facing them, nobody saying anything.

Finally Sandy broke the silence. "You're the ones that came here; don't you have something to say?"

"No," Peewee said, "you do."

"I knew Shrimp here was bullheaded." She wrapped her robe tightly around herself and sat back, pulling her bare feet up under her. "I found that out the other night. What exactly would you like me to say? Did Will tell you about it?" Her hair was still completely covering her face, her voice drifting out through the black, silky shroud.

"Said you watched a Joplin DVD. Didn't indulge me with the rest of the story, yet. Why haven't you been at school, or answering your phone, texts, emails . . . the door? What's up?"

Sandy quivered slightly. Although they couldn't see her face, they could tell she was starting to cry.

To Will's amazement, Peewee slid over and put his arms around her shoulders and hugged her. She leaned into him and put her hand out toward Will. Will knelt in front of the couch, taking her hand.

After a few moments she stopped shaking. "Time to talk," Peewee said. "Whatever it is, both of us are here for you."

She leaned away, shook her hair back off her face, her eyes red. "That's just the problem," she whispered.

"How can that be a problem?" Will finally asked, though he knew the answer.

She left Peewee's arm around her shoulder and held onto Will's hand but sat up straight, looking back and forth between the two of them. "I can't win," she finally said. "It's a setup."

Both scrunched their eyebrows but didn't say anything.

"I would have made love to you that night, you know," she said to Will, and then looked at Peewee. "What would you have thought of that?"

Peewee didn't respond.

"Well?"

"I don't know," Peewee said.

"I wanted to be his first. The first woman to make love to him. I love him. He said he loves me. So . . . ?"

"I'm afraid I love you, too," Peewee said. "I knew the day Will introduced us."

"So there you go. You see? I can't have either one of you, if I can't have both."

All three sat there, speechless, now not daring to look at each other.

Sandy finally looked up at Peewee. "Have you ever made love?"

Peewee's big Adam's apple bounced up and down. He looked down at her. "No, not made 'love.' You?"

"No," she answered with a guilty little grin, "not 'love.'"

All three sat quiet, Peewee's hand still around Sandy's shoulder; Sandy still holding Will's hand. "We're going up to Peewee's uncle's place up north," Will said, speaking for the first time, "as I'm sure you know. Leaving tomorrow after work for the long weekend. Naturally we want you to come with us."

"I've still got some thinking to do," she said, dropping Will's hand and shaking Peewee's arm off. "Please leave me to it. Please."

"See you in school then tomorrow?" Peewee asked.

"We'll see. Now please leave."

Peewee told her they would stop by after school to pick her up whether she was in school or not. They left but couldn't think of anything to say to each other, Peewee afraid to ask anything, Will not sure what to say.

Oct. 12

Well, I'm writing this on the strange night we got back from trying to convince Sandy to go with us to your uncle's place on Burntside. I have no clue as of writing this whether she came with us or not. Obviously, you know, of course. I understood her conundrum, as I'm sure you will as well . . . and am, I hesitate to say, flattered. Maybe we should just grab her, throw her in the van, and haul her up there kicking and screaming if we have to? I feel like we're dealing with predestination. Here we are worried about Sandy . . . and us, and what to do with her, yet I know you're sitting there, maybe together, reading this. I'm fairly confident my plan has worked out. No new item, but, I want to reiterate, it was MY plan, not Sandy's.

CHAPTER FIFTEEN

SHE HADN'T SHOWN UP AT SCHOOL the next day or answered her phone. Neither Peewee nor Will had brought up the Janis Joplin night; neither knew what to think or say. If she wasn't going to go with them, they didn't know what they'd do.

They left school early Wednesday and drove out to Sandy's. The gates were open, but no cars were in the driveway again. Of course it was a five-car garage, so they had no idea if Sandy, her brother, or parents were home. They walked down to her door and could see her on the floor in front of the fireplace playing with her little brother. When they knocked, the brother dove into Sandy's lap and wrapped his arms around her, burying his face in her hair. She stood and, carrying her brother, walked to the door, and slid it open.

"Are you packed?" Peewee asked. When she didn't respond, Peewee said, "We'll be back in two hours. We've got all the food. Bring some warm clothes."

Will and Peewee went home and finished packing. Will found an angry note from his mother asking where the hell he was and that she and Walter had gone to visit Will's sister at her college. Will thought, *Great! One battle scene we can avoid.*

Peewee came early to pick up Will. On their way back to Sandy's, neither said a word. They often rode without talking, but the silences were always comfortable. This one wasn't. When Peewee drove past the turn to Sandy's, Will looked over at Peewee. "Where we going?"

Peewee didn't answer.

"You gonna tell me where we're going?"

"Nope," was all he got for an answer.

In a mile Peewee turned south on a gravel road, which wound into a heavily wooded area. It got hilly, and small lakes were visible through the trees. After a couple miles Peewee slowed and turned left onto a rutted driveway. There was a metal sculpture that held a mailbox at the entrance. Will could see two names out of the corner of his eye as they passed: P. Kovak and H. W. Mitty.

Will looked again at Peewee, his wheels spinning faster than the van's. "What's this?"

Peewee glanced over and smiled. "You'll see."

The driveway, two parallel ruts, wound up a grassy hill, through some oaks at the top, and headed back down toward a little lake. Will started shaking. He could see a green roof through the trees.

The ruts ended behind a little house that looked more like a cabin. Peewee got out, but Will just sat there. "You coming, Shrimp?"

Several scenarios scampered around Will's brain, but he couldn't settle on one long enough to make sense of the situation. Was Peewee renting this place? Why were their names on the mailbox?

"Would you get your skinny little ass out of there and follow me?"

Will climbed out and followed Peewee along the side of the

graying, unpainted cedar shake cabin. There were three small windows along the back and three more, larger ones, on the side. The roof was green shingles, covered in browning moss. At the corner there were steps that led up to an open, covered porch.

Peewee went up the steps and disappeared. Will stayed at the corner and looked out at the lake. The sun was behind them, illuminating the far shore in the yellow afternoon light. Peewee reappeared. "Are you coming?" he asked through a suppressed grin.

"What . . . what is this?" Will asked.

"A cabin."

"Yeah, yeah, I know it's a cabin. But . . . "

"You notice the mailbox?"

"Yes, but I don't understand."

"Well come on in and I'll show you your bedroom."

Will walked up the stairs onto the porch. Straight ahead, halfway down the decking was a screen porch that wrapped around the far side of the cabin. He turned toward the water. A wide series of steps led down off the decking to a path, which led to the lake. Someone had trimmed the lower branches of the oaks so that the water was clearly visible through the trunks.

Peewee's head stuck out a front door just in front of the screen porch. "You lost?"

Will looked up at Peewee. "Tell me what's going on, right now." He leaned against the porch post for support, his eyes beginning to well.

THEY DROVE BACK TO SANDY'S, not at all sure she'd be up for or ready for the trip . . . not daring to even talk about it. Both were holding their breath as they approached the side door. Will hoped Peewee would use some of his magic on her if necessary. He really couldn't remember a time when Peewee really wanted something to happen that he didn't make it happen.

She surprised them by meeting them at the side entrance with her suitcase. She told them to shut up, walking brusquely through them, bumping them out of the way on her way to the van. Will and Peewee looked at each other and grinned.

Once again Will sat shotgun, Sandy in the back. Will had offered her shotgun, but she had declined again, reiterating that that was his spot. No one brought up her mysterious absence. So far, so good. Will was really happy that his parents had been out of town. He knew there would have been a knock-down, drag-out fight if his mother knew he was leaving for the weekend. He wasn't sure what side his father would have been on, but mother was the predominant wind.

"What'd you tell your mom?" Sandy asked Willy as they got underway heading north.

"That I had to help Peewee with homework," Will fibbed. "Trying to get him to finally graduate."

"Well, gee-golly, thank you," Peewee's attempt at sarcasm, "but I'm not interested in graduating, as you well know."

"Why the hell are you still going to school?" Sandy asked. "And why do you get there late and leave early every day?"

Will was brimming with excitement, but Peewee had asked him to keep the cabin their own secret for now. "Gotta look out for Shrimp here, until he graduates," Peewee answered.

"Will, you know where he goes?" Sandy asked.

"He's kept it a mystery."

"Oh, hell. You must know. You two don't appear to have any secrets from each other. You get along so well."

"Not always," Will answered. "Peewee doesn't like to be pressured. Me either, I guess." He tossed a glance at Peewee.

"The closest I've seen to him losing his temper is when I press him about shit."

"Like what kind of shit?" Sandy asked. "Have you ever seen him lose his temper? I can't imagine. Does he turn green?"

They all laughed. "Later," Will said. "Everything will be clear later."

Peewee looked over at Will. "Later?"

"What's your uncle's place like, Peewee?" Will asked, subtly, as usual, changing the subject.

"Yeah, where exactly is it?" Sandy asked.

"You've heard of the BWCA . . . Boundary Waters Canoe Area?"

"Of course," Sandy said. "But never been there."

"Well, Burntside Lake is on the edge of the Boundary Waters. It's beautiful. We'll take a little paddle in a canoe, and maybe even a kayak if the weather permits."

"Isn't the water a little cool for canoeing this late in the year?" Sandy asked.

"We're not going to be *in* the water," Peewee said, a second surprising spit of sarcasm for him. "On top is drier."

Sandy reached over and slugged him. "Hey, I'm the sarcastic one. Shut up. Besides, a canoe'd probably sink with you in it."

"Kayaks aren't tippy are they?" Will asked. "I've always wanted to try one."

"Nah," Peewee responded. "Less than a canoe . . . you're sittin' right on the water in a kayak. Closest thing to being a duck."

Suddenly both Sandy and Will started quacking. Peewee just shook his head.

"You said your uncle's not going to be there?" Will asked.

"No. He and Helen, his girlfriend, are in Washington DC

trying to get the attention of the federal government about the copper mine they're planning up there."

"I thought they mined iron ore on da range?" Sandy said. "What's your uncle upset about?"

"If we don't want to listen to the little guy with the big mouth for the rest of the trip, we better change the subject. It is the *Iron* Range, but this is copper—precious metal—mining, which is, apparently, a different ball game. He says he's afraid the mining is going to happen—too many people up there with mining in their genes. Too many unemployed miners worried about now, not later, as I'm sure Will will gladly rail on about if we encourage him. My uncle, although he feels it's absurd they're willing to risk polluting the Boundary Waters, just wants to make sure, if the mining contingency prevails, that it's done with as little environmental impact as possible . . . *if* it's gonna happen."

"Meaning there's going to be some polluting for sure," Will interjected, pleasantly surprised at Peewee's awareness of the issue. "Good luck with that. And, as you implied, there's the boom and bust . . ."

"You talking about my tits, again? You know," Sandy said to Peewee, "I tried to give him a peek at my boobs that night . . . since he was such a gentleman the night of the fiasco. I don't know, I just felt, you know, this was on my own terms, but . . . no, he still wouldn't look. How about that?"

Peewee glanced over at Will, who ignored both what Sandy said and Peewee's look.

"I mean," Will started in anyway, "they're threatening the long-term sustainability, livelihood, of the entire area—it being a huge wilderness and recreational destination—for twenty years of a few jobs. Shortsighted. Stupid."

"'Sustainability,' eh? He always talk like that?" Sandy asked.

"I told you not to talk about it," Peewee said.

"What? I changed the subject. No wonder he wouldn't look at them, he doesn't even want to talk about them."

Will leaned around his seat and looked at Sandy. "Well, in that case . . . "

"No. No. Too late. That's two strikes. One more you're out of here."

That made them all chuckle and shut Will up.

They made it to Hinckley, sharing nothing but some attempts at clever small talk. Will was actually the funniest. With his squeaky but interesting voice, almost anything he said sounded funny. Peewee had always thought that Will was a riot, even as a little kid. He especially liked his lisp, which was absent a lot more lately, especially with him and Sandy of course. But the lisp threw everybody else off. They underestimated him and expected him with his diminutive size, squeaky little voice, and lisp to be simpleminded. Will didn't mind. Peewee loved to see Will manipulate doltish people. To watch it dawn on them that they were the simpleminded ones.

Sometimes he used his shortcomings to get out of trouble. He could easily evoke pity. Sometimes Peewee would play along, like he was a big slow-wit himself. They'd had many good laughs, especially when they had put something over on an especially condescending or officious asshole. It threw most people off to interact with two people of such vastly different proportions . . . especially when one was as shrewd as the other. If a real asshole came into the store, Will and Peewee would get him or her so befuddled that by the time they left, they would have forgotten why they came in. Mr. Kovak would try to act mad, but he'd eventually break out laughing . . . probably aware that he could be a victim if he wasn't careful.

Peewee was funny, too, in a relaxed kind of way. Peewee

was the most confident person Will knew. His confidence, Will was sure, was at 100%. You couldn't possibly be more confident than Peewee. Will, himself, was confident that Peewee would fulfill his responsibility, not only to the planet and humanity but to Will's will. Peewee'd initiate things that would make the world a better place. He may not believe that now . . . but things would change. Peewee just didn't know it yet.

Suddenly Sandy sprawled out, hanging her elbows back over the arms of her seat, pushing her breasts front and center, and spreading her perfect legs out between the two boys, one on the edge of each front seat. Tight denim leggings did not mask their rather pleasant shape.

Peewee had the best view, his seat set back so far that he was almost parallel with Sandy's legs. After Peewee snuck what he thought was a clandestine peek, he looked up into his rearview mirror, and there she was staring at him. She smiled and waved. Caught.

"You know," Sandy started, "I have to say it . . ."

"Oh, you really don't," Will interrupted, turning, not looking at anything specific but taking the entire enticing vision in, like one might a moonrise.

"Oh, yourself. Looked to me like you are suddenly able to peruse my body. What's up with that?"

"No, I saw nothing spethific." Just the way he said it got both Sandy and Peewee laughing almost hysterically. "But, you don't really have to thay it," Will continued when the laughter dissipated. "I think we all know, Mith Thandy Thickner."

"Why in the devil are you lisping?" Sandy said, still laughing.

"I just like the moniker Mith Thandy Thickner. It's how I would have pronounced it when I first met you."

"He's a master at diversions, Sandy," Peewee said. "I think

he's afraid you're going to get sentimental. He's not good with sentimental. He's afraid he's gonna cry."

"The hell with him then. I may not need to say it, but I *want* to say it. So cry your little eyes out, Shrimp. I'm really glad I met you guys. I mean I saw both of you the first day of school. You know I'm in Shrimp's class . . . and you," directed at Peewee, "rather stand out. Can hardly miss ya. Anyway, I made it through every day knowing that I'd be meeting you two eventually. And becoming friends. If it weren't for you two, I wouldn't be in school. Thanks."

Peewee looked over at her. "You haven't been in school. You know you scared the shit out of us? No more vanishing acts. Not without telling us what's up. You can't just disappear."

"What!" she said, acting indignant. "I needed time to think. I got a little dilemma to deal with, remember?"

"We gonna deal with that elephant now? Maybe we should toss it out the window, send it home this weekend. Enjoy our platonic threesome," Will suggested.

Peewee rolled his eyes, and Sandy let out a shriek. "Threesome! He often come out with shit like that?" she asked Peewee.

"Oh, yeah," he said. "Sometimes he even says something intelligent."

"I said 'platonic' for crying out loud."

"Well, it's fine with me," Sandy said. "Out the window."

"Your mom and dad know you're coming up here with us?" Will asked over his shoulder to Sandy.

"Yeah, I texted them."

"*Texted*? That all?" Will asked.

"They're very . . . blasé, let's say. They allow me to do what I want."

"Wait! That's an oxymoron!" Will shouted.

"Oh, shut up you moron," Sandy shouted back.

Peewee laughed. "He's right. But even like not going to school? Hiding from the world? They wouldn't care if you didn't graduate?"

"Look who's concerned about graduating!" She leaned forward and punched him in the arm. "But, the answer's no. They believe it's my life to live."

"What are they like?" Will asked. "Do you love them?"

"Yeah, I do. We've got an arrangement that works. We care."

"What about your little brother?" Peewee asked. "Your stepdad's son?"

Sandy paused. "Yes, with my mother. He's autistic. They have an au pair, more like a governess, to take care of him most of the time. He's pretty severe. I love the little shit. He's seven, but I have no frickin' idea how to relate to him. Just hug him and kiss him and love him. That seems to keep him happy."

Peewee leaned forward a bit, snuck another sideways peek at the lovely limb stretched out next to him, and looked over at Will who was doing the same thing, both thinking that'd keep them pretty damn happy, too.

"How'd you get out of the house, dude?" Peewee asked Will.

Will looked at Peewee, nodding toward the luscious limbs and crossed his eyes. Will and Peewee chuckled to themselves. It was only the second time in their lives that Peewee had called Will "dude." "My parents are visiting my sister at college. She's depressed, again, poor little thang."

"So they don't know we're going up north?" Peewee asked.

Will shifted in his seat.

"Well?" Peewee pushed.

"No, but I would have come anyway. There just didn't need to be a battlefront this way."

"What is your dad like?" Sandy asked. "He seemed pretty

quiet. I think you said he was distant or something?"

Will chuckled again. "Really distant. In another world at times. Talk about me being in my head. It's almost like he has a secret life. He drifts off at times, smiles vapidly, stays there awhile. It just irritates my mom to no end."

"Vapidly? Holy shit, Wordsworth. Not sure what that even means," Sandy said. "So she's pretty overprotective towards you, you said?"

"Yeah. I think you know the story; she tries to protect me from everything . . . she thinks I'm going to die any old time anyway. I'm moving out as soon as I graduate." Will reached over and gave Peewee one of Sandy's little punches in the arm and choked up a bit. "She doesn't mean harm, but she'd never let me 'be' something. She'd want me to metamorphose into a stool nobody can sit on, a toilet nobody can shit in, a . . ."

Sandy laughed. "Ok, I get the idea. Hey!" she said, naturally poking Peewee's arm. "Why'd you have to take off so suddenly the other night?"

Peewee shifted his weight. Scratched his head.

"That's what he does when he's nervous or embarrassed," Will said to Sandy.

"What? Scratch his noggin?"

"Yup."

"So, you don't lisp, you scratch instead? Why are you nervous, big guy? Your parents? They big? Where'd you get your size? Have I told you . . . you're huge?"

"Ah, no. You haven't mentioned it."

"Figured you oughta know."

"Well, thanks."

"So . . . ?"

"My parents are normal size. Couldn't have children, so they adopted me."

"Really?" Sandy exclaimed. "You're adopted? No shit. Ain't that weird? You got no idea whose genes are crawling around inside you? They could be gorilla genes."

Both Peewee and Will laughed.

"Nope. No idea."

"So can I ask?" Sandy said. "What happened that night?"

A silence settled.

"Sorry," Sandy finally said.

Will turned, looking around his seat at Sandy, placing his hands just above her knee to lean over. He felt her thigh clinch, pleasing him, and she raised her eyes at him, smiling. "Peewee's mom is really cool. She's younger than Mr. Kovak. She was working on her PhD in psychology at the U when she met him. Mr. K. was a good high-school athlete and had gotten a decent job right out of school selling parts to distributors."

"Parts?" Sandy asked.

"Yeah. You know, like stuff they need in hardware stores. Got it right out of high school. Made pretty good money. Got married when Mrs. K. graduated."

"Then what?" Sandy asked.

Will glanced at Peewee for approval. "He didn't want her to work. Felt it was a knock on him. Like he couldn't support them. Actually, I think he didn't want her to work so she would be dependent on him. Couldn't leave him when he went into one of his abuse rants. She's smart and attractive . . . a definite flight risk."

Sandy looked over at Peewee. "You ok with this little analysis?"

"Can't argue. I think it exacerbated his insecurity that he was traveling so much for business."

"So what happened?" Sandy asked.

"He retired, bought the hardware store, and stayed around,"

Will said. "Of course Mrs. Kovac was accustomed to quite a bit of independence with him gone all the time. So it put stress on the marriage with him home . . . and drinking." Will looked to Peewee: "Pretty accurate?"

"Yip."

"No. I mean the other night."

"Oh, umm . . . well, and I'm just guessing." Will responded, "Peewee didn't actually tell me all about it, but Mr. K.'s really into sports . . . and drinking beer while he's watching. When his team doesn't do so well, he takes it out on Mrs. K—if he's had too much to drink."

"No shit?" Sandy said. "And you get caught in the middle?" aimed at Peewee.

Peewee just shrugged.

"Who called that night?" Sandy asked.

"Mom," Peewee said, quietly.

"What'd she say?"

"'They're losing.'"

They were all quiet for a while.

Peewee looked at Sandy in the rearview mirror. "Why don't you see your genetic father?"

"Know that song, 'Mammas, Don't Let Your Babies Grow Up to Be Cowboys'?" she sang.

Will and Peewee laughed.

"He was a cowboy. Got my mom pregnant with me . . . apparently she was attracted to cowboys at that time . . . but had no idea of settling down. He was a drinker, gambler, a 'rambling' man. Then she settled for stability and security with my stepdad."

"Funny how helplessly affected by our parents we are," Will said. "Peewee is the most compassionate person I know so as not to be like his father. I refuse to be passive, controlled, like my father." Will looked back at Sandy, a smirk on his face. "Don't get me wrong, you seemed to have been following in your mom's footsteps with your attraction to the country club cowboys . . . until you came on to me in the hallway. Now you've got a traditional relationship loving two guys."

Peewee just shook his head; Sandy screamed and bopped Will in the head.

"Well," Will said, rubbing his head. "I guess we'll throw that elephant out the window., as well."

"And don't forget it, Shrimp . . . 'country club cowboys,'" Sandy said, giggling.

Again, they were quiet.

Will broke the silence. "I can't get it out of my mind. What are we going to do about Bret and his fuckin' phone?"

"I've already taken care of it," Peewee said.

Sandy pulled her legs back and sat up. Both Will and Sandy looked at Peewee with eyebrows raised. "How?" they both said at the same time.

Peewee explained the call as it had gone:

"Hello, Mr. Piper?"

"Yeah. Who's this?"

"A friend of Bret's."

A pause. "I don't think so. I'd recognize that condescending voice anywhere. You're that animal that almost ruined my son's sex life."

"Odd you'd say 'sex life,' not 'ability to procreate.'"

A pause. "What you want?"

"I don't know what your son told you about the other night, but he and three of his asshole friends physically and sexually abused a man and woman, putting the man in the hospital . . ."

"What about Bret?" Mr. Piper burst into the speakerphone.

"He's still in the hospital. His life is ruined. That bitch almost bit his whole damn tongue off. He can't talk or even eat. Goddammit."

"If he hadn't stuck his tongue in the young lady's mouth, she could hardly have bitten it off. And no, she didn't ask for it. Two of Bret's buddies were holding her."

Mr. Piper started to sputter.

"Mr. Piper, just listen. The worst of it, for you and Bret, is that they took a photo of it . . . an explicit photo of the assault . . . on one of their phones. If that picture gets out on the internet, not only will you lose a lot of money but Bret will end up behind bars . . . which, by the way, may be the safest place for him."

"What? Are you threatening my son?"

"Let's just call it intuition. Your son's not the brightest bulb, as I'm sure you're aware. If you don't intercede, you know you will be very sorry. You're going to have to get all three of those guys together, along with Bret, and delete that photo from their and any other phones or whatever it may now be on. You do understand the ramifications?"

There was silence on the other end.

"Well?" Peewee finally said.

"Yes! Yes. I understand. It'll be gone. What's it to you?"

"You do understand if you don't make sure it's gone from any phone or computer or wherever, you'll be haunted by the prospect of ruin all your life? You do know if that image gets out this would ruin you, your family, Bret . . ."

"Yes, Goddammit. I understand. You . . . you . . ."

"Goodnight, Mr. Piper."

When Peewee was done reliving the call for them, they were all quiet. Before Peewee took the turn off 35N onto Highway 33, which would take them north through Cloquet onto 53N, up to 169 which wound through a dense forest to Ely and on to the east side of Burntside Lake at the end of the road, Sandy yelled, "I'm starving!"

"If Gordy's High Hat is still open in Cloquet," Peewee said, "we'll stop for a burger. If they've already closed for the season, we'll stop and get walleye fingers at the Steak House in Ely. It's a couple hours from Cloquet."

"So, your walleyes have fingers up here? Ok, sorry," she said when they both looked blankly at her. "Too lame to warrant even a smile, I agree." Will and Peewee silently agreed. "How long have you two known each other?" Sandy asked through a yawn.

Will peeked around the edge of his seat. "He's been protecting my sorry little ass since kindergarten."

"Really! Cool. Real cool. Cool, cool."

Peewee looked at Will. "Ya think she thinks it's cool?"

"Not sure," Will said. "You can never tell if she's being sarcastic, and you can't ask her because that'd definitely not be cool, according to her."

"What? You're awfully full of shit for a little fart," she shot back.

This got them all laughing again. Sandy said almost everything with a tinge of caprice, like she was mocking what she was saying herself. It was impossible to tell if she was ever serious. If you didn't love her, she'd have been quite irritating.

"So," Will started, "your aunt and uncle are in Washington to fight the mining?"

"Just copper and precious metals," Peewee said.

"The water gets contaminated for like five hundred years. Or more! That's one of the stupidest . . ."

"Will!" Peewee cut him off. He looked at Sandy, who was now lying on her back, her butt pushed against the back of Will's seat, her long legs crossed over the top of the seat, dangling over his head. "Don't encourage him," Peewee said, adjusting the rearview mirror so he could still be looking at Sandy. "I'm sure he knows all the facts and all the implications to our planet. If you get him going, it will turn into a rant . . . uh, you actually comfortable like that?"

"Yeah, ya got a problem with it?"

"It certainly doesn't look comfortable."

"That's cuz you couldn't do it."

"True." He looked over at Will, who was looking up at her bare feet floating above him.

"Hey, Hau," Sandy said. "Why you worried about something five hundred years in the future?"

"Somebody's got to worry about more than where we're gonna eat."

"Well, there goes Gordy's," Peewee said as they drove on through Cloquet. "Closed for the season. So I'm now thinking way into the future, to the Steak House."

Will smiled to himself. He could kid about it now.

CHAPTER SIXTEEN

WILL AND SANDY LOVED THE CABIN. It was a two-story log lodge that had been constructed around the turn of the century by one of the asshole northern Minnesota lumber barons. It faced west, snuggled in the tall pines, which of course had been preserved around the baron's home, overlooking a little cove. Two high points almost came together out front, leaving an inlet big enough for boats to get through. The opening perfectly framed an island in the distance. On each point sat stunted Jack pines that looked like they were growing right out of the ledge rock. From the points, the land fell away with big water showing through the pines. At least a dozen islands, illuminated by a full moon, were visible seeming to float above the calm water.

Peewee and Will decided to sleep in a bunk bed on the sleeping porch. The wind had died down with the sun's setting, and, although only a screen porch, it was cool but comfortable. Will insisted he get the top because, he claimed, his life could be cut real short with Peewee's mattress collapsing on him in the middle of the night. Of course Peewee had to toss Will up onto the top bunk. Sandy got the guest bedroom, although she whined about being cold, and here she was with two guys she wanted to have babies with and she was sleeping alone. Of course they didn't know if she was serious or not. Will more inclined to think so after his experience. After getting settled they built a fire in the stone fireplace in the living room, had a snack, but went to bed early. Will was especially tired.

They awoke to a cold wind coming off the lake, blown down from the border to the north. The wind was howling through the screens on the porch. Peewee found Will sniffling, curled up in a ball under the blankets. Peewee bundled him up in one of his uncle's old wool jackets that looked more like a robe on Will, built a fire, and, with Sandy's assistance, made them all a good, warm breakfast.

It appeared the day would stay windy and cool, but Will argued that after a good breakfast he would be fine and they should go out on the lake anyway. Peewee hesitantly agreed. He knew Will would not want to deter any of their plans because he didn't feel well. It had been that way all their lives. Or, heaven forbid, that he would be too small to handle some waves in a canoe.

Peewee grabbed a kayak for himself, Sandy and Will in an old aluminum canoe they had found tucked behind the boathouse. Sandy in the bow, Will in the driver's seat in the stern. It was calm in the protected cove, but almost as if a line had been drawn, curling waves roiled just past the two points. Will loved the way it looked, coming out through the calm into the big white-capped water. He yelled over at Peewee that he should remember this. That in his life a similar passage was going to happen. Peewee yelled back that he wasn't interested in things that were *going* to happen and that Will should concentrate on his canoe.

When they got out past the point, Peewee turned them to the right, heading directly into the north wind.

After paddling hard for a ways, Sandy yelled, "Why the devil we paddling into the wind? Wouldn't it be easier to paddle with the wind?"

Will immediately figured out why Peewee had headed them that way. He told Sandy it was probably safer to head out into the wind than to have to paddle back against it. That always trying to take the easy approach was a tragic flaw.

She froze for a moment and quit paddling, and Will could tell by her body language that she took the comment as a slight and immediately regretted saying it . . . not having meant it that way, just, ironically, trying to impress her with . . . with what he wasn't sure. Finally she turned sideways, swung her paddle, and tried to splash him with it, missing him but almost capsizing the canoe. Will dropped his paddle, grabbing the gunwales with both hands to balance the canoe. Then he leaned quickly to grab his paddle before the waves washed it away. At the same time Sandy reached for it . . . and over they went into the frigid water.

Sandy came up cussing, Will gasping for air, holding the paddle, his lungs screaming.

Peewee paddled swiftly over. Both had refused to wear life jackets. Peewee knew Will wasn't the strongest swimmer, but when he had asked Sandy, she said she had lived on water all her life and swam like a mermaid, that Will would be safe with her.

Peewee yelled for them to stay with the canoe, which had initially rolled over but came back upright, half-filled with water. When Peewee got there they were both hanging onto the canoe with difficulty, choking. Both had gotten mouthfuls of water, with waves having immediately washed over them when they emerged. And, to boot, the wind, frequently a wily adversary in the north woods, had changed to the west and increased in velocity, blowing down the length of the big bay.

It being mid-October, the water was as cold as it looked—dismal, deathly slate gray. With the water as rough and cold as it was, Peewee was concerned and mad at himself for letting them get into this predicament, but he managed to keep Willy and Sandy from panicking. He had to convince Will that they needed to abandon the now partially submerged canoe. With the kayak bouncing in the waves, it took Peewee a while to get both Will and Sandy mostly out of the freezing water and precariously lying on top of the kayak. Sandy had slid up on the front, trying to hold her paddle and stay calm, balancing her weight across it. Will was so light that Peewee just grabbed his arm and hefted him on to the kayak behind him, Will still grasping his paddle as well. Fortunately neither Will nor Sandy had panicked, even though they were choking and spitting water. They were both able to balance their weight lying across the kayak. But now in the brisk air, they were wet and growing colder, unable to keep their feet and legs completely out of the water.

Peewee paddled back as fast as he could, the wind actually aiding them, now blowing them back toward the cabin. They felt like they were surfing, as one wave then another lifted them and tossed them forward, making it more difficult for Peewee to maintain balance, frequently almost tipping.

By the time they got back to the cabin, both Will and Sandy were violently shivering and chattering. Will had started a hacking cough. Both their legs were so cold that they could barely walk. Peewee immediately built them a fire while they got into dry clothes. Sandy lay on the rug in front of the fire and pulled Willy into her, spooning and hugging him. Willy pointing out that wasn't it best if they were both naked. Sandy saying, "Nice try, you little perv."

Peewee covered them in wool blankets. With Sandy's arms around him, his back nestled between cozy breasts, Will, although shivering and coughing, figured he felt as good as he could possibly feel for as bad as he felt. Peewee took the outboard and went back after the canoe.

Will stayed bundled up in front of the fire for the rest of the day, but by night his cough had gotten worse—more persistent—and he couldn't stay warm, shivering almost uncontrollably. Peewee had the three of them sleep in Sandy's bed this time . . . Will tucked between Sandy's spoon and up against a very warm, very large back.

SUNDAY MORNING WHEN THEY GOT UP Will didn't look good. They decided to leave right after breakfast. They bundled him up and set him in the passenger seat, where he hunched up in the wool blankets, hugging himself. Sandy leaned against the back of Will's seat, rubbing and caressing his head, Peewee keeping a close eye on him while he drove; Will drifted off. For some reason the mining issue started bouncing . . . bounce, bounce, bounce against his skull.

Will's head slumped. Sandy stopped massaging it and peeked at his face. "Is he asleep?" she whispered to Peewee.

Peewee glanced at Will. "He's either asleep or off in his secret life."

"I did this to him," Sandy said.

"Did what?"

"Something's wrong. His voice is raspy and his breath is shallow. I can hear a rattle."

"You didn't do it. The wind did. Canoes are tippy if a big wave hits you broadside."

"I leaned too far to reach his paddle, and I caused him to drop it."

"I saw you. You both leaned suddenly at the same time as the canoe drifted sideways to the waves. Anyone can tip in a canoe in that kind of wind. If anything it's my fault for letting us go out in that weather."

"Yeah, but I leaned way over trying to grab the paddle, and that's when it tipped. He dropped his paddle because I almost tipped us trying to splash him."

"So? You were just goofing around. You didn't know he'd drop his paddle."

Sandy didn't respond. Suddenly, through tears, she said, "I splashed him because I can't handle criticism. I'm just like my mother. I don't even know if he was really criticizing me. What if he dies? I killed him," Sandy wailed.

Peewee looked down at Will, who hadn't stirred in spite of her wails. When he glanced back at Sandy, her eyes were watery and red. "Relax, will ya?" he told her. "He ain't dying. He's little but he's tough."

She sniffed and wiped her nose with the back of her hand. Looked around for something to wipe the snot on and found Peewee's pants. "How susceptible is he?"

"Nice. Thanks, there," Peewee said scowling at the smear. "Susceptible?"

"Yeah. Like his lungs and heart. Maybe we shouldn't have come up here. Maybe we shouldn't have gone canoeing."

Peewee took a deep breath. "If he can't do stuff like this . . . well, he's going to do stuff like this. I don't want to say he doesn't care if he dies. But if he worries about shit like canoeing . . . well, let's just say he isn't going to not do something because he's susceptible to some kind of ailment."

"But what if he's sick? What if he dies?"

"If you want to act like his mother and see how he likes that, be my guest. If I were you, I'd make sure he gets as much enjoyment out of life as he can, while he can. I'm guessing we're the two people he's gonna rely on most for that. So stop it."

Will stirred and opened his eyes for a moment. Peewee thought he caught a smile as Will again closed his eyes and tucked his chin back under the blankets.

PEEWEE HAD HESITANTLY AGREED to attend a meeting for Will, who said he was still ailing and insisted that Peewee appear in his place. It was a public meeting at the DNR office in Ely, a gateway to the Boundary Waters Wilderness Canoe Area. The meeting was about the proposed precious-metal mine near the Boundary Waters. Peewee agreed primarily out of interest for his uncle. When Peewee entered, he found the room full to capacity and a panel of officious-looking men in front facing the packed room. He stood in the back in case he would need to make a fast exit. He didn't trust his devious little friend. He noticed that the placards on the typical Formica fold-up tables identified a DNR guy, an EPA representative, and most prominent, in the middle, two precious-metal-mining dudes. There was an empty chair at the end of the table.

The DNR honcho, apparently the moderator, announced that first on the agenda was a Mr. Peewee Kovak.

Peewee froze. Will had not informed him that he was on the agenda. He considered bolting before anyone noticed him in the back of the room. If Will had been there, he would have killed him. He was well aware of the mining issue due to his uncle but had no idea what he would say to what looked to be bullheaded pundits in the front or to the audience, whose feelings would be strong on the issue. They would be split between pro-mining and pro-environment. All he knew was that the sides would never agree on anything. He strongly considered leaving and throwing Will down the nearest mineshaft.

"Is Mr. Kovak present?"

A loud clearing of the throat echoed throughout the room. When everyone turned to see the source, a round of hushed "Ahhs" filled the room. With everyone else seated, Peewee was a towering presence.

The DNR guy's eyes opened wide. "Are you Mr. Kovak? Would you please step up to the microphone?"

What the hell, Peewee thought, *I'm here*. He walked to the front of the room, all eyes following him. He slid the mic stand aside, not needing amplification. "I have a few questions," he directed at the faces at the table, his booming voice startling everyone. "I have been coming up to the Boundary Waters all my life and am well aware that the Iron Range is mining country. Iron mining. Are there now or have there been other mines of the type you are proposing up here?

"Well, no," answered the DNR fellow.

"But we have other similar mines in other areas," interjected the burly miner.

"Like Mount Polley in the Canadian wilderness?" Peewee countered.

The mining guy squirmed, his meaty neck turning red.

"The mine that just spewed billions of gallons of contaminated sludge, permanently polluting millions of acres of pristine lakes, streams, and rivers?"

"Yeah, but," the skinny mining guy with black-rimmed glasses jumped in, "there were no people living in proximity to that mine."

"Not like here, you mean? The most frequented wilderness area in America with thousands of residents living nearby in surrounding forests and lakes?"

The burly miner whispered, a little too loudly, for the skinny guy to shut up.

"Well," Peewee continued, "I understand a failed holding dam caused the catastrophe. At least you haven't hired the same contractor to build your proposed dam here to contain the polluted sludge?"

A pregnant silence followed from both mining men.

"You didn't?" Peewee said. "My God, you did!" Peewee turned to the crowd. "If your neighbor's house blew over, would you ask for their contractor's name to build your house?"

A few laughed; a few shook their heads. The absurdity slapped everyone in the face.

Peewee turned back to the panel. "That's ridiculous. Are any of these types of mines not polluting?"

"Of course," the burly guy, his neck now resembling rare meat, answered unconvincingly.

Peewee walked near the EPA guy. "Is that true?"

"Well, not entirely," he answered.

"Look!" the burly guy spit out. "We'll meet all the standards the government requires."

"Like at Mount Polley?" Peewee countered.

"Yes, of course. We . . . " the skinny guy started. The meaty guy told him to shut the fuck up.

"Tell me please," Peewee started, "this dam that's supposed to contain all the polluted sludge from the mining . . . how long does it have to last?"

The skinny guy chuckled nervously. "Well, everyone knows—that's five hundred years."

"Why such a round number?" Peewee asked, smiling.

"Well, that's how far our modeling goes."

"I see," Peewee said, still smiling. "So it could be longer?"

"Well . . . " the skinny guy stammered. The burly guy told him he'd break his neck if he didn't keep his mouth shut.

"Look! You big a-hole," Meat Neck exploded with. "We'll put up money up front to cover the cost of maintaining the damn dam."

"Oh, I see. Maintaining for how long?"

The burly guy muttered some unintelligible swear words, knowing where Peewee was going with this.

Peewee turned to the crowd, all very wide awake. "First, you have to realize even five hundred years is ridiculous. You know these people won't be around for five hundred years . . . not even close." He turned to the DNR guy. "I'm curious, how can a government agency responsible for maintaining recreational areas for all to enjoy even consider this threat to the remarkable lakes and forests in and around the Boundary Waters?"

The DNR honcho smiled sheepishly. "It's jobs. Mining jobs."

"How many jobs and for how long?"

"Oh, about three hundred. The life of the mine is predicted to be about twenty years."

"You're not joking, are you?"

The DNR guy didn't answer.

"How do most of the people up here make a living?"

The DNR guy shrugged. "Recreation and tourism."

"How many jobs there?"

"Oh, hundreds, thousands actually. Most businesses up here."

"How long have these jobs been around?"

"Oh, pretty much forever."

"How long will these jobs last?"

The DNR honcho shifted in his chair. "Well, forever . . . as long as people keep coming."

"So unless something destroys the beauty and allure of this area, they'll continue to come? Three hundred jobs—a drop in the bucket—and a meager twenty years seem a fair trade-off? And the recreation and tourism money stays in the community." He turned to the crowd, all on the edge of their seats. "Do you think the mining profits will remain here or leave, filling the pockets of distant investors and speculators?"

When Peewee turned back to the panel, he suddenly noticed that a very Native American–looking man had filled the empty chair. No one apparently had seen or heard him slip in. The placard on the table read GLIFWC. "Well hello," Peewee said. "You're joining us?"

The man paused before he spoke. "I have been observing from the rear. But it's getting interesting. Thought I'd join in. To answer your question, certainly no Indian will see any of that money, nothing new, but then neither will many, if any, in this room either . . . well, except two."

"Sir, may I ask what GLIFWC stands for?"

The man, for some reason, grinned at Peewee. "Great Lakes Indian Fish and Wildlife Commission."

Peewee had heard of it. His uncle had told him it was the only apolitical organization dealing with the mine issue. "What's your commission's take on this type of mine?"

"Of course we're opposed. We're especially vigilant on the possibility of them trying to extract uranium as well, a byproduct of gold mining."

Peewee frowned. "I thought this was copper they were after?"

The man's smile returned, only sardonic this time. "Precious metals include gold. We know there are at least some gold deposits. You think they're going to overlook another profit? Next is uranium, a side product of mining gold. You'll never hear them say that, now. They are associated with a company that has hundreds of gold and uranium mines on Indian land. All, not some, *all* are currently polluting. This company has 3.5 billion dollars in fines currently in process."

"Look, Goddammit!" The miner's face was now as red as his neck. "None of this contaminated water that escapes will flow into your beloved Boundary Waters. If you bother to look at our environmental impact study, you'll see the leakage will flow either into the Saint Louis River or the Mississippi."

Peewee was starting to get pissed. "Excuse me if I don't take the time to look at a three-thousand-page document, which seems like a smokescreen to me. Didn't a company that you contract with put this study together?" Peewee walked directly over to the DNR and EPA men. "Tell me, this doesn't constitute a conflict of interest?"

The two men remained silent.

"You realize you two," he directed at the EPA and DNR guys, "could have the distinction of allowing the most damaging, widespread polluting mine in history? Let's see, the Saint Louis flows into Lake Superior through the Great Lakes and out the Saint Lawrence into the Atlantic Ocean, and the Mississippi flows into the Gulf of Mexico. And I understand they've used *old*, outdated water tables to argue that the contaminated water will not flow into the BWCA? Which flows through our concerned neighbor, Canada, to Hudson Bay."

"That's correct," the GLIFWC representative interjected.

"Well, imagine, you two and these mining men could be famous. What a legacy to leave behind! I can't even blame the mining guys. Their bottom line, all through history, has been greed, err . . . let's call it profit for shareholders, no matter the cost to the environment or humanity. That's a given, proven by history. Around the world. Destroying the earth for profit.

But you two," he directed at the DNR and EPA representatives, "your job is to protect people and their natural resources. In other areas, the fracking process in mining is causing tremors and earthquakes! And they keep on fracking! My God, talk about absurd.

"And I would be remiss to a friend of mine if I didn't bring up not only the threat up here to recreational water but to our fresh water, our drinking water. Water is our most *precious* commodity, not just here but everywhere. We should be a model for the world. The threat to clean drinking water around the world is critical. As my astute friend likes to say, 'We can live without coal, copper, gold, even money, but we cannot live without water . . . ' "

"WILL. WILL, WAKE UP." Sandy rubbed his head vigorously.

"Huh? Uhhh, God, that feels good, don't stop," Will said, his little voice scratchy.

Sandy gave his head a little slap. "I've been rubbing that noggin of yours for hours. How do you feel?"

He involuntarily coughed a couple hollow hacks. "Ok."

"You don't sound ok," Peewee said, watching him intently. "We're coming up to Hinckley. We need to get something to eat. We can either stop at Toby's or there are several fast food places. When are your parents going to be home?" Peewee asked.

"Depends on the depth of my sister's depression, I suppose."

"We're not just going to drop you off by yourself at your house," Sandy said. "You're either coming home with me, or we go to your doctor."

"I'll be fine," he wheezed, trying not to.

"You're not going home if your parents aren't there," Peewee said. "We either call your doctor, Urgent Care, or the emergency room. You don't sound or look too good."

None of those options sounded good to Will. And not having met Sandy's parents, he wasn't going to go to her house, although being taken care of by Sandy sounded pretty good. "I'd rather see if I can't improve before I get all doctored up."

Sandy looked at Peewee. "What if we just take him home, tuck him in, and stay with him?"

"Good idea," Peewee said.

"Who's going to deal with my mom?"

"I can deal with your mom, don't worry," Sandy said.

"That's what you think. She's not exactly enamored with our relationship."

"Your mom will go easier on you if I'm there when they get home, anyway," Peewee reasoned. "You know that."

"She's not exactly enamored with you at the moment, either. She'll be really excited about Sandy, especially if she's spooning me in my bed."

"Who said anything about spooning you, you horny little sucker?"

Will smiled. "You've set a precedent," he said, and stifled a couple coughs.

"Don't worry about your mother, Sandy said. "I understand motherly instincts. We'll get along fine."

"By the way," Will said, "I don't want to hear anything about guilt. Me getting this way is nobody's fault. It's just the way it is."

Sandy started to argue, but Peewee gave her the evil eye.

They stopped for a sandwich and ate in the car. Will perked up a bit when he got some food in him.

When they got to Will's house, his parents weren't home. Peewee and Sandy made Will go right to bed. Will started to argue but acquiesced when Sandy said she'd cuddle with him until he warmed up, quit shivering, and went to sleep.

Although he knew it would piss Will off, Peewee tried calling the family doctor. He'd been hanging around Will's house for so long that he knew where everything was, including the emergency numbers attached to the side of the refrigerator by a magnet. The doctor wasn't available, but they transferred him to the nurse's line. A perky voice told him to get Will to the emergency room immediately. Peewee decided to wait until after he woke up. He was worried, but he would rather his parents made the emergency room decision, unless Will got worse and they didn't get home.

Peewee wasn't concerned about Mrs. Mitty. She was going to be pissed, of course, but now that Will knew about the cabin, things would change. Peewee'd be straight up with her if necessary. He'd tell her about the cabin. Give it time to sink in before she and Will had it out. He was glad he had finally shown Will the place. Really, he didn't know why he hadn't before.

When he had turned eighteen he had bought the property. The cabin had been abandoned for a while and was in pretty rough shape. It had only had one bedroom, one little bathroom, and a kitchen open to the living area. He had added a larger second bedroom with a walk-in closet and its own bathroom.

Outside, he had added a cedar porch that was half open but covered, with steps down to the path to the lake. The other half was a screen porch that wrapped around the other side of the cabin . . . a summer sleeping porch he imagined. He had remodeled the kitchen and bathroom. It would be very comfortable for Peewee and Will. Of course, Sandy was now in their lives. He guessed she was going to want to be a part of the deal as well. That should be interesting, Peewee surmised.

SANDY HAD FALLEN ASLEEP while cuddling with Will in his bed and woke late afternoon. She found him feverish and shivering. Although his coughing had eased, his breathing was still scratchy and shallow. She went to find Peewee, thinking maybe they should bring him in. But Peewee wasn't in the house. She looked outside and no van; she looked in the garage and no car. She immediately panicked. Where the hell was he? She didn't trust her own judgment. Peewee would know what to do . . . if he were there. She figured if Will had a temp, there must be some kind of infection.

Just as she was going to wake Will and call a cab to bring him to the emergency room, she heard the van pull up. Peewee had gone to Urgent Care, since they hadn't answered the phone, to discuss what to do. They'd said if he had a fever, he needed to be looked at. They had also recommended the emergency room at the hospital Will had been to previously. After punching Peewee, hard this time, Sandy made sandwiches for them. Will had no appetite. She forced him to take a few bites. After waking, his cough started again. Although he was experienced at acting like he felt fine when he actually didn't, Peewee and Sandy both declared, regardless of what he said, that he looked like crap. They left, and Peewee noticed that Will was carrying a leather folder.

When they got to the emergency room, Peewee insisted they look at Will right away, ahead of some sniffling noses and a couple cuts and lacerations. The nurse at the station didn't dare argue. When they pulled up Will's chart on the computer, they sent him up to ICU immediately, put him on a respirator, and stuck him with an IV. They wouldn't let Peewee and Sandy stay with him, so they went back to the Mittys'.

Peewee found Will's sister's number in the address book, and Mrs. Mitty answered when he called. Peewee started to explain Will's situation, but she interrupted, wanting to know what shenanigans they had been up to. Was that girl involved? Peewee suggested that they could deal with that later. She didn't actually ever ask what was wrong with Will. She said they wouldn't be back until tomorrow and that Missy was in tough shape. Peewee's temper got the best of him. He said, "Whatever!" and hung up. How could one of Missy's little depressed moments take precedent over what could be a serious problem with Will? He knew he'd have hell to pay, but it pissed him off. Missy was at a state college a little south of town. They could be home in a couple hours.

Sandy insisted they go back to the hospital. But when they got there a nurse still wouldn't let them in to see Will. He was doing ok, but "family only." "What family?" Peewee growled under his breath, and the nurse shrunk away. They went to the waiting room. Although they had a lot to talk about, their concern for Will overshadowed everything. They just sat silently. Peewee knew Sandy was blaming herself. He wanted to convince her that Will would react to her remorse like he would his mother's incriminations. But Peewee was worried this time. He didn't want to talk.

About a silent, stressful hour and a half they were surprised when Mr. Mitty and the young doctor that had seen Will last time walked into the waiting room. The doc told them that either the last infection had come back or a new one had formed. When the doc asked what caused this new affliction, they confirmed what it turned out Will had been able to tell him. The young doc looked at Mr. Mitty and reiterated that Will needed to be more careful. Mr. Mitty shrugged and looked at Peewee. Peewee just said, "Maybe he should." The doctor told them

Will was sleeping and they could see him when they moved him out of ICU, probably the next day.

When the doc left, Peewee and Sandy thought for sure they were going to get a lecture from Walter. To their surprise, there was no lecture or even anger. Peewee asked him where Mrs. Mitty was. Walter said she was holding poor Missy's hand. She had been crying since they had arrived there. Peewee asked when the Mrs. would be showing up. Walter smiled and said she expected him to drive back the next day and get her. Then he sat down, chuckled, and said, "If she knew how fast I drove getting here, she'd have a hissy fit." With a goofy grin on his face, he then closed his eyes and drifted off somewhere. Like father, like son.

Oct. 16

Don't like the way this one feels. I'm concerned. Better get this entry in while I can. I keep falling asleep. So: Item #8: Sandy cannot blame herself for whatever happens to me. I know you understand. This was not her fault. I may have her straightened out by the time you read this. I imagine she'll want to read this, too. That's fine. Sandy, I loved you. Thank you for fulfilling my life. Through you and Peewee, I will live on. I expect to accomplish great things. The world needs great things to be done. There are no two people that I know in the world who are more able to help me accomplish them. Thank you. I love you both.

Whew. Ok. That being said, this entry will be a bit longer than usual. Peewee, I realize the first item – world peace – may be a trifle difficult. Yeah, I know you can bring up my feelings toward Bret and point out my hypocrisy. But I do hope you've rehabilitated the SOB by now. In spite of the difficulty of even envisioning peace in the world, is it not the end game? All you have to do is get the ball rolling, and the momentum will carry it on. If educating young people here, especially in our cities and around the world, so they can have hope for their future, is the long-term answer to gaining world peace, then start right here in our little corner of the world. Except for occasional a-holes like Bret, most of the violence in the world is a result of poverty, ignorance, and lack of role models. People's behavior is a result of their circumstances. If parents, like Bret's father, aren't able to provide positive role models, and schools through early childhood education or programs like Headstart here in the US aren't available or funded we have to provide these things somehow. Whatever is being provided now certainly isn't working. The trouble with schools here is that children with problems, without prospects, have no motivation to learn much less excel. Who likes to go someplace everyday where they're made to feel stupid? So they turn to gangs, to other lost people who need followers to validate themselves. Gangs, ISIS . . . same thing.

I've read that one caring adult in a child's life is what's needed. So get your "Army of Hope" started right here. (Quit rolling your eyes, you big baboon. You can do it.) Get veterans, especially disabled ones, involved in community service. It'll be good for them . . . win-win . . . give the veterans something to live for as well: make them feel good about themselves by helping kids.

Start getting the kids in sports right away . . . when they're young. Sports are great for breaking down barriers of race and other shit. If not team sports, then boxing, wresting . . . sports where they can vent yet learn discipline. Vets will have all kinds of backgrounds and skills. Get kids involved in cleaning up their neighborhoods. Turn empty lots into sports fields. Have one neighborhood team play, not fight, against each other. Plant gardens. Organize music groups, Acappella groups if getting instruments is a problem. Hold dance/hip hop competitions. Make videos. Have kids use improvisation where they act out situations in which they're angry, frustrated, happy . . . humorous scenes that make them laugh. Involve the community, too. Get them doing artistic things with the kids, like graffiti contests. Photography. Things that make the kids feel success not failure. Start as young as possible. The older they get, the harder it may be to convince them that crime doesn't pay.

I'll give you a specific example of involving them in something creative, enjoyable, that they can be successful at. I've read it's a great intro to photography : have them all shoot the alphabet. You know, an "A" might be a dormer, an "H" a goal post. An older neighborhood kid with his hands in the air could be a "Y". They'll love to be creative. The vets or neighbors can buy them cameras. The vets can get the police involved. Have the police buy musical instruments, cameras. Get the police interacting positively with kids in the neighborhoods.

Then have the disabled vets get other retired vets involved. Maybe in Big Brother, Big Sister . . . Boys' and Girls' Clubs – whatever. Then aim for the big picture. Have the vets get active military involved . . . maybe the National Guard. Rather than having them do ridiculous military exercises, have them fulfill their duties in poor neighborhoods. Can you imagine how many talented people would join the military if their mission, here and around the world, was to seek peace by community service . . . educating, helping people, not shooting them?

You'll need to franchise yourself. Like the pay it forward concept. You'll clone yourself over and over again. Yes, yes we'll still need soldiers of war, mercenaries to protect our Army of Hope role models around the world. (Yeah, I know Army of Hope is maybe a bit cheesy, so get your own name. Maybe Soldiers of Peace?) The point is to change the notion of soldiers as always armed with weapons of aggression. Aggression has never worked. Killing to achieve peace is an oxymoron that humans have failed to figure out. The "weapons" should be compassion, education, training. The need for mercenaries will diminish as generations of educated, fulfilled kids become role models themselves. You don't have to do it all yourself. Just get it started. Clone yourself over and over again until we have kind, peaceful, fulfilled armies of hope, soldiers of peace around the world.

Can you think of any better way, big guy? Sitting on a porch gazing at a tranquil lake while innocent people around the world are slaughtered might be a pleasant break, but it's hardly a fulfilling mission in life. I know you. You can't fool me. I know you care. AND, most importantly, you can do it.

CHAPTER SEVENTEEN

WILL'S STAY IN THE HOSPITAL was expected to be longer this time. The next day he was allowed guests for only short visits. The respirator had been replaced, again, with oxygen tubes clipped inside his nostrils. An antibiotic drip stuck into his arm. The first day Sandy came right after school but spent so much time crying and apologizing, Will kicked her out before his mother got there. He didn't feel up for a skirmish and was getting pissed at Sandy.

Peewee came by after work but unfortunately ran into Mr. and Mrs. Mitty on their way out. Mr. Mitty was almost cheerful, but the Mrs. only glared at Peewee. He wondered what Will had told her about what had happened and was happy not to discuss anything until he had talked to Will. Peewee wondered if the glare was because of the misadventure or because he had hung up on her. Both, he guessed. He couldn't remember ever being rude to her before, even though he had wanted to stick up for Will many times. Will had always told him not to, that it would just make life more difficult for all of them. Peewee had gained a new respect for Mr. Mitty after he bucked the Mrs. by coming up alone to check on Will but wished he had stuck up for Will more often. Not that they were bad parents. He just thought they didn't know how to love Will in a way that was good for him.

Peewee, in his selective view of the world, wanted to believe that if everyone had a decent family, everything in the world would be fine. Of course, Will had pointed out that that would be great if everyone did, but . . . Peewee had argued that he couldn't help that. He'd raise his own kids and they'd be fine. Just leave him alone.

When the Mittys left, Peewee went into the room, and he found Will agitated. It turned out Will had refused to tell Mrs. Mitty any of what had happened at Burntside. He recapped for Peewee; he had said he wasn't sorry about any of what had happened, that he wasn't going to be homeschooled, that he wasn't quitting his job, and that he was moving out right after he graduated. When she had asked Will just where he thought he was going to live, he told her that she'd find out in due time. Peewee now understood the glare, figuring that Mrs. Mitty would contribute this flare-up of independence to him, somewhat rightfully so.

According to Peewee, keeping the job wouldn't be a problem. His dad had actually apologized. Especially when Peewee told him that if Will goes, he goes. Of course, the store couldn't function without Peewee. Will had also told his mother that she might as well quit flapping her wings, as well as her mouth, since he had decided he was no longer under the influence of either. Peewee was amused at this, what he considered for Will, a necessary leap of independence.

After recounting his rant with his mother, Will had had a coughing spasm and trouble catching his breath. Peewee told him to calm down and pointed out that if he wanted to kill, maim, or castrate Bret, he'd have to get healthy.

"So what are *you* going to do about retribution?" Will asked

Peewee when the spasm subsided.

Peewee smiled. “You’ll see.”

It was now Will’s turn to smile. The image of Bret’s “Pit and the Pendulum” daydream popped into his head.

“What are you smiling about? You got something planned, you little weasel?”

“I’ve considered a couple things.”

“Oh? Like what?”

“Never mind. What you got? I need to know, now.”

Peewee frowned. “Well, like I was saying, since you intend to inflict physical vengeance, I thought I’d try a little psychological anguish.”

“Is he at home yet?”

“No. I found Derek before school today and we had a little discussion.”

“About what?” Will asked.

“His finger.”

“Uh, good idea. Think it worked?”

“His finger doesn’t anymore. The idiot stuck it in my face. Pretty sure that after he quit crying—it snapped and sounded like a pencil breaking—the powwow that followed did the job. I felt guilty hurting him but hope the asshole sees the light.

“He nicely informed me that Bret’s parents have him in a facility, kind of a sanitarium it sounds like, where they will be trying to rehabilitate his speech, among other things. The dude can’t even eat. He has to learn how to use his stub of a tongue all over again. I guess he won’t be force-Frenching any more women. Derek was kind enough to tell me which room was Bret’s. He has a window facing the parking lot. I dropped to Derek that I might head right out and check the place out, maybe have a little visit. I stopped at the store first and borrowed a pair of binoculars, and, as I thought, there was Bret, looking out his window, waiting for me. I looked at him in my binocs and there he was lookin' back at me through his. I smiled, gave him the finger, and headed out, walking toward the back of the establishment, hoping he'd think I was sneaking in. Sure enough, when I came back to the van, he wasn't at the window. I figure he's off cowering somewhere."

"Now what?" Will asked, thinking this was maybe the perfect retribution: driving Bret crazy.

"Figure I drive by again tomorrow, then every other day, then maybe randomly, to keep him on his toes."

Will laughed. "You'll drive him frickin' nuts. And since there's no physical threat, there's no reason for him to use the pics of Sandy as blackmail . . . if his dad hasn't gotten rid of them. "

"Exactly," Peewee said, knuckling Will. "You're a lot smarter than you look . . . or sound."

Willy's laugh caught in his throat, and his cough turned into a wheeze. It looked to Peewee like he couldn't get his breath, but when he went to push the nurse button, Will slapped his hand away. Peewee wasn't happy with how his little friend looked or sounded. Something sure wasn't right. Peewee was getting worried big time.

Eventually Will started breathing normally, although the cough hadn't completely gone. They talked for another hour. Peewee apologized for getting short with his mother and asked how it went with them after his rant. Will told him not to worry about his mother. Now that he knew about the cabin, he felt a sense of release, calm. He could be independent of her. He felt bad, though, because his health problems were causing a rift between his parents. He knew Walter wanted to side with him. Will figured he'd realized that Will needed to live, while Mrs. was afraid he was going to die. He couldn't really blame her, either. She was just going to have to learn to let go. Everything would be better if she could, especially for her.

Will explained that in the middle of his rant to his mother, Walter had addled over to the window, and Will could see in the reflection his insipid smile slowly creep onto his face. That the man was in his own thoughts. Will guessed that Walter had become a famous doctor and cured Will of all his ailments. Will loved him for his ability to find contentment in his secret life and hoped he could at least "fix" Will there.

Peewee left, worried.

Sandy stopped in after dinner and found Will dozing. He opened up his eyes as she sat on the side of the bed. He told her if she started crying again, she'd have to leave. She didn't respond or say anything but lay next to him in the bed and cradled his head, gently stroking it, rubbing her fingers through his hair. Although Will was rating this now as his number one sexual experience, with his head so delicately cushioned he was asleep in less than a minute.

Sandy might have stayed there all night, but unfortunately, both Peewee's dad and mom walked in followed by a nurse. Mr. Kovak crossed his arms and frowned; Mrs. Kovak smiled and said, "You must be the Sandy we've been hearing about."

Sandy's first urge was to leap up. But number one—it would have woken Will; number two—it would have made it look like she was doing something she thought she shouldn't; and number three—she didn't give a shit what anybody thought, anyway. She was consoling her friend.

The nurse was the cute Patsie of the 'too small to find' temptation. She apologized to the Kovaks, saying they should probably come back the next day, that Will needed his sleep. Mr. surveyed the scene skeptically; Mrs. said, "It's nice to meet you, Sandy. Peewee has never taken to another woman like he has to you." She looked at Will and said to Sandy, "Tell him to get well now, you hear? He's a special person. Peewee is beside himself with worry." She grabbed Mr. K.'s hand and dragged him toward the door.

Mr. Kovak looked back once and said in his pseudo-tough voice, "Tell him to get his butt back into work. I've been doing all the stocking. My worthless son is spending all his time here in the hospital or wherever." Just before he was dragged through the door, he looked back again, not speaking a word but saying plenty with his eyes. Sandy wasn't sure what exactly, but she figured she better make a better second impression. After they left, the nurse conceded that Sandy could stay for a while but reiterated that Will needed to sleep.

PEEWEE DROVE BY BRET'S FACILITY at about the same time the next morning. He parked in the same spot. Pulled out his binocs. There was Bret, once again looking back at Peewee through his. This time Bret gave Peewee the old finger. Peewee smiled at him and waved, causing Bret to raise his finger up and shake it at him in a rage, resulting in more animated waving from Peewee. Peewee then drove to the far end of the parking lot out of view of Bret's window, waited awhile, and when he drove back, Bret was once again gone. Peewee figured he'd take a couple days off. Let Bret stare out his window, stew and worry.

CHAPTER EIGHTEEN

SANDY CAME INTO THE HARDWARE STORE before dinnertime, tears streaming down her face. Peewee's dad was at the front counter. She tried to smile at him but the attempt just made her cry harder. Her nose was running, and she wiped it with the back of her hand and snorted. "Can I see Peewee?"

"What's wrong?" Mr. Kovak asked matter-of-factly but seeming concerned. He handed her a Kleenex.

"Nothing," Sandy answered and blew into the Kleenex.

"Always make that much fuss over nothing?"

Again she tried to smile, a little concerned about the second impression. She started to thank him for dropping in to see Will but broke out weeping again when she said his name. Fortunately it looked like nobody else was in the store. "Peewee?" was all she could manage.

A bell dinged and a couple old guys walked in. Mr. Kovak handed her a fresh Kleenex, pointed to the back of the store, and turned to the old guys. She found Peewee working on a lamp that looked like a lost cause.

He looked up when he heard her coming and came out from behind the counter when he saw the state she was in. "What's wrong?"

She threw herself at him and squeezed.

He squeezed back for a moment and then held her away from himself. “Tell me, please. What are you crying about?”

“They wouldn’t let me see him now,” she wailed.

“I assume you’re talking about Will?”

“Of course you idiot!” She beat him on his chest with both hands. “I just know something terrible has happened.”

“Calm down. Calm down,” he said, soothing her, hugging her again. “Let’s not assume the worst. What did they tell you?”

“Nothing!” she bayed.

He held her away again. “Calm down,” he said. “You’re not accomplishing anything by overreacting like this. Now stop crying.”

She took a few deep, sobbing breaths. “It’s all my fault.”

“Look,” Peewee said, holding her arms firmly, “You’re going to have to get over this guilt trip. You’re going to really piss him off, you hear? I don’t think you want him mad at you right now?”

“I know. I know.” She leaned her head against his chest, sputtered some snot, and wiped it on his chest, smearing “Shangri-La,” the T-shirt choice of the day. She kept shuddering with little hiccups that shook her whole body. So Peewee just held on for a while. Seeing her cry was difficult for him.

“Look. I’ll call the Mittys and see what they know.” He looked down at his shirt. “Thanks, again, by the way. They told you nothing at the hospital?”

She took a deep breath, tried to wipe the snot off his shirt with her snot-filled Kleenexes, spreading the smear, hiccupped, and turned away. “Nothing. ‘He isn’t allowed visitors’ is pretty much word for word what that old fluffy-haired witch told me.”

Peewee picked up his phone and called the Mittys’ landline.

Naturally, Mrs. Mitty answered. "Hello, Mrs. Mitty, it's me—Peewee. Has there been a change in Will's condition?"

Peewee heard nothing for a while. "Mrs. Mitty?"

"Peewee, I need to get to the bottom of this. You and I have to talk."

"I totally agree, we have things to discuss, Mrs. Mitty. But right now could you tell me what's up with Will?"

Another pause, then she said, "Listen Peewee, you and that girl . . . "

"Not now, please, Mrs. Mitty," Peewee interrupted. "We'll get around to the blaming when I come over to talk." He heard Mr. Mitty in the background tell her to quit yammering and tell Peewee what she knew. Peewee heard a loud "Walter!"

Suddenly Peewee heard his name being almost shouted into the phone.

"Yes, Mr. Mitty, how are you?"

Before he could answer, Peewee heard the indignant Mrs. Mitty say, "Walter. Give me that phone back."

"Peewee, it's me." Mrs. Mitty was back. "Will's heart started to fillibrate." He knew she meant fibrillate. "He's having trouble breathing. They've got him on a respirator again."

"Did you see him?"

"Yes. But he got all agitated and that young doctor made us leave. Nobody can see him, so don't try to get in there. I know you. You'll push your way in. Just stay away for now. He needs to rest."

"Yes, Mrs. Mitty, of course. Shall I come over tomorrow to talk?"

"No. No. That's ok. Not now."

"I apologize for being short with you the other day. I was just concerned about what to do about Will."

"Well, don't you think we all are? I am his mother, you

know?"

"Yes, Mrs. Mitty. I'm sure you are concerned about Will. So are Sandy and I."

"Sandy!" Her voice went up a pitch. "I don't think that young lady is good for Will."

"That will be part of our discussion. Please let me know when I can come over."

"Oh, Peewee. I'm so worried about that little guy."

Peewee had mixed emotions. He wanted to tell her that Will was not a "little guy," but her momentary flash of compassion stilled his irritation. He had no right to judge her as a mother, he told himself. "I'll talk to you tomorrow, Mrs. Mitty. We'll see how he does. I believe he's stronger than you think," he finished and hung up.

"What?" Sandy implored. "What's wrong?"

"Nothing," Peewee lied. He could feel that something bad was up. "They just want him to rest. So, no visitors right now."

She sniffed, wiping her nose again with the back of her hand, then wiped her hand on her standard black jeans, leaving a pretty juicy smear.

"Look. Go home and settle down. Can I come over tonight?"

She inhaled some more snot up her nose and answered, her voice breaking, "Yes. Of course. You'll be meeting the folks, though. They want to meet you."

"Good," Peewee answered. "Is around 8:00 ok?"

Still sniffling she said, "Yeah. Good. See you." She sniffled down the aisle and tried to smile at Peewee's dad as she went by but again broke out in tears and ran out the door. She feared the worst, and, no matter what anybody said, she felt responsible.

AT 8:00 PEEWEE RANG THE DOORBELL at the cavernous front entrance, worried how he'd be received. In a few moments an attractive, slight, dark-haired woman with Sandy's eyes opened the door. She looked up at Peewee, smiled lightly, and said in a voice much like Sandy's, "It looks like we'll have to readjust our security lens for you. All I could see is, I think it says, 'Shangri-La' in the camera. I can see the reports of your stature have not been exaggerated. I'm Sandy's mother, of course—Loretta. Please come in. I think Sandy expected you at the side entrance."

"Felt like I'd be sneaking in, Mrs. Stickner. I've been looking forward to meeting you and Mr. Stickner."

She smiled. "Well, Jack's not home yet. But he will be. He's rather a worker bee."

He followed her through a stone-tiled foyer into a room that, similar to Sandy's apartment, opened up with a wall of glass looking out over the water in the distance, the deep yellow light of the fall sun lingering on the treetops on the far shore. She stopped at an intercom and told Sandy that Peewee was here.

She turned to Peewee and surprised him when she placed her hand on his arm. "Before Sandy gets here I'd like to ask something of you."

"Yes?"

"Please be cautious with Sandy. Her history with men has been . . . well, not the most beneficial to her, emotionally. She can be very vulnerable, especially at the moment with your friend, Will, being in the hospital."

"I understand, Mrs. Stickner. I hate to just drop this on you on our first meeting, but I love Sandy. So does Will."

She grimaced and looked Peewee in the eye with those dark, penetrating eyes she had passed on to Sandy. "I've gathered that. I am concerned. She has made it clear that she feels she loves you, both of you, as well. And I'm sorry to say, loving two men doesn't seem to me to be a terribly stabilizing predicament."

"I understand completely, Mrs. Stickner. I'm sorry I don't have a more comforting response. It is what it is. When you meet Will, you'll understand why Sandy loves him. He's an exceptional person."

"Exceptional how?"

"In about every way: the way he looks, talks. He's highly intelligent and irritably well informed. You wouldn't guess it, probably, looking at him, but he's completely grounded, secure. His only hang-up is that he wants to save the world, but I'm afraid doesn't have much more time to do it. But neither he nor I would ever do anything to hurt Sandy. I'm afraid we've adopted her."

"Adopted? That's a strange term to use."

They heard Sandy's bare feet slapping down the tile hallway that led from her stairs. When she emerged into the big family room, both Peewee and her mother, still facing each other, followed Sandy with their eyes. She stopped abruptly. "You two both look like you're guilty of some indiscretion. Been talking about me?"

"I'll go and fix up some munchies," Mrs. Stickner said. "You can give this 'little' friend here a tour if he likes."

"I'd love one," Peewee said. "This is a fantastic place. I understand you're a decorator, Mrs. Stickner. It sure shows."

"Thank you. That's kind of you," she said as she disappeared around a corner.

"Heard any more about Will?" was the next thing out of Sandy's mouth.

THE EVENING WENT WELL. Mr. Stickner got home; he was pleasant but remained a little distant. Mrs. Stickner was, as Sandy had said, a competent hostess: polite, though a little formal. Peewee understood. From the little Will had finally told him, they had a right to be skeptical. But they both said, as Peewee left, to let them know when Will could have visitors, that they would like to meet him and wish him well.

SANDY AND PEEWEE STOPPED by the hospital over the next couple days. They still wouldn't let them in to see Will. Surprisingly on the second day, Sandy, on her way out, ran into Big Betty. When she asked Betty what she was doing there, she had looked embarrassed and told Sandy it was none of her business. She paused then asked Sandy why she hadn't been in school. She had felt like telling her "none of your business," but instead said it was because of Will. Big Betty paused for a while again, leaving them awkwardly facing each other. Then Betty admitted that she kinda liked the little guy and felt bad for being mean. She asked if Sandy would apologize for her. Sandy told her she'd have to do that herself. Betty whined that they wouldn't let her in to see him . . . yesterday, either. She didn't know how he was. She actually sounded sincerely concerned. Sandy just started to cry, patted Betty on the shoulder, and walked away.

PEEWEE MADE ANOTHER SWING by Bret's window a couple mornings later. There he was, watching. Peewee just waved and rolled by. Out of curiosity he drove by during sixth hour and started feeling guilty when there Bret was, at his window. He assumed he must sit there all day, watching. Peewee had considered sending Bret some threatening emails to increase his anxiety . . . but relented. He was starting to feel sorry for Bret.

Will's recent insistence that Bret's behavior was due to his father and the way he had been raised was starting to make Peewee question what he was doing. It was really pretty wicked—deserved but still wicked. Will had suggested that he go talk to Bret. Peewee wasn't sure he was ready for that yet.

The fourth day with no visitation, Peewee made an appointment to meet with the doctor after he did his last rounds. Peewee had continued to call the Mittys for updates, but Mrs. Mitty would always answer, say that this was Peewee's and "that girl's" fault, and hang up. Peewee was irritated since he thought they had shared mutual empathy last time they talked. But he tried to understand her frustration. It was as if Sandy was the catalyst, bringing about what Mrs. Mitty had feared since the moment Hau William was born. He couldn't really blame her.

Peewee and Sandy were in the waiting room when the doctor came in and sat down. He looked contrite. "We're at a loss. His lungs are not operating at full capacity . . . and probably never will again. He breathes fine with the oxygen tubes, but we have to sedate him pretty heavily at times. He will come out of a deep sleep and start yelling, expounding . . . which causes his heart to fibrillate and flutter wildly. His heartbeat has become seriously irregular."

Sandy, who had started crying, blurted out, "Is this all because he fell into that lake?"

The doctor looked at Sandy. "Listen, I love the little shit. When he's coherent, he's incorrigible. The nurses have all fallen for him. I can tell he really enjoyed life and would make a great friend."

She wiped her nose with the back of her hand and nonchalantly wiped the snot on Peewee's pants.

"I can get you some tissues," the doctor said.

"That's ok. He has endless places to wipe . . . for Christ's sake, why did you say "enjoyed"? Is he going to die?"

"Just 'living' was always going to be a problem. The only way to protect him would have been to lock him in a room. That, I'm guessing, would have killed him a long time ago." He smiled compassionately at Sandy. "By the way, he told me if you asked that question—if it was your fault—to tell you he'll refuse to see you. You best dump any guilt you're feeling. Get it out of your system."

Peewee had been quiet, his face stony. He was afraid he couldn't talk. "Doc," he managed. "You're talking like he may not recover?"

"He may recover, but he won't be the same. He's lost both heart and lung function . . . and his kidneys aren't the greatest. Believe me, this was inevitable. It's a testament to his willpower that he's done as well as he's done . . . all his life, really."

"Do his outbursts," Peewee asked, having to take breaths, "have anything to do with water?"

The doctor looked surprised. "That was the first one. 'Water!' he'd yell. 'You can't frickin' live without water!'"

"Anything about the United Nations?" Peewee asked, smiling sadly.

The doctor laughed. "The nurses say he's really pissed about the United Nations. Oh, yes. From what I've heard he's pretty upset about how 'pathetic' their attempt at gaining world peace has been. The nurses all gather at his doorway, listening. I don't think he knows we're there. It's really quite fascinating."

"Anything about mining?"

The doctor laughed. "Oh my God. The nurses called me in today. He was yelling about copper, precious metals and, of course, that got tied into 'water' as well. I have to say, I agree with him on that one—I'm an avid canoeist, absolutely love the Boundary Waters—and probably agree with all of his rants from what I've heard, if you want to know the truth. And there have been others. He's surprisingly well informed. He wakes up enough to spout off, and then drifts back away when he runs out of steam. It is really quite remarkable. There is certainly a passion built up inside of him."

Peewee shook his head. "You have no idea. When will he be ok for a visit?"

"Well, we've tried to let his parents in, but as soon as he sees them his heart rate increases, he gets upset and has trouble breathing, goes into coughing fits . . . and we have to sedate him."

"Is this," Peewee started, and hesitated. "When his mother starts in . . . ?"

The doctor looked at both Peewee and Sandy over the top of his glasses. "I've talked to her about it, but Mrs. Mitty can't seem to accept what's happened to him. She is usually silent at first, but you can see she's pent up. Will's dad will usually ask the ordinary, mundane questions. 'Feeling any better?' Etcetera. But Mrs. Mitty can't control herself. She just has to 'get to the bottom' of what happened to him. Apparently he won't tell her the story. That's when he goes into a rage, even starts to lisp. He's such a literate, articulate kid . . . witty and clever . . . but when his mother starts in he becomes very upset. I think, really, he could have a stroke. It's a risk. So we're very hesitant to let him have any other visitors."

Peewee cleared his throat and scratched his head. "It sounds like you are aware of what's happening. Will's mother loves him but is going to blame herself for, she believes, having allowed whatever she imagines happened happen to him. And it's obvious Will's not going to tell her, which she'll never accept."

"No. You're right. He has told me the story, but he says he'll stick my stethoscope up my ass if I tell her. I think he's serious. I promised, although I'm not sure I should have, that I wouldn't tell her."

"I imagine you also know that if we visit with him, it'll calm him? Probably better than sedatives?"

It was the doc's turn to scratch his head. "Look," he said hesitantly, "by 11:00 we have a skeleton crew on, most patients are asleep. They say he's usually awake then, and he's usually scribbling in a notebook he keeps hidden. The nurses say they've gotten similar threats if they disclose his hiding place. Although the threats aren't taken seriously—the nurses all love him, even Shirley—none of them would give him away."

"Shirley's the one with the big, fluffy hair?" Sandy asked.

Doc laughed. "Yes, that's Shirley, and although she generally takes no crap from anybody and tends to be a bit pedantic, Will had demanded they have a heart-to-heart, and they've been fine—actually more than fine—ever since. No, all the nurses, even Shirley, have a tender spot for him. He's actually very charismatic. Oddly, at first he lisped considerably. Now—infrequently."

"He only lisps when he's nervous," Peewee explained.

"Well, good. That means he's more comfortable with us all now. Look, I wish to hell there was a magic pill I could administer. The kid's tough. You may not know, . . ."

Peewee just smiled sadly. Sandy started to cry, again.

". . . but he just wasn't born fully developed. With every breath he took, he knew it. He knew he wasn't going to last long enough for him. By the way, what does the word 'hau' mean? That word pops up in his rants at his mother."

Sandy started to cry harder. Peewee had trouble, his voice breaking. "It's a Hawaiian flower that blossoms and only lives one day. It's actually his first name."

The doc took off his glasses. "Jesus. Who'd . . . ?"

"I just found out a little while ago what it meant. Don't bring it up with him," Peewee said.

"Well, damn!" The doctor pinched the bridge of his nose. "Anyway, I have to tell you that you can't see him, but 11:00 would work. But I didn't tell you that."

Oct. 20

This is my fourth day in this frickin' place. I don't know where you two have been. A little rule has never stopped you before. I got a feeling I'll see you two tonight. I'm having difficulty staying awake long enough to get much written, but I feel better at the moment. I'm guessing this may be the last entry in my will. Peewee, the only regret I have is that I won't have a chance to live in the home you created for us. I would have loved that. Thank you. Just knowing it was there freed me more than you know. I can go out my own man. It would have been interesting to try Sandy's little scenario ...but as they say, "three's a crowd." But don't think you're done with me. I'm still going to be making noise. That scare you? Well, you'll know what I mean, if you don't already. You can graduate now and get on with your life, accomplishing bigger and better things than protecting my little ass. You'll have a much more attractive one that I'm guessing's going to need a lot of protecting as well. You'll need my room in the cabin, anyway. Even without me there you're going to have your hands full as I'm sure you now know. Thank you Peewee. Sandy, I love you. Thank you, again, for loving me. You have no idea.

CHAPTER NINETEEN

PEEWEE PEEKED AROUND THE DOOR before he opened it all the way, concerned about disturbing the Shrimp. He found Will gazing at him, sitting up in his bed, the oxygen hose lying by his side, smiling a goofy smile. A notebook in his lap.

"Just the man I was hoping to see," Will said.

Peewee walked in, grabbed the heavy chair with one hand, and set it next to the bed. Sat. Looked at Will. Said: "I don't like the sound of that."

Will quit smiling. "We gotta talk."

Peewee looked at him with one eye. "What we 'gotta' talk about? I don't want to talk if I 'gotta' talk. I don't think I want this conversation."

"Fine," Will said. "Don't talk. Just listen. I have a will, you know." He held up the leather-bound notebook. "I've made my last entry."

"You got a will? Really. What the hell for? And what do you mean by your 'last entry'?"

"What you mean why do I have a will? I got something really good to pass on."

"Pass on to who . . . sorry: to *whom*?"

"Very good." Will was trying to smile, "To you."

"I don't think your jeans will fit me."

"I'm not talkin' about 'shit.' I wouldn't will you shit for crying out loud. No, I'm leaving you something valuable."

"Sandy?"

Will tried to laugh and it got caught in his chest and he started coughing. Peewee waited until the spasm passed. He didn't like the sound of it.

"Sandy?" Will choked out when he was done hacking. "Although definitely 'valuable,' she's hardly my possession. Matter of fact, I think Sandy's done being possessed. Sometimes I think she is 'possessed.' Probably not good material for an actual spouse. She could be difficult to live with, I'm guessing."

"You'd take your chances if . . . if she proposed to you."

"Damn right!" Will punctuated his outburst with a hack. "So would you. Now shut up and listen."

Peewee saw the look in Will's eye and knew it wasn't a time for humor. Although he'd rather keep going with the banter they'd done all their lives, he shut up. But he feared what was coming.

"I've willed you my will."

"I don't want it," Peewee answered instantly, knowing where Will was going.

"No, not like a piece of paper but like in 'power.' Willpower."

"I know what you mean. I don't want your willpower. I'm doing just fine with my own."

"There are covenants in my will," Will continued, nonplussed.

Peewee just shook his head. He had to acknowledge to himself for the first time that Will was a funny color. His face was definitely ashen, anemic. He looked tired, worn out. "Ok?"

"The very first covenant: if a person is willed something from the non-material, spirit world, he can't refuse it."

"Spirit world?"

"Peewee. I don't feel like I'm coming back from this. It just feels like the lungs are leaving and I'm going with them. I don't think I could live fettered to a bed."

"Then you get a lung transplant or something artificial to help you breathe. This isn't like you."

"I don't think my heart would make it through any kind of an operation. Wouldn't that be cool, new lungs but no heart? And even if my heart makes it, my kidneys are not exactly the bee's knees either, you know. I feel like it ain't going to ever be the same. Not even alright."

Peewee was going to argue, of course, but he was having difficulty not crying because he believed Will. Will, with his blasted willpower, would never say what he had just said unless he felt strongly that it was true.

"The doctors told you that?" Peewee choked out and cleared his throat.

"No. But they said no big surgeries. It would be a big risk that they are not willing to take. So, since I won't be here to make the changes that this planet deserves, I'm leaving that in your hands. Very capable hands."

Peewee was going to have trouble talking, so he didn't want to. He could feel his eyes starting to water. "I've been able to choose just what this planet needs all on my own, thank you," he managed. And then he tried to summon anger. "You want me to solve all these problems? Like where? In the Middle East? They've been fighting forever. Forget it. A waste of time." He took out a Kleenex and blew his nose. "Or how about Africa! I suppose you want me to go rescue all those young girls that were kidnapped? Then how about the next batch that are kidnapped? There is no putting an end to that shit. I want nothing to do with that. I don't even want to know about it. I wouldn't if it weren't for you, you little shit. I have plenty of clean water for Christ's sake. So will *my* children. Then, of course, here we have inequality, injustices, greedy assholes leeching our money, companies not caring if they destroy the earth, government assholes who hate our president because he's black. I want nothing to do with that shit. You hear? Nothing! You want to spend your life trying to fix shit that can't be fixed, then don't die on me. You do it. I can't fix the United Nations. Yes, I would love peace in the world. I have peace in my world. I love you. I love Sandy. That's all I need. So don't give me this shit about fixing the world. If everyone just fixed their own little world, there would be peace in the universe. I want to be happy! You hear me? You want to spend your life getting frustrated trying to fix shit . . . then stick around . . . don't frickin' die on me. Don't . . . " He burst into tears. The only person that had ever seen him cry was Will, and that was probably in first grade.

Will closed his eyes, calmed himself, and waited for Peewee to look back up. "I know you. You know that. You have to face up to the fact that you were given your gifts for a reason. I'll feel like I died for nothing, if I don't . . ."

"Please don't," Peewee pleaded. "I just want to be happy. Don't do that to me."

"Think of Sandy. You think she'll continue to be satisfied and love you if you sit around on your ass, contemplating your frickin' navel?"

Peewee gave up on Kleenex and wiped his nose on his shirt sleeve. Will noticed when his shirt, again worn like a cardigan, separated that his T-shirt said, "Ely: End of the Road" on it.

"She's not going to stand by and let you 'apathize' into serenity."

Peewee sniffed again but tried to smile. "Nice try. 'Apathize'?"

"It works," Will said, and he closed his eyes. "Oh." He opened them suddenly. "There's more than one covenant in this will."

"No? You don't say."

"I made a mistake; I almost forgot to tell you."

"A mistake?"

"Yeah, I had you tell the United Nations that they should put together a global force to deal with problems like Boko Haram. Christ, Boko Haram; it sounds like a frickin' musical group. But I think you left the impression that that force should be military."

"*I* left? What the hell? So, is that where you go inside that head of yours? You do go and solve the world's problems?"

"No," Will corrected, "*you* solve the problems. You can. I can't. So, you see, the United Nations has to change things but not by aggression. Wars never really end. Nobody really wins. It's just who's left at the end of the day. It's been that way since the beginning of time. Aggression doesn't work. History has certainly shown us that killing doesn't convert. It's rather an oxymoron."

Peewee rolled his bloodshot eyes and wiped his nose. "Yeah, right. So . . . ?"

"Can you imagine armies of nations not armed with guns but reason, reason being the only weapon. This is all in my will. I've been writing it for some time, now."

Peewee wiped his eyes. "My dad thinks the displaced Muslims are spreading throughout the world to take it over. What if they all have the same interpretation of their Koran and are infiltrating every city of the world with the ultimate agenda of apocalypse?"

Will attempted a laugh, and it brought on another round of hacks. "Well, I guess that doesn't surprise me coming from your father. If true, that would qualify as the cleverest most colassal conspiracy in history."

Peewee couldn't help but notice Will's usually comical high-pitched voice was now exceptionally weak and scratchy.

They were both quiet for a while. Peewee wondering how to discuss with Will what he hoped wasn't happening. "Do you believe in heaven, or an afterlife?" he asked Will, mostly to change the subject. This is something they had always avoided talking about. Peewee had always feared this day.

Will laughed quietly so as not to spur on another spasm. "I have no frickin' idea. Obviously it's a mystery and I don't have much choice in the matter. One of the two ways that I can feel I have an afterlife is if I will you my will. You do understand?"

Peewee didn't want to listen; he bowed his head and slowly shook it. "I wish you wouldn't do this to me."

"I'm not going to say sorry. I'm not. Well, I guess I've said and written that, but I didn't mean it. I avoided pushing you too much to have a bigger view of happiness while alive. Can't avoid it when I'm gone. You know that in no time there won't be enough food to feed the world's population. They'll use up or destroy what good water we have left trying. Then what? I think of the world as an aimless ship, adrift. It keeps picking up more passengers, but provisions are running out. There is no captain to guide it. Everyone's just scrabbling for anything they can get. Soon this ship will be on its endless loop, going round and round with a boatload of bones."

Will attempted a smile. "How's that for one of your allegories?"

"Cheerful. Real uplifting," Peewee said, blowing his nose.

Will tried to laugh, but it got caught before it came out and he started coughing.

Peewee leaned back, resigned, the chair creaking, and

breathed deeply, knowing his life was going to change. He couldn't even imagine no Will. What would he do without the lisping little wiseass? Bugging him, making him laugh, keeping him honest? There never was nor ever would be anyone like Will. He almost lost it, then took another deep breath, wiped his nose, again, on his sleeve, and composed himself. "I got a will, too."

"Oh, really?" Will hadn't anticipated this turnabout. "Let's hear it."

"I will you Sandy. Maybe she can convince you to keep trying, you with all this willpower. Keep it. Use it yourself. Don't burden me with it."

"What's that supposed to mean?" Will looked away. He was doing his best to hold up, but a heavy fear was crushing his lungs, lying like lead in his heart. It was really just hitting him that he was saying goodbye. He closed his eyes.

Peewee waited. He first thought that Will had gone to sleep. Then his heart skipped a beat when he wondered if . . .

"So," Will said, almost in a whisper, his eyes partially opening, "a will, like 'last will and testament,' only takes affect after you die. You plan on dying before me, you'd better hurry."

"That's not funny," Peewee said, and wiped his eyes. "Call it a revocable, living trust, wiseass."

"How the hell do you know what those are?"

"What? You think you're the only one who knows shit? Anyway, while I'm alive and so are you, Sandy's yours as far as I'm concerned."

Will opened his eyes wide and stared at Peewee for a moment. "Seems like that should be Sandy's decision."

"I said 'as far as I'm concerned.' But dude, make the most of it, guilt-free."

"Why would I feel guilt?"

"This is not the time to start bullshitting. Why didn't you accept her invitation that night?"

Will took his time answering, then closed his eyes again. "I don't know," he said, and sighed. Will was totally aware of what Peewee was trying to do, almost as if he knew Will's plan. But what he most wanted was to assure that his will would be validated. He reached under the mattress, coming up with the leather folder Peewee had noticed earlier.

Will tried to sit up straighter. Peewee helped him, startled at how light he felt. Will handed Peewee the folder, Peewee taking it hesitantly, knowing what it was.

"I'd like to know, before I take my last breath, that you assent to follow the wishes of my will." He burst into a fit of shallow coughing that didn't relent. Peewee laid him back and went and got a nurse.

They made Peewee leave. He called Sandy. Sandy said she'd be right there. Her parents had just gotten home. "If he dies," she said, "I'll never forgive him."

THEY MET IN THE WAITING ROOM. Sandy couldn't quit shaking. Peewee told her that they wouldn't let them see Will. They sat silently, side by side, Sandy holding onto a handful of Peewee's shirt. After a couple hours, Peewee said he had to leave but would be back in the morning. Sandy said she'd stay, hoping to see Will.

Nurses continued to show up every half hour saying, "Not yet."

At 3:00 a.m. the ward was silent, like it had gone to sleep. Nurses seemed to be off doing whatever they do. As Sandy peeked around the corner, the only nurse in sight, sitting behind a counter in the main nurses' station, got up and headed for the restroom.

Sandy darted past and down the hall to Will's room. She quietly opened the door and peeked around to find him gazing at her, an anemic smile on his face. The breathing tubes were again by his side. He motioned for her to come in. She looked both ways down the hall, saw no one, and slipped through the door. "You ok?" she asked as she leaned over him.

"No. Not really."

"What's wrong?"

"Everything but you."

She leaned on the bed, gently setting her forehead against his. She had promised herself that she would keep it together. No easy tears or she would fall completely apart. "You really think you're dying?" She almost choked on the words. "You sure there isn't something here they can do? You can't die. You hear?" She could see by the look in his eyes what he thought.

"Peewee said he has a will," Will said, his voice vague. "Actually it's a living trust. Are you aware of what it says?"

"I'm not," she whispered, nose to nose with Will. "I have no idea what a living trust is. What's it do?"

"It bequeaths to me what he thinks I most want in the world."

She stood up and sat on the edge of the bed. She peered at Will for a while, then took a deep breath, pulling herself together. "What is it?" she managed.

"You."

She remained quiet, staring intently into his eyes. Finally she said, "Shouldn't that be something I decide?"

That's what I told him." When she didn't immediately respond, he added, "He knows it's what I'd most like before I die. I think he was trying to eliminate any guilt on my part . . . just in case."

"So, that's why you wouldn't let me make love to you? Guilt?"

"Probably."

She had never experienced or had these kinds of loyalties before, had friends dear enough that she would put their feelings first. Was Will really dying? She almost lost it at the thought and gave him a quick, soft kiss to distract herself. "It wasn't the easiest thing for me, you know?" she whispered, losing her voice. "I could have been hurt by your refusal . . . I actually was, as I'm sure you've figured out. I do love you, you know?"

"I'm sorry." He turned his head. Refusing her that night had been the hardest thing he had ever done in his life. "But the time wasn't right . . . then."

She couldn't let him die . . . not without confirming for him that she loved him. Maybe making love to him would keep him alive . . . give him something to live for. She reached over, cupping his face, and turned it toward her. "So, is making love to me the thing you most want in the world, now?"

He tried to turn away again, but she wouldn't let him.

She placed one arm across him, leaning over, looking down into his face. She tried to smile. "What about world peace?"

He tried to smile back. "Peewee can take care of that, just like he will take care of you. I guess right now it's my peace I'm more—"

"What'd I tell you?" She kissed him. She spread his lips softly, slowly flicking her tongue and Will figured out the rest this time.

She found herself immediately ready. Before, with other men, she had never felt ready. She eased his pajamas off, surprised at the size of his erection. He hadn't been kidding. She slipped out of her clothes, Will watching this time, and she gently climbed onto the bed and straddled him. She leaned forward and kissed him. This time Will took a deep breath at the vision. Of course her breasts were perfect. He falteringly reached his hands toward them. Sandy grasped his hands and pulled them to her. When she leaned back, he felt himself slide inside her. She was warm. She gasped. He held his breath. He knew if he breathed, he would start coughing. He felt himself go deeper, warmer. He felt he was becoming part of her.

Her breaths became brief and intense. She was so beautiful. She rose up and gently lowered, breathlessly whispering, "I'm going to have your baby. You'll live on."

It felt like heaven to Will. He had never, before meeting Sandy, hoped to make love, especially to a beautiful woman he loved. He felt he was being pulled whole inside her, like she was a keyhole into which he would vanish. She rose up, again, and slowly settled. Although she had had sex before, it had been nothing like this. This was more than sex. She felt like she wanted to encompass him, draw his entire being inside her. She gradually intensified . . . rising and settling, rising and settling. She wanted to scream out. She had never felt like this before. It was like Will, inside her, filled an empty space she had always had. She closed her eyes and almost seemed to ascend.

Will opened his eyes. She was so beautiful. He felt he was so close to heaven. Then he went there, letting himself go, as Sandy screamed.

PEEWEE WAS SOUND ASLEEP. He had taken one of his mother's pills because he couldn't get to sleep worrying about Will. He was dreaming that his cell phone was ringing. Finally he realized it wasn't a dream. Groggily, he answered it.

Before he could say anything comprehensible, Sandy's voice leapt out at him like it had claws: "I killed him!" she screamed.

"I killed him." Then sounds of weeping smothered the phone.

"Sandy," Peewee said, shaking his head to clear the fog. When she continued to wail, he said much more firmly, "Sandy. What do you mean? What's happened?"

"Oh, God," she moaned. "Will's dead. He's dead. I killed him."

Peewee instantly became alert. "Where are you?" When she didn't answer, he said again more firmly, "Sandy, where are you?"

"At the hospital," she managed, still weeping.

"I'll be right there."

PEEWEE FOUND SANDY IN THE WAITING ROOM. She flew at him and clasped on for dear life, burying her head in his chest weeping profusely. Peewee held her and let her cry herself out.

Finally she pulled away and started beating Peewee's chest yelling, "I killed him! I killed him!" Peewee let Sandy vent, and when she tired, her fists slowly relenting, he led her to a chair.

He sat next to her and held both her hands. She wouldn't look at him. "Sandy, tell me what happened. Is Will really dead?"

She finally looked up at him. His heart almost stopped. There was nothing in her eyes. They looked almost hollow, like black holes.

He asked her again to tell him what happened. Between short breakdowns of angst, she told him.

"So, does the staff know . . . know what happened, exactly?"

"No, I fixed him so it looked like he had been asleep. I knew he was dead. I dressed quickly and ran to get a nurse, but . . . I knew he was dead." She started to cry again.

Peewee was holding himself together pretty well, surprising himself. He figured he had to for Sandy. He couldn't imagine what it would be like without Will in the world. He could painfully feel an emptyness. Will was like air. He had always been there. It was like it hadn't really happened; he couldn't be gone. Gone? What does 'gone' mean? It wouldn't sink in. Will had been his life since he was old enough to remember. Nobody could replace Will. Not even Sandy. There simply was and never would be someone like Hau William Mitty. Before he knew it, tears were draining down his face. Sandy noticed, pulled herself together somewhat, and sat sideways in Peewee's lap, hugging him.

Her composure did not last long, and she started shaking, her body heaving in sobs. Peewee stood, picking Sandy up, walked over to a table, and sat her on it. He kneeled on one knee so that he was face to face with her. He smoothed her hair back and used his thumbs to clear her face of dark, salty streaks.

"Listen to me," he started, swallowing back emotion, fear. "Although I can't really grasp that he's, he's . . . I knew this was coming. Will knew it was coming. It doesn't really make it any easier . . . but . . . I really can't imagine not having the little shrimp around. But, he wasn't coming out of this. You could tell from what the doc said. Things were not going to go back to normal. You didn't kill him, you released him. You gave him what he most wanted out of life. You gave him love, and love in its most majestic form. Making love to you would have been the most wonderful thing in his life. He was not coming back, and rather than going through a long, painful, embarrassing, disagreeable, exasperating dying, he went out the way he would have wanted. Seriously, you didn't kill him. You gave him his heaven."

CHAPTER TWENTY

FOUR MONTHS LATER, on a warm winter day, sitting side by side with Peewee on the front porch of the little cabin, watching snow float down over (not so) Long Lake, Sandy punched him in the arm. "You haven't even noticed!" she accused.

"What, that you're preggers?"

"You know?"

"Of course. How oblivious do you think I am?"

She punched him again. "I didn't think I was showing yet. I've been cleverly wearing loose-fitting winter clothes, assuming that like most men, you *were* oblivious. Why didn't you say anything?"

"Sorry for my lack of 'obliviousity' . . . sounds like something the Shrimp would say . . . anyway, I figured since it's you that's doing the carrying, it should be you that's doing the telling."

"Oh, is that so?" Sandy watched him chew on a long, sweet sprig of grass, where it came from she had no idea, squinting into the morning sun. "You know it's Will's?"

"Well, of course I know it's not mine. I don't know why you haven't wanted to talk about it. You look like you're about four months along, so unless you've been active, I'd say the timing is right. I assume it was a doctor's appointment you were at yesterday? So what did she say?"

Sandy's eyes watered up. Normally she'd have punched him for his "active" remark, but all she could say was, "He's small."

CHAPTER TWENTY-ONE

FOUR MONTHS LATER, on a humid spring afternoon, Peewee and Sandy sitting barefoot, side by side again, on the covered porch at Long Lake.

"After I have the baby, I want to move out of my parents' house and in here with you. We haven't talked about it. What do you think?"

Peewee stared out at the water, the far shore veiled through the heavy air. "You'd be moving from the lap of luxury you're accustomed to, to a pretty primitive lifestyle."

Sandy punched him in the arm. A habit of hers that he didn't mind. "You're what I'm accustomed to. I love this place. So will the baby. So would Will have—man that would have been great, huh? The three of us? I can't believe you did this all by yourself. Guess it explains first and sixth hours."

He smiled at her. "I did most of the actual work on weekends. Principal Smith knew what I was up to, anyway."

"He condoned it?" Sandy asked, surprised.

"Well . . . I wouldn't say he 'condoned' it, but I brought him out here when he stopped me one day when I was leaving after fifth hour and asked me what the hell I did with those two hours every day. So we drove out here and I showed him."

"No shit. What'd he say?"

"Any fish in the lake?"

Sandy laughed. "So . . . can we move in?"

"Sure. Naturally I was hoping you'd want to. But that's over a month away."

Sandy smiled, apprehensively. "No, I don't think so. Doc says any day. I can tell, too."

Peewee looked from Sandy to the lake, not really seeing it, and back to Sandy. "So, one month premature is ok, right?"

CHAPTER TWENTY-TWO

FOUR MONTHS LATER, a fine fall Sunday morning, Peewee sitting on the porch steps Sandy sitting on a rocker, the rising autumn sun casting diamond sparkles that flicked around on the water. Sandy nursing the baby boy they had named Shrimp. A choice that raised many an eyebrow. Both had been quiet.

"Hey," Sandy broke the fragrant morning stillness, "think it's time? Doc says it's ok. I've got a feeling little Shrimp here's going to need a protector. What you think?"

Peewee's eyes inadvertently watered up. "Thought you'd never ask. Really ready for another so soon? What about a ceremony?"

"Let's put it this way. I've wanted a baby with you since the day Will introduced us. I'd say it's about time." She had told him that she wouldn't "accept his seed" unless it was to get a baby.

Peewee smiled at the lake, the water in his eyes causing the sparkles to flicker even brighter. "I suppose," he managed.

Sandy quit nursing, threw little Shrimp over her shoulder for a burp, got up, walked over to Peewee, and kicked him gently in the butt. "Don't act so excited," she said, and sat next to him. "I don't care if we get married or not. You really going to quit the hardware store?"

"Either I take over ownership or I find something where I can make more money in fewer hours. This thing at the Capitol is going to take up a lot of my time. I'll be doing my most favorite thing: meeting with politicians. You can thank Shrimp's daddy for that."

"They really going to start sending soldiers into the bad neighborhoods? Here and in other cities?" Sandy asked.

"Yip."

"What exactly are the soldiers going to do?"

"Well, they enlisted not to fight but, along with the vet's and police, to work with all the kids. Create positive relationships, get all kinds of shit going: some sports, some music, some community-type jobs the kids get paid for. Just what Will ordered."

"Cool. Yup, cool, really cool. Cool."

They all three started crying . . . Sandy and Peewee because of the Will remembrance, baby Shrimp because his parents were crying.

"So today the cities, tomorrow the world?" Sandy said, wiping her nose with her hand then wiping the snot on Peewee's pants. She hugged baby Shrimp. "You will be proud of both your daddies." Shrimp looked worried but quit crying.

"Yeah, yeah," Peewee said. "That little pecker had some pretty good ideas, I guess. Simple solutions to complex problems, he used to say. I just wish he were here. The little SOB is probably having a great old time up there watching us . . . if there is an 'up there.' Him with his blasted will."

"He willed you to straighten Bret out, I read? That's why you been talking to him?"

"Yip."

"How's that goin'?"

"I'm not holding my breath."

"Hmm. Good luck. I think it's too late. He's been an asshole too long."

"Yeah, well . . . it was Will's idea—this is one with no simple solution."

"One simple idea I did like was getting the mayors, who aren't all tied up in party politics, involved," Sandy said. "Isn't that how you got things started in the city?"

Peewee smiled at Sandy. "Hey, you're smarter than you look."

This warranted an extra hefty slug, which caused Shrimp to burp but left Sandy muttering, "Shit, shit, shit," and shaking her hand, which got Shrimp crying again.

Peewee reached down and gently rubbed Shrimp's hairless head. "Wouldn't it be weird if he never grew any hair? God, I hate those soft spots. There's nothing but a thin layer of skin between life and death. They're so vulnerable. I can just hear Shrimp Senior say, 'See, I knew you'd worry. Want a better world for our baby? Do something other than gaze at your navel, pretending everything is hunky-dory.'"

Peewee leaned down and kissed the soft spot. Shrimp whimpered, sighed, and closed his eyes. "Listen," he said to Shrimp but looked at Sandy out of the corner of his eye, "I don't want you to be talkin' like your momma, you hear?"

"Well, darn. I wish you had a soft spot I could punch," Sandy half-whispered, still shaking her hand.

Peewee shook his head. "The first word the kid says is going to be a cuss word."

"Uh uh. He's too little to remember." They both looked down at him. He was staring intently at his mother, and a little sound slipped out of his mouth that sounded a lot like "shit."

They looked at each other, mouths open. "Too little, huh?

Remember who his father is. I don't think Will ever forgot anything he ever heard. Of course the gene pool is a trifle contaminated."

Sandy started to wind up for a slug, and then stopped, reached over, grabbed a rattle, and whapped Peewee with it.

Shrimp's eyes jerked open at the noise and wandered over to Peewee, who leaned down and, in a highly incongruous baby voice, said, "I know it's going to be hard for you to believe in peace in the world with your mother whopping me with your toys, but we'll try."

This got Peewee another whap with the rattle, and Shrimp started crying again. Peewee reached over and took Shrimp, balancing him in his cupped hand, making him look half his size. "It's ok. Mean Mommy can't hurt Daddy."

Sandy teared up immediately. Which happened every time Peewee held Shrimp.

"See, your momma's so sorry she hit your Daddy she's crying." Which got another rattle rap.

Sandy sniffed, wiped her nose with her finger, and nonchalantly smeared it on Peewee's pants, once again.

Shrimp contentedly settled in the palm of Peewee's hand.

Sandy leaned her head against Peewee's shoulder.

Peewee looked down at Shrimp, who looked back. The baby was almost purring as Peewee gently swayed him in his hand. Peewee smiled, and Shrimp appeared, for the first time, to smile back at him. To Peewee's alarm . . . he was suddenly aware that it was unmistakably Will's smile. It hit him that the crying actually had Will's squeaky tinge. *God*, he thought, *what if he lisps?* Then baby Shrimp closed his eyes, Will's smile remaining on his face as he drifted off.

"Ah crap," Peewee mumbled to himself. "I'll never be able to rest again."

ACKNOWLEDGMENTS

Wise Ink Creative Publishing with Dara Beevas and Patrick Maloney for putting it all together.

Erin Heep McKensie at Bee's Knees for typing and oversight.

Marlene Straley, an old friend and associate who has provided much constructive criticism over the years, for an initial reading and feedback.

Kelsey Lundberg for my websites and first round of editing on Will.

Erik Hane for copyediting.

The reliable assistance from my daughter-in-law, Lisa Munkeby, whenever I run into a glitch.